THE

TRIGON

RITUALS

NCP

Be sure to check out our website for the very best in fiction at
fantastic prices!

When you visit our webpage, you can:

* Read excerpts of currently available books
* View cover art of upcoming books and current releases
* Find out more about the talented artists who capture the magic
of the writer's imagination on the covers
* Order books from our backlist
* Find out the latest NCP and author news--including any
upcoming book signings by your favorite NCP author
* Read author bios and reviews of our books
* Get NCP submission guidelines
* And so much more!

We offer a 20% discount on all new ebook releases!
(Sorry, but short stories are not included in this offer.)

We also have contests and sales regularly, so be sure to visit our
webpage to find the best deals in ebooks and paperbacks! To
find out about our new releases as soon as they are available,
please be sure to sign up for our newsletter
(http://www.newconceptspublishing.com/newsletter.htm) or join
our reader group
(http://groups.yahoo.com/group/new_concepts_pub/join) !

The newsletter is available by double opt in only and our
customer information is *never* shared!

Visit our webpage at:
www.newconceptspublishing.com

The Trigon Rituals is an original publication of NCP. This work has never before appeared in book form. This work is a novel. Any similarity to actual persons or events is purely coincidental.

New Concepts Publishing
5202 Humphreys Rd.
Lake Park, GA 31636

ISBN 1-58608-709-6

NCP books are available at special quantity discounts for bulk purchases for sales promotions, premiums, fund raising, or educational use. For details, write, email, or phone New Concepts Publishing, 5202Humphreys Rd., Lake Park, GA 31636, ncp@newconceptspublishing.com, Ph. 229-257-0367, Fax 229-219-1097.

First NCP Paperback Printing: 2005

Printed in the United States of America

THE
TRIGON
RITUALS

Angelia Whiting

Futuristic Romance

New Concepts   Georgia

Prologue

CalyTron Galaxy: Cosmic date: 252 Epochs

Tren ot Dmor sat cross legged, on a large, plush cushion, cradled within the serenity of the temple walls. His eyes were closed, his arms were bent, his fingers and thumbs formed the delta, held mere inches from his face. It was the position of prayer, more than symbolic in nature. It summoned the flows of cosmic energies to inspire wisdom, seek tranquility and harmony, and to move into alternate states of consciousness. Revered as the locus to spiritual awakening, the delta was part of all sacred rituals, but the one that Tren desired the most was the Triconjugal ceremony, the first mating between the Trigon males and their virgin female mate.

More than two sun phases had passed since being summoned to the Trigon, but it was a time that Tren remembered well. Rjant ot Pel'r, his Trigon brethren, was young when they first made contact. He was only seventeen phases of age back then and ten phases Tren's junior. At first, Tren worried that Rjant would lack the maturity significant to the Trigon mating. Most warriors his age still had a taste for escapade and craved variety in the carnal flesh. Tren was anxious to claim their female. He had thought of little else since being called forth. It could have taken many phases before Rjant was ready, and Tren was loath to wait.

Tren was pleasantly surprised however, when he learned that Rjant was a noted paragon in battle, leaving his home on Terta Minor, taking up the fight with the fiercest band of warriors known to the CalyTron galaxy, when he was just fourteen. Rjant was a mighty and respected leader among his regiment and demonstrated integrity well beyond his phase age. He had proven his worth as a warrior, working his way through the ranks to become Chief Loyal, second in command, of his fleet. In Tren's mind, it was a perfect match. Tren himself was High Chief, elected to the position by the Mahatma Tribunal. He'd earned the position by merit of his warrior skills, accelerated academic performance and leadership qualities. Tren was the first Commander, leader of the sentry forces from the planet of Tertia. Rjant would fit nicely as next in rank. Not only was he a mighty warrior, he was born on the sister planet in the Third Ward. Rjant was a full-blooded Tertani male, raised within his own culture. His position would be well accepted by the populace on Tren's planet, and their new She'mana should be much pleased to be joined with warriors of such high status.

Presently, Rjant was in the Fourth Ward leading his sentries to impede the advancement of the Krellian radicals who were planning an assault on the planet of Dormoth. One of the allegiant planets on the perimeter, it was still untouched by the devastating disease that was driving the galaxy's inhabitants into extinction. Though Tren agreed that Dormoth needed the protection, he had grown impatient for Rjant's military sect to gain control and develop the perimeter patrols the planet desperately needed.

That dawning had finally arrived.

Tren received word from Rjant's superior that they were overtaking the Krellian radicals. A new Chief Loyal for the First Ward was trained, and the patrols were being established. Rjant was soon to be released from his duties and would return to the Third Ward to take his place.

At last.

They could now claim their woman and bring her home.

Their mate.

Tren's loins ached to be between her thighs and only her thighs. No woman had ever been able to completely satiate his lust, no matter how often he pounded her flesh. His sex urgently needed their chosen female. Only then would he truly feel complete. Such was the nature of the Trigon males, loyal to their She'mana until death. Once mated, they were stripped of desire for any female, save their mate.

And it had long been said that the life force shared during Triconjugal mating brought satisfaction like no other. No one had to tell Tren this. The looks of contentment that seemed to always grace the faces of the mated triples in his acquaintance, told him all he needed to know.

His balls tightened just thinking about it.

Rapt in his meditative trance, Tren thanked the Mahatma Divinities for their blessings. He recited the mantra and beckoned the mystics to bring Rjant safely home. In a mighty gathering of power he channeled his benediction across the galaxy to reach his Trigon brethren. Rjant was thick within the throes of combat, and too far away to communicate with, but Tren could sense the violence and death that surrounded him. It was the same dreadful tumult that he, himself, had witnessed and fought against, on more occasions than he cared to recall.

Tren stiffened.

Rjant was struggling, but not against a warrior. It was a female that taunted him. Rjant's shudder reached clear to Tren's bones. He could almost smell it--Megberry, a potent aphrodisiac that not only induced a frenzied lust in any female that ingested it, but caused her to release an excessive amount of pheromones that drove any nearby male into sexual insanity.

And this particular female was drenched with it.

The fruit was used as a combat tactic by the Krellians and their radical supporters, to gain advantage over their foes. It took great might to resist these heavily drugged females who were turned loose on the battlefield. Even the strongest of warriors were known to throw down their weapons to viciously rut on the woman, only to meet their deaths when the radicals quietly crept up and slaughtered them.

Fight it, brethren.

A battle cry pounded inside Tren's head and he could feel Rjant's strength building. A vision of Rjant's talon arc slicing through the woman formed in his brain.

Rjant had killed her, and Tren could feel his brethren's agony at being forced do so. Tren's heart also saddened at the loss. Collateral misfortune was often a bitter consequence of war. Alas, she would have died anyway, being torn asunder by the warriors who lusted on her body, and if that didn't kill her, the drug eventually would have. This was by far a more dignified way to die.

Drawing his thoughts away from Rjant, Tren deepened his reverie. He stretched his mind toward their outer galaxy female, to a planet discovered three sun phases back--her home world, tucked into the far-reaches of the universe, innocent to the tragedy of his dying galaxy and unaware of the catastrophe of the epochs-long war.

They had prior knowledge of her planet and its location, because of the previous Trigon males who embarked on the arduous task of charting the intergalactic route to the distant star system. The planet was in unexplored hinterlands well beyond the Wards, well outside of the CalyTron galaxy. The existence of her planet was a well guarded secret known by only a privileged few. It was imperative to keep it safely hidden from the grips of the radicals who would wreak havoc on it if its presence was revealed.

Now that the stars had been properly mapped, it would take only four sept-dawnings to reach it, a lunar cycle--*one month*. Originally it had taken three lunar cycles to find the planet, but it seemed well worth the effort. The Trigon males returned home with their woman, a beautiful, feisty female who gave them exhilarating pleasure during the Triconjugal hunt. Tren did not partake in the ceremony, reserved only for mated males, but he'd heard that the Tina Karen eluded her Sh'em for three dawnings before they finally captured her and won her heart. Tren hoped the Tina Alea would prove to be just as spirited.

The vibration resounded along Tren's fingertips. His breathing moved rhythmically with his heart. He released his physical being to the ebb and flow of transcendental consciousness. His pulse beat hard and steady as the essence of their future She'mana hummed through him, but without Rjant he could not reach her thoughts. The first time he and Rjant yoked in transdelta meditation, they'd located her. Several times afterward, while Rjant was in reprieve from battle, they'd entered her mind as sleep images. The next time Rjant returned, he and Tren would finally be able to fully engage her. The link would be weak, given the vast star systems that separated them, but nonetheless, she would feel their presence, and it would grow stronger as they neared her world. They could complete the Edification, the priming of the Tina--virgin female--to receive her Trigon mates.

Tren looked forward to the Edification, a period during which the triad became acquainted before the marriage took place. It was a necessary ritual, particularly with otherworld females whose experience and knowledge of the Tertani customs was limited. It was not unusual for the female to become hysterical with two overpowering warriors intent on ravaging her untouched body. The ritual served to accustom her to her mates' touch, and to decrease her apprehension of the upcoming Triconjugal ceremony--to prepare her for her first sexual breaching. During the Edification, the Trigon males, Sh'em as they were called, would become familiar with their Tina's body, come to understand what pleasures she enjoyed, and how she responded to their fondling. Bringing climax to the female was highly encouraged. Kissing, licking, stroking and suggested acts of copulation were allowed, but actual penetration and nudity was not.

Tren released a controlled breath as he allowed his body to return to full awareness. He tensed as he rubbed his crotch. His cock had swelled to an agonizingly rock hardness with the thought of actually touching their female. Grabbing the rhyton at his side, he took a long, hard swallow of grata, a favored brew of many Tertani dwellers. Tren stood, ignoring his arousal, and stretched his muscles, shaking out the stiffness from sitting motionless during his long meditation. He pulled on his boots and approached a rack along one of the temple's walls, lifting his baldric and buckling it into place.

"Commander."

The voice behind Tren startled him. With quick reflex he yanked his talon arc from the sheath at his back, and spun around, ready to strike. The figure in the temple's doorway took one wary step back. "Sir?"

Tren relaxed and sheathed his weapon. It was only his steward. "Forgive me Gorsch. I'm not yet fully dispelled of my trance."

"Of course, sir."

"Why do you seek me here?"

Gorsch slithered through the door. Tren watched his steward as he walked, his eyes following the strange lateral curvatures that Gorsch's body formed. With long, slender bodies that snapped from side to side in an S-pattern as they moved, the inhabitants of Junpar were odd looking creatures, but they were a gentle breed and they made excellent servants.

Forming the delta with his hands, Gorsch nodded. "I beg your pardon for the interruption, but three Tertian warships are docking. I thought it best you be informed."

"Yes, good man. Thank you." Tren nodded as he brushed passed the Junparian and out into the open air. He straddled his hover cycle and revved the engine. Within a quarter dial he arrived at the depot. Tocol, one of his top-ranking warriors, was helping the healthteks disembark the wounded.

"All ranks!" Tocol shouted when he spied Tren approaching the platform. Several hundred sentries fell into position. Tocol stood rigid, presenting the delta salute as Tren came to stand before him. Tren returned the gesture and then scanned the squadrons. They looked weary, but otherwise, well.

"How many dead, Chief?"

"Twenty-two, Commander."

Twenty-two. Tren closed his eyes to absorb the information. *Twenty-two mighty warriors gone. And for what? A mass of radicals who could not think beyond their madness.*

Tren opened his eyes and refocused his attention on his Chief-at-Arms. Tocol was charged with maintaining discipline aboard ship and on the battlefield. In addition to his field duties, he was also senior ranking officer aboard one of the warships that just arrived. He was one of Tren's most trustworthy and capable warriors despite the fact he was Krellian. Not that Tocol cared much to be reminded of his ancestral bloodline. He had never been to the planet of Krell and kept no desire to be linked to his origins. Tocol was raised on Tertia, in one of the several villages established two epochs past to give refuge to fleeing Krellian citizens--those who escaped from the grips of that wretched virus.

Brits Scorn.

There was no cure. And no one fully comprehended the impact of the disease when it was discovered, but by the time it was recognized, it had spread to epidemic proportions. Of the fifty-two inhabited planets in the galaxy only twenty-two remained untainted. The Krellians controlled six of the tainted planets and sought to conquer more. Patrols guarded the rest of the infected planets under Allegiance control, not only to keep the radicals out, but to prevent the inhabitants from leaving and further spreading the disease. Persistent scanning of the inhabitants had been ordered by the ISDS--the Intergalactic System for Disease and Sickness Control, in the hopes of eradicating the disease before it completely consumed those planets and the rest of the CalyTron galaxy.

It began on Krell, a distant planet in the First Ward, about three hundred phases back. A patriarchal society ruled by a king, they were known for their ferocious battle skills, but the Krellians were not typically prone to unprovoked violence. All of that changed when Jonhi, the king's son, became enamored by Windi Britny, enchantress queen from the planet of Geminus. The queen wanted no part of Jonhi and persistently rejected his affections. Jonhi, angry and humiliated, snatched her away to a secluded outpost. He raped her, thinking that by dictate of his planet's laws, the taking of a female's maidenhead legally gave him rights to her.

He was fatally mistaken.

In her fury over being violated, Windi Britny cast a fog around Geminus, and put her people to sleep. She cursed all Krellians and gave decree for their doom, throwing down her wrath with tainted spores let loose in the Krellian atmosphere. In a slip of mercy, or perhaps she had some other mysterious intent, she allowed Jonhi to warn his people and some escaped. And before she died of hemorrhage from her own virginal blood, Windi Britny cast her faerie seed into the cosmos, promising that in the future, a redeemer would be their salvation. More than three epochs later, the redeemer had not come and Brits Scorn was running her wicked course.

No one ever knew what became of Jonhi.

"Have you more to report, Chief?"

"Sir, the perimeter around Dormoth is in the process of being secured, but we will have to order re-testing for all inhabitants. The radicals were able to transport to the surface."

"Damnation," Tren mumbled. *Not another planet.*

"We don't believe the radicals were there long enough to infect anyone, Commander, but they did steal away with forty-two women."

Tren raked his fingers through his hair. More women taken. More fertile wombs for the radicals to breed upon. Will this madness never cease?

Madness. Brits Scorn was an unforgiving disease. Infected males typically lived to their life's full expectancy while the disease slowly ate away at their minds, making them violently aggressive, but no less intelligent. It was not unusual to see one of these males frothing at the mouth when in a full-blown fit of excitement. Adult females, when infected did not become aggressive, but many died within three to five phases, usually after a sudden attack of seizures that assaulted them until their hearts succumbed to exhaustion. Other females became carriers and could pass the disease to any male they bedded. The unborn babes of tainted women were prone to a hodgepodge of anomalies while developing within the womb, and were examined carefully at birth. Offspring who were fully infected with Brits Scorn typically died within the first phase of life. Others were merely carriers and grew to adulthood, but they were isolated from society, forced by the ISDS to live on Puratan, a system of secured colonies, where polluted souls were banished. Those who were free of the virus were seized and placed in communes to be raised. Of these, female babes were sterile, but their male counterparts were not.

On Krell, fewer and fewer fertile females were being born and this put them in a dire situation, one that threatened to drive them to extinction. For this reason, they looked toward other planetary establishments to save them. Thus, in their madness, they began their reign of war, spreading Brits Scorn throughout the galaxy, instead of turning to the Galactic Allegiance for help.

Tren inhaled deeply. His next question was a difficult one to ask, but he needed to know. "How many warriors were tainted, Chief?"

"Only twelve this time, Commander."

Tren's nostrils flared and he fought to control his anger. He wanted to believe that each and every one of his sentrymen was strong of will, but it was not to be. "Where are they now?"

"Sent to Puratan, sir."

"Have their families been notified?" Shifting his gaze beyond Tocol, Tren focused on the hatchway of a docked warship. Larimon, one of his sentries, was emerging from the ship. He was grasping the upper arm of a very shapely female.

Tocol looked over his shoulder to see where Tren's attention had gone. Larimon approached and stood in front of Tren, releasing the woman to acknowledge his Commander with the delta. Then he began to shuffle from side to side.

Tren's eyes shifted from Larimon to the woman and back to Larimon again. The sentry's nervous behavior told him something was amiss. Again his attention re-focused on the female. Her eyes were turquoise, the same as Tren's but slightly deeper in color. She was a Tertani, revealed by the characteristic rim of gold that circled her irises. There was a worried expression on her pale but beautiful face.

Tocol spoke first. "Sir, we had to make port at the

Venuvian outpost."

"For what reason?"

"This female was there." Tocol gulped, apprehensive of how Tren would react to the truth.

"This rescue couldn't wait?"

Rescuing fugitives and providing sanctuary was not uncommon within the Allegiance, but there was something suspicious about this particular situation. Tren's Chief-at-Arms had disobeyed the direct order to come straight home.

"We insisted he go there." A warrior that Tren recognized, but did not know well, approached. Tucking his helmet under his arm, he came to stand behind the woman and placed a hand on her shoulder. His chin lifted and he looked as though he was ready to do battle as opposed to recovering from it. He did not offer the delta and Tren crooked an eyebrow at the sentry's defiance.

"Since when do you follow the orders of your subordinates?" Tren turned his head toward Tocol, his stare lagging on the warrior before snapping to meet Tocol's eyes.

"He had no choice, Commander." The second warrior interceded on Tocol's behalf.

Tren became impatient. He rolled his shoulders but could not contain his irritation. "Speak your name, warrior, before you speak to me!"

His voice grew deep and loud. The woman shrank behind Larimon. She looked frightened. Tren relaxed a bit, taking pity on her. Tertani women did not frighten easily. What had happened to this one to make her so timid?

"Bjead, of Tertia Minor, sir." The sentry finally bowed and offered Tren the delta. The gesture was not returned by Tren. "Who is this woman, and why is she here?"

"We wish to mate with her," Larimon said.

Tren did not miss the look that passed between Bjead and Larimon. They were communicating, touching each other's minds--linked. Tren was suddenly aware of what was happening. They had been summoned to the Trigon and this female was their Tina.

Tren folded his arms across his chest. Being summoned was a sacred occurrence. He would never interfere with the mystic event. "And this is a problem, why?"

Taking a deep breath, Tocol readied himself for the explosion he was certain was about to occur. "The Venuvian outpost is tainted."

"What!" Tren's well-controlled temper blew apart. Several nearby sentries stopped what they were doing and looked over, but returned to their tasks immediately as though pretending not to hear. "You took my sentrymen to a tainted post! I suppose next you're going to tell me that this is where those twelve men were polluted!"

Tren took one long, angry stride toward Tocol. His Chief-at-Arms stood tall, but his eyes averted downward, giving Tren his answer.

"Damnation, Tocol! How could you risk my men?" Tren grabbed the woman's arm and pulled her from behind Larimon. Both warriors growled at Tren's rough handling of their future She'mana. Tren ignored them. They would not dare strike their superior officer or he would put them to death.

"Has she been scanned?"

"Yes, Commander. We all have. She is a Tina, sir, and I assure you, she is not infected." Larimon reached out and attempted to pull his Tina free of Tren's grasp.

Tren's arm shot up and he stopped the sentry with a firm hand to his chest. Was this woman really a virgin? How could she be, living on a tainted outpost with infected males?

Releasing the female, he swung about. He stalked three paces before stopping abruptly and drawing in a deep breath. Tren hailed the Mahatma divinities, forming the delta with his hands, and bridled his anger.

He understood.

Once the Trigon males located their mate, they were nearly unstoppable to claim her. Being denied her would have driven them to an insane urgency--as insane as he was feeling for being denied his own woman.

Tren turned back to his sentrymen. They eyed him warily.

The female's face paled further and she looked as though she was about to faint.

Sacred damnation! Tertani females were stronger than that. He would like to kill whoever had broken her spirit.

With his composure regained, Tren drew up his chest and walked back to the group, exuding the controlled command expected by a warrior in his position. He halted in front of his Chief-at-Arms. "You defied an order, Tocol."

Tocol opened his mouth to speak, but Tren held up a hand to hush him.

"You understood when you did this, that you would be punished."

It was not a question.

Tocol nodded.

"Report to the gridmaster for a full dial of zapping."

"Yes, sir." Tocol gulped and strode away, feeling fortunate that he would not have to endure the voltaic shocks for a longer period. His Commander was being more than lenient. He would suffer no more than a bad headache for a dawning or two, and maybe vomit a few times.

Tren watched Tocol disappear from the platform and then turned toward the female. "Come to me, Tina."

Bjead and Larimon moved together, placing the female behind them, standing shoulder to shoulder to protect her.

Rolling his eyes, Tren blew out a gust of air. *What did they think he was going to do to her, string her up by her lovely toes?* "Separate yourselves. I'm not going to harm her."

When they didn't move, Tren bellowed. "That's an order, sentries!"

They parted immediately.

Tren's eyes fell upon the Tertani woman. He crooked a finger, beckoning her toward him. She took on wary step forward and began to tremble. Cupping his hand under her chin, Tren lifted her face upward.

"What's your name?" Tren softened his voice to ease her fear.

"Bligh, sir." Her whisper was barely audible.

"How did you escape with your virginity intact?"

"My mother hid me while she serviced the men to feed me, sir."

"Your mother hid you? For how long?"

"Most of my life, sir."

Tren released her chin. "Most of your... but where?" He could not disguise his surprise.

"In the sub-compartment of our dwelling."

Tren shook his head. It was no wonder the girl was so frail-minded. By nature, Tertani women needed to roam free. Though most had become civilized and somewhat settled over the epochs there was still an innate wildness in their blood. Caging one would be more than enough to fracture her spirit.

"Is your mother polluted?"

Bligh nodded.

Tren swallowed his disgust. All of the galaxy's inhabitants who knew they were infected with Brits Scorn were, by law of the Allegiance, required to report to the ISDS for placement in the Puratan colonies. Her mother had acted irresponsibly and that, he could not tolerate. How many men had she infected? She was a criminal and would be put to death for it.

"Where is she now?"

"Commander, if I may." Larimon stepped beside Bligh. "Her mother surrendered herself to us when she realized that we were her daughter's Sh'em. We turned her over to the ISDS."

"What about your fathers?" Tren asked Bligh.

There was no mistaking the fire that instantly lit in her eyes. If Bligh were a male, Tren might be a bit frightened.

"I hate them. They infected my mother and threw her aside. She raised me alone. If I ever find them, I will kill them."

Humph. Perhaps remnants of wild, female Tertian blood remained in her after all.

"And you are barren because of it?"

"Yes!" she hissed. "And for that I will torture them first!"

Admiring her pluck, Tren couldn't help but smile Yes,

she was a true-natured Tertani woman. Though it burned him that this Trigon would produce no children because of Brits Scorn, he could nearly admire Larimon and Bjead for still having desire for her. Tren could not honestly admit to the same, should his Tina turn out to be sterile.

No. His woman would bear children. Otherwise, there would be no reason for the Divinities to send him and Rjant to the outer galaxy to claim her as a mate.

"Take your Tina and go home." Tren heaved a heavy breath as he turned to make his leave. A discernable sigh of relief was expelled from the three of them in unison.

"Bjead, Larimon." Tren turned back.

"Yes, sir!" The two sentries snapped to attention.

"Your Triconjugal ceremony will not take place until after mine. I would be pleased to be one of your Prowlers."

"Yes, it would be an honor, sir," Bjead responded and Larimon nodded his agreement.

Chapter One

Earth: Present Day

"Can I borrow that sweater?"

Alea looked down at herself, then back to her roommate. "The one I'm wearing?"

"Yeah, I like the way it makes my breasts look."

Alea smirked and shook her head. Sometimes it wasn't easy living with Beth and her audacious spirit, always on the prowl for the ultimate lay. In Alea's eyes Beth was the sum of all Alea wished she could be--easy going, sociable, confident. Even Beth's unabashed promiscuity fascinated Alea. Not that she could picture herself engaging in one casual relationship after the other as Beth did, but it was her attitude about grasping all of life's pleasures while the chance was there that Alea admired.

"Don't you have an exam tomorrow?" Alea really couldn't fathom how Beth managed. She was a straight "A" student, another of her admirable assets, yet she seemed to barely put any effort into her studies, whereas Alea always had her nose in her textbooks--except when she was running. Working on her master's thesis and running on the university track team left little time for anything else, let alone socializing.

Running was the reason that Alea enrolled at the university. Recruited on a full sports scholarship, Alea had jumped at the opportunity to better herself.

"How do you do it?"

Beth turned from side to side examining her body in the full-length mirror, plumping her small, perky breasts and readjusting her thong underwear. "Do what?"

Alea pulled off her sweater and tossed it at Beth. It landed on the floor near her feet. "Party all night, sleep all day, yet you're graduating next month with full honors."

"Talent my dear, pure talent." Beth grinned and picked up

Alea's fuzzy pink sweater, right-sided it and slipped it over her trunk. She sauntered toward her dorm buddy and tsked. "You're so pretty, Alea."

Beth unabashedly scanned Alea's body, stopping to admire Alea's breasts. "And your boobs are so big and round." Her hands came up and she squeezed Alea's bosoms like she was testing a couple of melons at the grocery store.

Alea laughed and swatted at her roommate's hands. "I swear, Beth, if I wasn't so sure of your hankering for men, I would think you had a taste for women."

"Oh, I don't know." Beth strolled over to a chair in the corner, shook out a pair of jeans bunched on the seat, and put them on. She then plopped into the chair and threw a leg over one of the arms. "I might sleep with a woman some day."

Beth waggled her eyebrows at Alea. "Do you wanna have sex with me?"

"No." Alea pressed her lips into a smirk. She knew Beth was only teasing her.

"I give good head, so they tell me. A lickin' might do you some good."

Alea folded her arms across her chest and tapped her foot on the floor. "And what would you do if I said 'yes'?"

Beth squirmed in the chair. "Oh, baby."

"Change the subject, Beth."

"What's the matter? Am I making you uncomfortable?"

"No. I just don't feel like talking about my sexuality."

"You never do, but fine, I'll change the subject."

Beth refocused on Alea's breasts. "What do you do with your boobs when you're running? They always look so flat when you're on the track"

Ugh! Alea flopped backward onto the mattress. Not exactly a change in subjects. She and Beth had been rooming together for nearly six years and she'd wondered when Beth would get around to asking that question. "Easy, I bind them up."

"Ouch! Doesn't that hurt?"

"It just makes me run faster, work harder. No pain, no

gain you know. Besides, the faster I move, the quicker I can free them up."

Beth burst out laughing. "I know a few guys who would like to see that."

Alea smiled. She was used to Beth's bold ways. They were good friends despite their polar opposite personalities. When they first met, they liked each other immediately and their friendship was instantaneous.

"Hey, I have a great idea!"

Closing her eyes, Alea groaned. *Here it comes.*

"Why don't we hit the strip tonight and rid you of that pesky virginity you like so well?"

Alea propped up on her elbows and gave Beth the once over. The sweater did mold her breasts, giving her a plumped up, rounded look, sexy enough to arouse a eunuch.

"I'll pass, too much competition." She waved Beth off with the back of her hand.

Dropping to the floor, Beth began crawling around on her knees. She pulled a chunky-heeled, black leather ankle boot out from under the chair. She located its match between the mattresses of her bed. "Hmm, now how did that get there?"

She shrugged and rolled to her bottom to pull the boots onto her feet. She then stood and headed for the door. Beth spared a glance over her shoulder towards Alea. "Are you sure?"

"I'm sure. Go have fun. I'm just going to curl up with a book."

"Gag." Beth stuck her index finger in her mouth, feigning a choking sound. "Okay, but if you change your mind, you know where to find me."

The door slammed shut. Alea stared at the closed door for several seconds before finally getting up and locking it. She stripped off the rest of her clothes until she was down to nothing but her powder blue, lace, bikini panties. Her eyes scanned the books on a small unit above her bed's headboard until she found what she was looking for. Removing the book from the shelf, Alea traced the gold embossed letters on the drab green front cover with her finger--*Finding Your Spiritual Self.* The hard covered text looked expensive, but Alea really only paid a dollar for it at the Dollar Days store in the nearby plaza. The title alone was enough to deter her rowdy, college buddies. They wouldn't touch a book that reeked of religious fulfillment with a ten foot pole. It was a great hiding place.

It was why she bought it.

Alea pressed her lips into a smirk. *If only they knew.*

Indeed, if only. They would rush her off to the nearest swinger's club to get her laid. Not that *that* was anything new. Ever since her friends learned she was a virgin, they assigned themselves to the relentless task of getting her cherry popped. At age twenty-four, almost twenty-five, Alea was an oddity to her campus sisters. Her chastity was the target of much conversation, though Alea always offered the typical excuses.

I've just been too busy with my studies and running... the right guy just hasn't come along... no, I'm not a lesbian.

Karla, who lived in one of the dorm rooms just down the hall, badgered Alea constantly. *Just pick up some stud and let him stick it in you, Alea. It will be over before you know it. Don't be such a good girl.*

Alea wasn't a good girl. She liked men. She wanted to get laid, but she couldn't risk it.

Fear preserved Alea's virginity.

Not fear of the pain, or a broken heart, or some misguided notion that it should be saved for marriage. It was the fear of what she would become, what she might not be able to control once she surrendered. There was no way to make Karla, Beth, or any of her other friends understand, so she didn't bother to explain the truth.

Flipping the book open, Alea removed a CD, minus its plastic case, tucked inside of the pages. She tossed the book on the bed, and settled beneath the bedspread, her pillows plumped behind her, and her lap top perched on her thighs. She booted the computer and inserted the disc.

This book contains explicit sexual material intended for adult viewing only. All material contained is under copyright by....

Alea scrolled down. Her eyes roamed along the bodies of the two male forms displayed in the e-book's accompanying picture. Bare-chested, but clad in very tight jeans, they were both so profoundly gorgeous and sinewy that the picture made Alea's entire body ache with longing. She could almost see the muscles ripple with male, arrogant pride.

No one looks that good.

Alea's nipples stiffened as her eyes drifted to the woman caught up between them, looking as if she was being consumed with ecstasy. Her hips were tightly pressed against the groin of one male as he grasped her buttocks. Her back arched into the arms of the second male, his eyes staring with lust at two breasts that threatened to pop free from the low-cut shirt she wore. Alea's breath quickened as she stared at the picture and visualized the carnal pleasure they would give the woman. She loved a good picture on a book, resisting the general consensus that a book shouldn't be judged by its cover. The art on the cover was often what drew Alea's attention to the book, especially if it had two men on it--and one woman shared between them.

Unconsciously, Alea's hand came to her breast. She gently caressed it and plucked at her nipple before skimming her palm along her belly to dip beneath the elastic band of her panties. She found her clit and started pleasuring herself with a finger.

With her other hand, she scrolled further down the page until she came to the title. *Buy One Get One Free.*

Great title. Alea closed her eyes and arched up into her own hand, but settled back down as she rotated her index finger against her bud. She released a heavy breath and began to read, imagining herself as being the woman described in the pages of the book, realizing her need for a vibrator.

Thank goodness for women's erotic romance websites and plain package wrapping.

Without them, Alea didn't know where or how she would find release or delve into her fantasies. Contrary to her friends' beliefs, she ached for sexual stimulation and the penetration of a good, stiff cock.

Or two.

And therein lay Alea's secret. One that she told to nobody.

Alea's finger moved faster as she continued to read. After bringing herself to a mediocre climax--it was a poor substitute for the real thing she guessed--she abandoned her reading and slid her cherished CD back to its secure hiding place. She yawned and looked at the clock.

Was it midnight already?

Her classes started late in the afternoon the next day, so sleep wasn't an issue, but Alea wanted to get up early in the morning to run. Running was what she did best. She had been running all of her life, not just in the physical sense but mentally, as well, mostly out of fear of what she might become if she ever gave freedom to her desires--desires she kept covertly secluded within the safety of her mind, like the e-books she hid within the volumes of the pages.

At first, Alea thought that she might be frigid, and she despaired over that, not fully understanding why. She was attracted to some of the men she dated, but never aroused. Perhaps she was one of those girls who needed to be in love before giving her body freely. But as she matured, Alea came to realize that single men just did not turn her on.

Emphasis on *single*.

Not in the unmarried sense of the word, but as in *solo*-- one man, by himself--*alone*. She tried to deny it, but finally had to admit that her cravings went a step beyond those of other women. During her pubescent years, it spurred many late-night, sleepover talks that gave way to fantasies and lots of girlish giggles. Alea always remained aloof from those conversations, trying to sort through her own feelings, and what that meant to her future.

It was a startling discovery, reflected in so many ways on so many occasions, whenever Alea thought of the perfect relationship. *Double your pleasure, double your fun* was her private motto. At nightclubs, while her friends flirted with the available men, Alea had her own private brand of scrutinizing--in pairs. *I'll take that one... with... that one.*

Then there was the time that she and Beth rented the DVD *Tango and Cash* and they sat and watched it over a bottle of wine. They both drooled in open pleasure at the sight of the well-muscled, naked butts of Sylvester Stallone and Kurt Russell as they sauntered away from the shower. Alea nearly creamed her panties with that one. When Beth had commented that she would pay a little *cash* to do a *tango* with that pair, Alea strongly agreed. What she dared not admit to was that she could not imagine having one without the other--would not even be turned on. Men could only arouse her in the plural form. Oh, she wanted what every girl wanted, the white picket fence, children to care for, the love and adoration of two ravishing men.

Two?

Alea wasn't ashamed of her unusual need--well she was at first, until she learned to accept it, but she was also determined not to act upon her hidden passions. And so, Alea set her mind to a lifetime of chastity. Having sex was not even a consideration, lest she become like her mother.

Charlotte, Alea's mother was beautiful, that is, until a lifetime of abuse chipped away at her beauty. She had shimmering auburn hair with natural golden highlights, a tiny waist and slim but feminine hips, long sexy legs with just the right amount of muscle, and a firm round butt--a runner's body. Alea resembled her like a clone with the exception of Alea's much larger breasts--a trait she assumed was inherited from her father's side of the family--whoever that might be. She didn't know, and neither did her mother.

Her mother. She had probably been found dead in a gutter by now. Such a shameful loss of a stunning woman. Charlotte was a looker and could bed any man who tossed a glance her way, and she did--for money. Alea's mother was a prostitute--a slut, frowned on by society. But more than that, she was the worst kind of whore, one who was willing to peddle her daughter's wares, and began pressuring Alea to do so at the tender age of twelve. Because of that Alea was forced to run away, to escape from the dismal life that the streets offered and one that she wanted nothing to do with.

As luck would have it Alea was caught by the police, running away from the scene of her crime, packing a grilled hotdog that she'd stolen from a street vendor. She was hungry after all. She had to eat and would not peddle her body to feed her empty stomach. Alea was apprehended and taken into custody by social services. They placed her with the Miltons, a kind, old couple that fostered her until she came of age. Alea never looked back.

She didn't dare look back.

The Miltons died four years ago, within six months of each other, but Alea would never forget the love they shared, with each other and with her. She dreamed that someday she would find that kind of love, but resigned herself to the reality that it was likely never to be. One man would never please her enough to keep her satisfied, and she didn't want to lead some secret hedonistic lifestyle. And marrying two men, well, that was against the law. Besides, what two men on Earth would agree to such a thing?

Ignoring her unfulfilled urges, Alea sighed and turned off the light. She tossed and turned a few times before falling asleep.

Chapter Two

Hell.

She was living in hell, and nothing anyone said could convince Alea otherwise.

They came to her again last night, and their visits were becoming more frequent. Not that she thought they were real. It was just a dream.

If only it was *just* a dream. Alea was having a horrible time with the effect they had on her body this time. She couldn't shake it. Even after two cold showers.

This morning Alea awoke in the worst state of arousal feeling like a cat in heat--feeling like she could have humped the eighty year old janitor if she crossed paths with him in the hallway on her way to the track. She needed to get fucked.

She chose to run.

Alea pressed her feet harder into the track. Pushed herself to run faster. Something had to pound out her sexual frustration.

Running wasn't going to do.

She ran faster.

Her heartbeat raced and felt like it might burst. Yet, she urged her body to move along the track. The neurological response of opiates began filling her bloodstream--the runner's high--and then a soothing calm took over. She lost count of how many laps she'd done around the track.

Alea's mind began to wander to her younger years, to the nights long ago, remembering how the sounds of passion seeped to her bedroom from the room on the other side of the wall. Snuggled with her stuffed tiger and wrapped in her blankets, she would listen, as the laughter turned to moans of ecstasy and then to heavy breathing, and Charlotte would cry out her pleasure. Sometimes there would be one man and sometimes two, but the fact that her

mother enjoyed what she was doing did not escape Alea.
Her mother couldn't control her passions, and Alea had her
mother's genes.

It was the reason Alea fled the bar that night, about two
and half years ago--the night that reality reared its ugly
head.

Karla had fixed her up, and Alea relented to the idea of
giving up her hymen, convincing herself that it was merely
a piece of flesh separating the girl from womanhood. She
was twenty-two years old and it was time. Alea was tired of
waiting for the right man to come along and blow her
away. Obviously, it was never going to happen.

Dressed in her best hip hugging jeans and a tight midriff
top, Alea hit the bar scene, her cheering section of Beth,
Linda and Karla in tow. He was a friend of Karla's and a
hunk, to say the least, with neatly cropped sandy, brown
hair and a firm, athletic body--*funny Alea couldn't
remember his name.*

Alea sucked down two glasses of wine and let Karla
introduce them. Karla hung around until Alea and her
cherry picker had a comfortable conversation going, and
then quietly slipped away. Karla's friend smiled and
scanned her body, looking quite pleased with her, and then
he promised to fuck her silly. When she reminded him that
she was a virgin, Alea could swear his chest puffed up a bit,
as though he were letting her know that he was the right
man for the job. He tongue kissed her openly in the bar, as
he hugged her to his body, his hands roaming over every
inch of her. Alea actually liked his touch, finding a little
hope with that. Still, something was missing. Despite
enjoying his company, he was like the rest. Nothing in her
stirred.

He was one poker short of the fire.

And then his friend showed up. Her hormones went
berserk. Before she knew what was happening, Alea was
perched between them on the bar stool, taking turns kissing
and running her hands along both of them, as her stupefied,
but not totally discouraging friends watched.

You go girl. Beth whispered at one point, as she casually

brushed by.

Awareness hit Alea quickly, however, and she escaped before they took her to the nearest motel. She blamed it on too much wine and faulty genes. Alea swore off alcohol and men forever, threatening her friends to never speak about it or she would tell the entire campus about all of their dirty little secrets.

The dreams started shortly afterward.

There were two of them, of course. What wet dream would be of any good if it didn't tap into your fantasies?

It always began the same way with Alea being called from the darkness of her slumber by the ghostly images of two sets of hands forming the shape of a triangle they called the delta. They spoke incomprehensible words, though with each dream, it seemed Alea was able to understand them more and more. Although their characteristic features were indistinct, they radiated an essence so effectually potent that Alea was helpless to do anything but yield to whatever they wanted to do to her.

They touched her--light feathery touches that made her feel wantonly weak. They kissed her lips and her body, but they never undressed her or themselves, and still, it felt good--arousing. But they always faded before she could cum. Most mornings after, she would be horny, but a quick titillation in the bathroom would usually take care of that.

Last night was different. Their images were much more vivid--solid, instead of the ethereal figures they'd been before. She could actually feel their heated flesh and muscles flexing. She could feel their cocks, thick and hard as they stroked against her. They nearly drove her over the brink, licking at her pussy through the lace of her panties, suckling her breasts through her cotton top. She ground against them and they ground back. Four male hands worked at her until she was near bursting, and still, they didn't take off her clothes.

Please, Alea begged them and they chuckled back.

Ickqu--soon, they told her.

When? Tell me when.

Hucm ickqu--very soon.

And then they disappeared.

Waking almost immediately, Alea was drenched in sweat. Her heart was thumping, her nipples were erect, and her clit was throbbing like she had never felt it throb before. She nearly screamed in frustration, but she didn't want to wake Beth. She tried to give herself an orgasm, but she was so tightly coiled with sexual tension she couldn't even accomplish that task.

They did it on purpose. Something deep inside of Alea told her so.

Who was she kidding? She did it to herself. Even in her world of dreams, Alea's fears were denying her pleasure. She needed to get a grip.

She needed to stop reading those books!

Alea dug her heels into the dirt and began to slow her pace around the track, cooling herself down, as if that were possible. She was sweating and gulping air as she came to a stop. Her coach approached, holding a towel and a water bottle. Ignoring his offer, Alea instead bent forward, propping her hands on her knees, panting heavily.

"What's gotten into you?"

Nothing, that's the problem. "Why?" Alea gasped out.

"You beat your own time by a mile."

Still gulping, attempting to ease her hard breaths, Alea took the towel from her coach. She patted her brow and then draped the towel around her neck. Her legs started to quiver. Reaching for the water bottle, Alea took a small drink, swallowing hard.

"I guess I was a little motivated this morning."

"A little? I've never seen you run so fast, drive yourself so mercilessly. I swore you were going to run straight into another dimension."

Through her pants for air, Alea laughed. An alternate dimension where she could be free to explore her innermost desires was exactly what she needed. Perhaps that was where her dream lovers were from.

Alea stood upright and arched her back before ambling to the grass and dropping to her bottom. She could feel the beginning of shin splints straining at her lower legs.

"Call it quits for the day, Alea. Hit the showers."

"In a minute." She drew a long breath of air and blew it out quickly, swiping an arm across her sweaty forehead. She bent forward to massage her shins and calves. "I need to do some stretching."

"Well, I'm done for the morning. See you tomorrow."

"Sure thing, coach." Alea watched her coach leave and fell back to the grassy surface. She was unaware of the two pairs of eyes that watched her. And she did not hear the quiet groans incited by the sight of her knees falling apart as she lay in the grass.

After several minutes of catching her breath and calming her shaking muscles, Alea finally sat up, straightened her legs and stretched forward, reaching for her toes. A strange, pleasing scent floated through the air and tickled her nostrils. It was the same scent that taunted her last night and lingered in the air around her for most of the morning. It had to be her imagination--the result of being over-aroused and under-fulfilled. Alea wrinkled her nose and rubbed a finger against it. Ignoring the scent, she concentrated instead on the smell of the grass beneath her and the smell of her own sweat. She twisted and arched and bent, flexed and extended, finally losing herself in the blissful sensation of softening and loosening her aching muscles. Satisfied she was limber enough not to pull anything, Alea stood and walked to the bleachers to retrieve her duffel.

A slight movement at the curve of the track caught Alea's eye and she turned to look. *God help me.*

The most beautiful example of a man she had ever seen was standing there, staring at her with his lips curved up revealing a dazzling white smile. He was... perfect--tall, very tall, maybe six and half feet or more. His hair shimmered with a golden-yellow color, with hints of bronze intertwined. It was wavy and long, hanging just to his shoulders, and was such an unusual shade that Alea had to wonder if his carpet matched his drapes. He had thick biceps, rippling abdominals and narrow hips, supported by powerful thighs. His broad, muscular chest was bare except for a thick leather strap that crossed in front of him and then attached to a belt around his waist. There appeared to be some kind of stick sheathed at his back. He wore black leather pants that seemed so tight Alea thought they might burst.

She wished they would burst.

He was checking her out too. His gaze zigzagged along her body, stopping at her breasts and then finally fixating at her crotch. How could she blame him? Alea knew her shorts were clinging between her legs and outlining her labia--the result of running hard and spandex shorts too tight--*camel paw*.

It was there for all to see--for him to see, and he *was* looking.

His ogling didn't make Alea uncomfortable. She was staring at his crotch too, or at least she was, until she noticed his attention had gone elsewhere. Alea followed the path of his gaze across the track.

She gasped. There was another man standing there. He was dressed in a similar manner, looking at her and grinning. He was an equally extraordinary specimen. His brawny chest was dusted with black hair that looked so soft Alea's fingers itched to graze through it. His shoulders were broad, his hips were slim. He had a body so finely honed it said *lick me*.

He looked delicious.

His hair was even longer than the blonde's, hanging nearly to his waist. It was straight and thick and such a lustrous ebony, it reminded Alea of black satin sheets.

One blonde, one brunette and satin sheets. Now there was an interesting thought.

Considering what happened in her dream last night, this was much too overwhelming.

The rational side of Alea's brain rang a bell. Her libido refused to answer.

You're supposed to be celibate, dumb head.

I'm just looking. Now go away.

The two men locked gazes. Their hands formed the delta and they nodded. The dark one pulled a strap from a pocket in his pants and tied his hair back behind his head. Then, with long, heavy strides, they began stalking toward each other, looking like two wildcats ready to clash. They drew their weapons--long sticks, curved like an archery bow, with a wicked looking, pointed blade at one end and a glowing, green tip at the other. They met in the center of the track and then lunged at each other with the bows raised high. The dark-haired one struck first and the blonde parried, deflecting the advancing weapon with a mighty, overhead swing and the clatter of metal hitting metal.

Alea's mouth fell open at both the sight of the delta and their intense sparring, but with quick rationalization she deduced that they were part of some campus martial arts group. Yes, that had to be it. Alea had seen an exhibition at sometime, probably at the Renaissance fair she visited a few years back, and she integrated the delta into her nighttime musings. She might have even seen these guys before. There was something vaguely familiar about them.

With that thought settled, Alea relaxed and enjoyed the show.

* * * *

Rjant swung his talon arc low to the ground. *Ka! She's spectacular, Tren.*

Most spectacular, Tren agreed, springing off the ground with two feet as Rjant's blade passed below. *And did you see how fast she could run?*

Tren retaliated by swinging his talon arc at Rjant's head. Ducking, Rjant hooked his weapon behind Tren's knees, knocking him to his back. *It's going to be great fun tracking her during the hunt.*

Tren arched, thrust his hips and legs into the air and propelled himself to his feet, while simultaneously striking his talon at Rjant's chest. Rjant was ready and drove his weapon upward, halting Tren's attack with the end of his own talon arc.

That was impressive, Tren remarked.

Thank you.

Rjant pushed Tren back and in one sweeping motion, brought the blade of his weapon up toward Tren's groin. Tren blocked the blade with a downward thrust just before it made contact. He shot a laser sphere from the talon's opposite end. It whizzed by Rjant's left ear and the smell of burnt hair invaded his nose.

That was uncalled for, brethren.

Don't ever threaten my noogies.

They moved with swiftness making ground across the field, holding their weapons with two hands... one hand... striking and blocking, blade to blade, tip to tip... vertically, horizontally, overhead, sparring like they had something to prove.

And they did.

Like two proud peacocks swank with their plumes, Rjant and Tren were engaged in the *Flaunting*, an ancient Tertian dance, part of the Trigon Rituals, meant to demonstrate their masculine prowess--to pique the female's interest in them as her mates.

Alea was mewing her own peafowl cries of approval. She was doubly impressed, until that is, they crossed the field and came dangerously close to her with their blades swinging. She closed her eyes, frozen in place, and prayed they were as skilled as they looked. She could hear the weapons whirring and striking, to the left of her head, low near her right hip, in front, over her head.

Oh! Did a blade just pass between her legs?

There was one final clash and all movement stopped. Alea could hear nothing but heavy breathing. Slowly her eyes fluttered open and she found herself encircled between the elliptical shape created by the concaves of their weapons. One to the front and one to the back.

Now what? Alea wondered as she stared at the heaving chest of the dark-haired one in front of her.

Definitely tasty looking.

The blonde was behind her. She could feel his hot, panting breath on her neck. Maybe she should say something, like *thank you* and *please take me to bed.*

Celibate, pinhead.

Stuff a sock in it. I'm still only looking.

Lifting her hand, Alea ran her fingers along the curved weapon held level to her chest. The surface was warm, and it appeared to be made of some kind of smoky, gray metal. She examined it from end to end looking at the razor sharp blade where it lay athwart over the blade on the other weapon. She ran her hand along the curvature and down to the end with the glowing green tip. Alea touched it.

And got zapped!

"Ouch!" Alea reflexively yanked her hand away and cradled it against her chest. The blonde behind her chuckled, a rich, deep sound that caused Alea's breath to catch in her throat and to forget her hurting fingers.

"Uh…" Alea started awkwardly, "Nice rods, fellas."

Oh-my-God.

She did *not* really just say that, did she? Could she have said anything more stupid? Blushing profusely, Alea hoped they missed her double innuendo.

The dark one in front of her smirked, his eyes sparkled and his pupils dilated, letting her know that he'd heard her loud and clear. It was then that Alea noticed his eyes. They were such a beautiful turquoise color that Alea had to lean in for a closer look. *Wow!* The irises were rimmed with gold. She stared at them for several seconds before swinging around to look at the man behind her. His eyes were a stunning aqua shade, also rimmed in gold.

Alea blinked and brought her fingertips to her lips.

"Your eyes…" she gasped with astonishment.

No one on Earth had eyes like that. They had to be contact lenses.

"Tertian eyes, Tina." The dark-haired one leaned in and whispered in her ear. His silky voice slid along her senses. His accent was exotic and sexy.

Foreign exchange students from… where? Alea never heard of the place.

And who was this Tina?

Whoever she was, Tina was definitely a lucky, lucky girl. Alea made a mental note to find this Tina person and become her best friend at once. At least it explained why these guys were on the track. They thought she was someone else.

Alea would have to tell them… eventually.

"Rjant ot Pel'r." The blonde one sheathed his weapon, formed the delta and nodded.

"Nice to meet you." Alea held out her hand, assuming he was giving her his name, and not some foreign phrase. He cupped her hand between both of his own and took a step closer.

"Tren ot Dmor, Tina. I'm very pleased to be in your presence," the dark one said as he slid his hands along her hips and then down the front of her thighs. The one called Rjant released her hand, smoothed his palms against her shoulders and began grazing her body with his eyes. Before Alea could consider their actions, Rjant leaned his head toward her and brushed his lips against her mouth. He then pulled back and lifted his hands to cradle her head, his thumbs caressing her cheeks, while the one called Tren nuzzled his face against her neck from behind.

Somewhere from deep inside her brain's pleasure center, Alea heard the mating cry of *hubba hubba*.

Times two.

Her heartbeat also chimed in with a heavy pounding of *thumpity, thump, thump, thump... thump.*

_Times one hundred... *and two.*

She inhaled deeply in an attempt to calm herself and was assaulted with the blending scent of virile masculinity and sensuous heat that radiated from their flesh. An olfactory explosion erupted in her brain sending a riptide of tremors dancing along her spine. It was intoxicating. She could become addicted to that scent. She could become addicted to *them*.

"Interesting fragrance, guys. What's it called?" It was the same fragrance that teased her all morning. They must have been visiting in the dorm last night and the smell of their cologne lingered.

Rjant leaned forward again and pressed his lips to her ear. "Pheromones."

Alea gulped. She knew what those were. Probably had a few herself.

"Come with us, Tina," Tren said.

It didn't sound like a request. It sounded more like a

summoning.

I'd love to. Alea was silently amused by the hidden meaning, but her amusement was quickly replaced with concern. She was losing herself--losing control. Alea wasn't just looking anymore, she was feeling... feeling....

...feeling like she'd better get out there and fast!

This was getting way too weird. Who were these guys?

She's getting edgy. Rjant sent the thought to Tren.

Yes, I know.

Despite the fact that Alea's hormones were beating her mindless, a wave of uneasiness spread through her. Had she lost her marbles? These guys might be crazy, or part of a cult, or something. What if they wanted to hurt her? Alea knew she had to get away from them, but she was trapped between their bodies--*sandwiched.*

Stay calm, Alea. Keep talking and then run, she told herself.

"It was, uh... nice meeting you guys, but my name isn't Tina and I really have to go."

She's going to bolt. Rjant sent the thought to Tren

She won't get away. Keep her talking, Tren answered mentally.

"Did you enjoy the Flaunting, Tina?" Rjant asked her.

Flaunting? That was a good name for it. At least they admitted to showing off.

"Uh, yes. It was... interesting." Alea forced her feet to move and she stepped out sideways and away from them. They watched her closely.

Get ready, brethren, Tren said silently.

"So," Alea said, watching them just as closely in return. She began backing away. "Why do you call it the Flaunting?"

Did she really want to know?

They separated and started circling her. This wasn't good. Alea felt like trapped prey, ready to be pounced on.

"It is meant to entice our mate."

"Really?" She tried to appear composed. "And who is it exactly, you intend to mate with?"

"You."

Alea leapt toward an open space, but they came together swiftly, pressing her between their bodies again causing air to expel from her lungs.

It didn't hurt.

Rjant was behind her now. He swiftly wrapped his arms around her ribs and pinned her to his body. Tren grasped her wrists, imprisoned them with one hand and then he stepped on her feet.

Her friggin' feet, for God's sake!

It worked. She couldn't move. It was amazing how well they seemed to work together, a thought intriguing enough to explore further, if Alea wasn't so scared at the moment.

Scream, Alea!

She opened her mouth and let it fly.

Tren pressed a red stone on his belt. "*Critais,*" he said.

Transport.

A peculiar vibration surged through Alea and an out-of-sorts feeling came over her. Blood rushed to her ears as the ground beneath her feet dropped out and she was falling. Her vision faded to black.

Chapter Three

Alea was still screaming when something solid slammed against her soles. With a heavy *oomph* her scream was silenced. Her knees gave out and Tren caught her.

Thank the falling stars she stopped that bedamned screeching. I think my eardrums have blown out. Rjant stuck his pinky in his ear and wiggled it around.

"Are you alright, Tina?"

"I'm okay!" Alea snapped, immediately realizing she was hugging Tren's chest, her cheek resting against his pec muscle. It twitched against her face. Startled, Alea jumped back, lost her balance and was caught by Rjant who was still behind her.

"Is it hot in here?" She pulled free, only to lose her balance again.

Not wanting to feel like a ping pong ball she tensed, stiffening every muscle that was willing to fire, and fought to gain her equilibrium. She found the nearest wall instead, braced her arms against it and dropped her head, resting it atop her overlapping forearms. Her eyes examined the floor. *Tiles.* The floor was made of small tiles. She closed her eyes and took a few deep breaths.

I'm in the locker room. I ran too hard and then these guys showed up. I must have fainted and they carried me into the shower to revive me.

Alea opened her eyes.

It wasn't tiles, but a grid of some sort, and there were colored lights blinking through it. Alea's head snapped up. Spinning around, she plastered herself against the wall, arms outspread, fingers splayed. She was *not* in the locker room's shower stall.

"Where am I?"

"In the transport room," Tren answered her.

"Transport room?"

"Yes. We couldn't land without being detected. It was safer to transport."

"Land what?"

"Our vessel, the *Stardancer*," Rjant said.

"I'm on a boat?" Well, that would explain the rocking in her head.

"Not a boat, a space cruiser."

"Huh? R-i-g-h-t." Alea elongated the word, as she spoke, nodding slowly and looking at them as if they were out of their minds. Hers eyes darted around the room until she found what looked like a door. She had to get out of there. These guys were nuts!

Lifting a hand, Tren ran his knuckles along Alea's cheek. "I'm sorry if the transporting made you feel ill."

Alea pushed at his hand and moved away, but the small size of the room put her in closer proximity to Rjant.

Rjant crooked a finger under her chin. "Do you need to lie down, Tina?"

"No, I don't want to lie down, and my name is not Tina." Alea inhaled and tried to stay calm. She was starting to get irritated. "You have the wrong woman."

"We think not." Rjant reached behind her and pulled the rubber band from Alea's hair, freeing her ponytail. He started combing through it with his fingers, spreading it around her shoulders. Alea started to tremble, half from his heated touch, half out of fear. Her eyes swung towards the door again.

No doorknob.

Alea slid away from Rjant, moving along the wall and closer to the door. "What do you want from me?"

"We told you, Tina. To mate," Tren answered and then he smirked. He was amused by her obvious attempt to escape. The Tina Alea was proving to be a fine example of a Tertani female, always trying to run from her mates.

The door was just behind her now. Reaching back discreetly, Alea tried to find a latch. "Mate… as in sex… with both of you?"

Her mind said *yeah baby!* but her mouth said. "I don't think so."

Just because she fantasized about this for most of her life, she couldn't be expected to just go ahead and do it.

"Not just sex, Tina, bonding."

"Like in vows… tie the knot… marriage?"

Rjant nodded.

"Look, I don't care how gorgeous the two of you are…."

She thinks we're gorgeous, Rjant. Tren burst into a beaming smile.

"I…" Alea's mouth snapped shut when Tren smiled at her. *Goodness, he's sexy.* She furled her brow. "What was I saying?"

"You were saying we're gorgeous." In one long stride Rjant was in front of her. He grasped her around her waist, pulled her close and lowered his head, plying his lips against hers until she stopped resisting and she opened her mouth to him. He slid his tongue inside and kissed her hard, as he turned her away from the door. Tren pressed up against her back. Both of his hands slid to her belly and then he slipped one hand between her legs. Through the spandex of her shorts, he ran his fingers along her labia, found her clit and started stroking it. Rjant released her lips and kissed her neck, moving lower to her breast, while Tren continued to rub her clit with his finger. His other hand meandered up her body until he reached her face. He grasped Alea's chin and tipped her head back. Tren's mouth found hers, and he nibbled her lips, licked them, thrust his tongue fully inside of her mouth.

Mother of stars, she tastes sweet!

I'll go mad before we're allowed to have her. Rjant slipped his hands under Alea's sports top.

Easy, brethren, Tren warned.

I'm not touching her flesh, just trying to find her breasts.

What?

She's got them squashed in something and I want to play with them.

Rjant found the Velcro fastening the tight cloth that held Alea's breasts bound and pulled it apart. He yanked the binder from her chest, dropped it to the floor and groaned as her breasts sprang free. But keeping to the dictates of the

Edification that her clothing not be removed, Rjant straightened Alea's top to cover her, and kneaded her breast through the cloth.

Alea was weakening with desire and the carnal scent from two men intent on giving her pleasure. She let her mind go and began to succumb to the orgasmic sensations that were beginning to bubble inside of her.

And then she started to panic. "Stop! Let me go!"

They both released her immediately.

"Don't you want to cum, Tina?" Rjant asked.

"Yes! No! You've kidnapped me!" This was getting confusing and very, very weird.

"Not kidnapped, Tina--claimed." Tren took a step toward her and Alea took a step back.

"I told you my name is not Tina! Now take me home, damn it!" Alea turned toward the door and dug her fingers at the seam near the frame, frantically trying to pull it open. It didn't budge.

"Help! Help! Help!" She pounded her fists against the door. "I'm being held hostage by two sex maniacs!"

God help her, she wanted them to fuck her. She had to run away.

She's going to pop a circuit, Tren.

"Calm down, Alea. We're not going to hurt you."

Alea stopped pounding on the door and turned to face Tren. "H-how did you know my name?"

Tren responded. "You told us your name."

"I-I did? Then why do you keep calling me Tina?"

"It's the Tertian word for untouched--a virgin." Rjant grinned. Alea did not miss his quick glance to the area between her legs. "You've heard the word before."

"I'm not a virgin!" Alea blurted, ignoring his last comment. If it was a virgin they wanted and she wasn't one, then maybe they would let her go.

Rjant's grin widened. "Liar."

Alea opened her mouth to protest, but was interrupted by a voice coming from a swirling, silver pattern inside a circlet, set within the wall.

"Commander."

"What is it, Calem?" Tren asked.

"Is the door to the transporter stuck?"

"No. Why?"

"Well, sir, you've been in there for a half a dial. We're awaiting orders."

"We're having a discussion with the Tina Alea," Rjant answered. "We'll be on the bridge shortly"

"Sir, I think it might be better if you come now. The Earthling satellites have detected us."

"Very well, Ensign, prepare to leave orbit."

The conversation between the voice and her two captors threaded through Alea's ears, foreign words, some of which she was able to understand.

How was that possible? She didn't know a second language.

Tren took Alea's hand. "Let's go, Alea. I don't think you'll want to miss your first trip through space."

Rjant pressed his hand against a bright yellow tile near the door. It illuminated and the door slid open.

Taking note of the door's mechanics, Alea stored it for later use. She said nothing as they led her through a series of corridors. Alea examined them carefully attempting to map their directions and a possible escape route. They reached what looked like two large, main doors. Again, Rjant pressed a yellow tile and the doors separated.

The first thing Alea noticed was the large window across the room. She was overcome with a surrealistic sight of outer space and the Earth at the uppermost, left corner. It was a scene right out of the Discovery Channel, but this looked much too three-dimensional to be just a TV screen. There was a bustling of activity inside the room. Several men were scampering around, all clad in the same clothing--uniforms--a few of them tossing glances her way.

Rjant and Tren seemed to be giving orders. Foreign words were coming from their mouths again, and as before Alea was able to decipher a few of them. It disturbed her that she didn't know why.

Tren approached and led Alea by the elbow to a chair at the far end of the bridge. She sat down without looking at

him. Her attention was on the blinking consoles and hands
that worked the controls with purposeful intent. Alea
shifted her gaze to the window again. There was a slight
swaying motion in the hull as they turned away from the
Earth. She heard a low pitched whirring, like the sound of
an engine being powered and felt a mild rush as the stars
they were now facing began to flash by. Closing her eyes,
Alea tried to swallow the reality that this was actually
happening. She was in outer space on an alien spaceship.

Alea was oddly calm about it, or perhaps she was just in
shock. Whichever was the case, the fact remained that there
was nothing she could do to change it, at least for now.

Do you think she's okay, Tren? Rjant looked down at her.

I don't know. She looks a little green, Tren answered.

Rjant drew his brows together. *She hasn't said a word
since we left the transport room.*

*Take her to the observation deck, Rjant. It's a bit less
hectic there.*

Yes, a much better place to enjoy the stars. Rjant agreed.

Furling her brows, Alea watched their unspoken
exchange. Rjant and Tren stood in front of her, but were
facing and staring at each other. Tren nodded, they both
gave her a worried glance, and then looked back to each
other again. Still, they didn't say anything. Rjant nodded
this time and turned to Alea, offering her his hand. Alea
glanced at his hand and then her chin went up a notch.

*Who do they think they are, snatching me from Earth
without even so much as considering whether or not I
wanted to leave?*

Alea decided right then and there that she would not give
them the satisfaction of thinking they could just do what
they liked to her. She stood, turned her back to them and
walked toward the double doors leading from the bridge.

Rjant caught up to Alea as she located and tapped the
square, yellow switch. She frowned when the door didn't
move.

"It isn't yet programmed to your touch identity, Alea." He
reached over her shoulder and activated the control plate.
The doors opened.

Alea flashed what could not be interpreted as anything else but a dirty look.

Rjant smiled at her. He liked her spunk.

A myriad of thoughts began whirling in Alea's brain as she followed Rjant through the corridors. She had a track meet in the morning... her finals were next week. Beth would be worried when she didn't come home. Alea was in outer space with two hot looking aliens who wanted to make love to her, who wanted to marry her, something she thought she would never have--especially the space alien part. Alea shook away the thought. She couldn't consider it right now. There were too many years of denial and avoidance tucked under her belt for Alea to believe it could be any other way.

Alea looked around the room that Rjant brought her to. There was a window on one wall, smaller than the one on the bridge, but still large enough to offer a nice view of the stars. Walking up to it, she stared out at the universe. It really was a breathtaking sight to behold.

Removing his baldric, Rjant hooked it over a knob on the wall. Alea looked over her shoulder to see what he was doing and watched as he moved toward a sideboard in the room. He tapped what appeared to be a code in a panel attached to the edge of it, and the surface, which looked like a tempered, cobalt glass, began to shimmer. A holographic image of two urn-shaped cups appeared and then materialized. Rjant picked them both up and offered one to Alea.

"Amazing," Alea whispered, accepting the cup from him. She stared at the sparkling, pink liquid inside. It looked like a wine cooler.

"It's called taw, comparable to your Earth water."

Swirling the liquid around, Alea ewatched the little bubbles in it pop. She sniffed it and found that it was odorless. *What if their food is poisonous to me?*

Alea set the cup down.

"Don't be afraid of us, Tina." Rjant took a sip from his own cup and then set it aside. He attempted to take Alea's hand, but she stepped back and turned around. She paced a few steps away from him before stopping.

"How can you say that to me?"

She turned to face him. Irritation began tickling at her emotions. "How can you expect me not to be afraid when I'm on a spaceship heading for a planet I didn't even know existed with aliens I've never met before?"

Her voice rose an octave as her temper threatened its way to the surface. She stepped closer to him. "How can you ask me to accept this, when you gave me no choice in the first place?"

Alea searched Rjant's face. "How can you...?"

Leaning in for a closer look, she noticed for the first time, the absence of aging lines on his smooth face. "How...?"

Alea tilted her head sideways, momentarily forgetting her train of thought. "How the heck old are you?"

Alea knew Tren was older, more mature. She'd spent a lengthy time studying him while encircled between their weapons when they were on the track. But Rjant--he looked so young.

"Nineteen phases, Alea. Almost twenty."

"Nineteen phases? Like in years?"

"It's comparable."

Alea's eyebrows lifted.

"Pft..." She waved a hand in the air. "I can't have sex with you."

"And why not?"

His expression told Alea she had offended him.

So what?

She wasn't done with her hissy fit yet, hadn't even gotten started. She wasn't done rebelling against what he and Tren were proposing.

"You're just a kid."

"I assure you I am not a child."

"Yes... you *are*."

Rjant's nostrils flared at her condescending tone.

"I assure you, *Tina*," he emphasized the word. "I have seen and done more in my short phases than you will ever experience during the entire span of yours."

"Hog wash! What could you possibly know about love

and satisfaction and pleasing a woman? Hah! You're barely grown up."

Rjant clenched his teeth and fisted his palms.

Alea didn't care that he was angry, she was on a roll. "In fact, it's so fucking obvious that you're ill-equipped and so ill-acquainted with the female body that you need Tren to help you do it!"

Uh oh.

Alea realized immediately that she stepped over the line. Rjant was furious and she was playing with fire. She had no idea how a Tertani male would react to being provoked and she most certainly had just done that.

Rjant rushed toward Alea and she scurried backwards until her legs hit the backless sofa that was in the room. Arching over her, he tumbled her onto the cushion, following her down and pressing his body on top of hers. His lips crashed down, forced her mouth to open and he kissed her like a hungry savage. At first Alea tensed, ready to fight, but something was happening to her senses. She was being kissed into a stupor. Her body softened, she reached up to lace her fingers through his hair and started kissing him back.

Rjant broke the kiss, and for a moment, Alea just laid there, her lips tingling, her mind absent of any lucid thought. Moving off of her, Rjant sat back on his haunches. He grabbed her ankles and pushed at her legs, causing them to bend at the knees. He then slapped her feet onto the seat cushion.

Alea's eyes fluttered open. "What are you doing?"

"Getting acquainted with my ill equipment… and yours." Rjant pushed against the inside of her knees and splayed her legs open, as he climbed over her.

He lowered his hips, settling them between her thighs.

With a long, slow stroke, he brushed his groin with her crotch and then pressed against her. Alea felt his cock thicken and lengthen, and her vagina flooded instantly. She sucked in a breath, held it for a moment and then released it slowly. It didn't matter that she still had her running shorts on, or that he was clothed. The effect Rjant was having on her wouldn't have been any more intensified if they were wearing nothing at all.

It gave Alea reason to reconsider the value of a dry hump.

Rjant stared down at Alea, watching the reaction on her face. Her mouth parting, her eyes glazing over, and then Alea moaned--a soft, feminine cry that let him know he was giving his Tina exactly what she needed. He stroked against her again, struggling not to lose himself as ripples of immense pleasure roared up his spine.

Alea felt the quickening between her legs first and it surged through her body. Her climax was building, swelling, consuming her. She tipped up her pelvis needing more pressure and then, yes, he was there, thrusting, teasing, coaxing her to the brink.

But just as the edge of ecstasy began to reach her, Rjant lifted away from her, denying Alea what she needed to drive her home. "It's not proper that you have your first climax without Tren present."

He shuddered as he stood, attempting to shake down his own arousal.

"You bastard," Alea gasped out angrily. Her body was trembling wildly. He had broken her control. But that's not why Alea was upset. She was angry because he left her dangling and aching with need.

Alea trembled a few more times and then her body went as limp as a wet noodle. Tren entered the room and his gaze fell to Alea. She was sagging face up on the bench, arms and legs falling over the edge on either side, watching him through lust-hazed eyes.

I appreciate your consideration, Rjant. Tren lifted his hand and rested it atop Rjant's shoulder. *I came as soon as I could.*

You heard.

Tren nodded. *Every word she said, you repeated in your mind. I received it all and then I felt it all.*

She questioned my manhood.

Yes.

"Since the two of you are so fond of staring at one another, why don't you just fuck each other and leave me the hell out of it!" Alea was standing now, somewhat recomposed, arms folded across her chest, and foot tapping.

Rjant rolled his eyes. *She's still in a mood.*

I think, brethren, that you're responsible for some of that.

Well, at least I didn't frighten her.

_"We're not staring, Alea. Rjant and I are of one mind. Linked."

Alea contemplated Tren's words for a moment and then her eyes widened. "Telepathy? Everyone here reads minds?"

She brought her hand to her mouth, mortified as a nun in a porn shop, as she quickly reviewed every thought she'd had that day. "Are you reading my mind?"

"No, Tina." Tren removed his baldric and hung it next to Rjant's. He then walked over to a circlet on the wall identical to the one in the transporter room, and waved his palm across the smooth, silver background. It began to swirl.

"*Uyo cledal*--Yes, sir?" A voice projected from it.

"*Ta het wiev aspec. Tond therob su*--We're in the observatory. See that we are not disturbed."

"Yes, sir."

Alea listened silently, understanding some of the words. She watched as Tren approached her. He took her hands and urged her to sit down on the sofa.

"The link is a gift bestowed on the males when called to the Trigon. It's strengthened during transdelta meditation, when it is time to find our mate," he said as he sat down beside her. Rjant joined them, sitting on Alea's other side.

"But why me? Why not someone from your own race?"

"The Trigon is as a much a spiritual joining as it is a physical one, Alea. The Mahatma Divinities found us a compatible female."

Tren lifted a hand forming half of a triangle with his fingers and thumb. Rjant met Tren's fingers, forming the identical, opposite pattern with his own hand. Their thumbs and fingertips touched forming a full triangular pattern, and the transdelta link was initiated.

"They brought us to you," Rjant said leaning over her

shoulder and pressing his cheek against hers.

Alea blinked a few times and then she became drowsy. Her eyes drifted shut and she started to fall asleep. They were there, in her mind's eye, Rjant and Tren, hands caressing her body, her sexual senses awakening, responding. She lifted her lids and fixed her gaze on Tren's eyes--exotic turquoise irises rimmed in gold. She turned her head to look at Rjant and was met by his alluring aqua irises rimmed in gold--alien eyes.

Ethereal eyes.

Familiar eyes!

Alea's mouth dropped open and her mind began to race--the delta, being taught their language, the feel of their touch--it all came crashing together like two trains speeding toward each other on the same rail.

Alea gasped. "I know who you are."

Chapter Four

"Come here, Alea."

"No." Alea looked at Tren for a moment and then continued her pacing. "And stay out of my head!"

Tren and Rjant watched her, their heads turning back and forth in unison, following her movements like spectators at a tennis match.

Rjant finally shook his head and then rubbed his brow. "It's part of the Edification, Alea, a way to make our presence known to you. And dreamless sleep is a time when the female is most responsive."

"Once we've breached you," Tren added, "we will no longer have that particular gift."

This is not the reaction I expected, brethren. Rjant scratched the back of his head.

I know. I thought she might be upset, but I expected fear, not anger.

Yes, instead she spits at us like a viper, ready to strike at any moment.

Tren chuckled mentally. *Like a true-blooded Tertuni woman.*

I think I'm in love. Rjant sighed.

"You're doing it again." Alea stopped her pacing and narrowed her eyes at them.

"Doing what?" Rjant asked.

Alea threw her hands in the air. "Talking behind my back."

"It's a natural thing for us. It can't be helped," Tren answered.

"Oh, there is nothing natural about any of this." Alea shook her head from side to side. "At least not on Earth."

Tren rose from the bench and stood in front of her. His hands came up and he grasped her by the hips. "You are no longer on Earth, Tina Alea." Yanking her toward him, Tren thrust his groin upward and against her mound before wedging his thigh between her legs.

Alea's senses were immediately assaulted by a wave of unsolicited desire, and her head dropped back. She groaned and began rubbing against his leg. Startled by her own untamed reaction, Alea jumped back, and turned away, walking right into Rjant's arms. His hands came up to cup her face. "We are Tertani warriors, called to the Trigon, and you are our mate." His mouth came down to hers, his tongue licking at the crease of her lips before delving within, plying her mouth until it softened and melded with his own. His hands swept around her, flattening her against him, holding her prisoner within his embrace.

Alea's libido went into overdrive and she nearly cried out for them to take her. She couldn't believe how horny she was getting and how bad the urge was to spread her legs.

No.

It was too much.

Their effect on her was bewildering and she didn't know how to handle it. Alea wasn't afraid, not of them--not really. She truly believed they wouldn't hurt her. She just didn't know how to let go, to break through the solid barrier she'd built between her desires and finding ecstasy.

Alea pushed Rjant away from her. "Good lord! Do you two walk around like that all day?"

"Like what?"

"With… with… with hard-ons." Alea waved her hands at their crotches.

Tren smiled arrogantly. "I don't have a hard on, as you call it, Alea… *yet.*"

I do. Rjant rubbed his groin, a painful expression on his face. Tren suppressed a grin, thankful that their jittery Tina hadn't seen that.

Alea gulped at Tren's words, and then, she couldn't believe it, she actually blushed. It was a little belated considering what they had been doing to her since bringing her on board their ship.

"Charming." Tren's eyes sparkled at Alea's sudden shyness. He brushed a knuckle along her cheek. "We're playing with you, Tina. Not trying to upset you." He moved back, leaned casually against the wall and crossed his arms.

"Yeah, like a cat playing with its food before moving in for the kill."

"Mmm. I like to *lick* my food before I eat it." Rjant craned his head and licked Alea under the chin before suckling at her throat.

"Stop it!" Alea jerked away. She raked her hands through her hair. "You're passing me back and forth like a football."

"A foot what?" Rjant asked.

"Oh, never mind." Alea started pacing again. Her emotions were riding her like an out of control roller coaster. She was horny. She was afraid. She was angry. She was calm. Alea couldn't take it anymore.

Run, Alea, her sensibilities screamed. *Run away and hide.*

"You have to take me home. You just have to." Alea's eyes misted. *For the love of Pete! Tears now?*

Rjant furled his brow at her tears. *We've overwhelmed her, Tren.*

Give her breathing space, brethren.

It was ordinary behavior for Trigon males to be aggressive with their She'mana, but Alea was a still a Tina, and she was not a Tertani female. The last thing Tren wanted was to see her become hysterical. This would be her first physical encounter with her future Sh'em and he wanted it to be pleasurable for her. They had to treat her with special care.

Rjant agreed and strolled over to the bench. He stretched out on his side and propped his head in his hand. "Why do you want to go home, Alea?"

His casual posture belied his true feelings. He was worried. What had he and Tren taken her away from to make her want to return so badly? A mother perhaps? He didn't like the idea of hurting her.

"I…" Alea began. *What was so important that she had to return home? Was it running?*

Nah. Running was and ingrained part of her character and she did love to run, but she could do that anywhere. *Was it the competition?* It wasn't that either. In fact, Alea hated competing. It was too stressful. She was always nauseous before a meet and only did it because of the scholarship.

She snapped her fingers. "My degree."

Yes, that was it.

"I'm supposed to graduate next month and I don't want to miss it."

"What's a degree?" Tren asked her.

"It's like an award you get for a special area of study. The degree says you are qualified to work in a specific field and maybe become successful in life."

"And what degree of special study will you obtain, Alea?" Rjant sat up looking genuinely interested.

Alea smiled, relaxing a little. Talking about school was making her feel grounded, a bit more stable emotionally. "Philosophy. My degree is in philosophy."

"Feel-us-offy? I have to admit I like the sound of that." Rjant grinned back at her, admiring Alea's smile. It was soft and warm and inviting--*lickable*.

"Philosophy." Alea laughed at his pronunciation and more of her tension drained. She walked over to the glass of *taw* and took a sip. Alea didn't realize how dry her mouth and throat were until she swallowed the liquid. It was soothing and Rjant was right. *Taw* was very similar to Earth water, except it felt lighter in her mouth and had a crisper taste. She took another large swallow before setting the cup aside.

Tren moved over to where Rjant was and sat down. "Sit with us, Tina. We won't do anything you don't want us to do."

Alea's gaze shifted between Rjant and Tren as they patiently waited for her to make the next move. She closed her eyes, wanting very much to be near them--between them.

One step at a time. She took one step toward them and then another, until she was there and sitting in the space they left for her, Tren on her right and Rjant on her left.

"What will you do with this degree, Alea?" Rjant asked.

That was a good question, and she could not answer it.

Alea figured she would graduate from college and get an apartment and a job. Beth was moving to New York to pursue a writing career and hopefully produce screenplays. She and Alea would email, maybe visit every now and then, until the long distance friendship became more of a pain in the ass than a pleasure, and they slowly stopped keeping in touch. Beyond that, Alea really had no other plans.

"I have no idea, but that's not the point."

What was the point?

"The point is," she continued after a short pause, holding up a finger. "I earned my diploma. I should be allowed to receive it and now you've taken that opportunity away from me."

"Is this degree really so important?" Rjant leaned forward, resting his chin on her shoulder. Alea started to tense, but forced herself to relax.

It was just his chin after all, affectionate, not sexual. Not so bad.

And *no*, the degree actually wasn't that important. Alea went to the university to run for the team, mostly because the scholarship provided a place for her to live and bought her time to figure out what she was going to do with the rest of her life. Loans, thousands of dollars in loans, took care of the rest of her keep--loans she would eventually have to pay back with whatever little money she earned.

"If we take you home and you get this degree, will it make you happy, Tina?" Tren studied her face as he smoothed his hands up and down her arms. He could tell by her forlorn expression what her answer would be, realizing she had not mentioned any significant someone that might make her want to return to her Earth. It saddened Tren to think she was alone on her world.

Have you lost your rockets, Tren?

She's not going anywhere, Rjant.

"No, not really." Alea whispered, admitting and accepting the truth. "There's nothing for me there."

"Stay here with us, Tina." Tren's lips touched her cheek. At the same time Alea felt Rjant's hands grazing her thighs.

But this time, instead of fretting over it, Alea willed away the urge to run and settled back into Rjant's arms. Her breathing deepened and a yearning assailed her. Their touch was familiar to her. For two years they'd primed Alea for this moment. Through the intimate path of her subconscious sleep, they gently coaxed her trust, slowly increased her level of comfort with being in their presence. Her response to them had grown to be a natural thing-- instinctive.

Accepting.

Alea realized there was something special about Rjant and Tren. They could each stimulate her sexually, one without the other. She didn't need them both together to awaken her lust, yet here they were offering themselves as one package.

Just the way she liked it--the way she'd always wanted it.

She had nothing to lose and everything to gain.

"Let us make you happy," Rjant said, wrapping his arms around her.

Tipping her head back, Alea looked into Rjant's captivating eyes. She saw nothing but sincerity there. "Yes, yes, I'll stay."

Her gaze shifted to Tren and he smiled, leaning forward to kiss her mouth, a tender peck at first, but then his kiss deepened. Alea responded immediately, molding her lips to Tren's, kissing him back. Rjant massaged her thighs, slowly easing them open. His hands moved higher until his fingers grazed her clit and he strummed his fingertips over it. Alea's female muscles clenched. Heat and then moisture flooded her pussy.

"No, wait, not yet." Alea turned her head away from Tren's kisses, her voice husky with her rising arousal. "I need answers first."

Tren craned his head back and looked at her. When first he'd seen Alea he thought she was pretty, but now here in their arms, hints of passion glowing on her face, Tren thought she was beautiful. "This first, Alea. Answers later. We've waited too long to do this for you and you've waited too long for it to happen."

Alea angled her head to look at Rjant and then turned back to Tren. "No sex right now."

"No penetration, Tina. Not this dawning. Not for awhile." Tren moved further back on the bench, pulling Alea toward him, splaying her legs until she was seated on his lap, straddling and facing him.

Rjant straddled Alea from behind. His hands held her hips, slowly rocking her, rubbing her pussy against Tren's sex. He stroked his own cock against her bottom in a smooth, even rhythm. "We'll only give you as much pleasure as you wish, Tina."

He nuzzled against her neck and then nibbled at her earlobe. His warm breath feathered along the shell of her ear sending a shiver down her spine. Tren rotated his pelvis, helping Alea find her tempo until they were all pumping and grinding against each other, moaning in an orgy of pleasure as their orgasms started to build. Tren's hand molded around Alea's left breast and he teased her nipple through her top with his thumb until it budded and stiffened. He brought his head forward and drew her nipple into his mouth and began sucking on it. Rjant massaged her right breast, stroking the nipple with the palm of his hand and then rolling it between his thumb and forefinger.

Alea was crooning, beginning the climb to her carnal summit until there was no turning back. Tren's scent and then Rjant's seeped into her nostrils, separate at first, and then mingling. Alea inhaled deeply, her arousal surging from the blended, ardently male bouquet taking root in her brain--branding her with their pheromones so that she would crave only them.

Rjant stroked harder, his breathing grew heavy and quicker. Alea moaned, pumping faster. Tren threw back his head and groaned as his ejaculation burst forth. Alea cried out her climax riding on the sensations from Tren's pulsating cock and Rjant's hard thrusts behind her, and then Rjant too, was grunting out his orgasm.

Tren fell back onto the sofa. Alea collapsed on his chest, and Rjant fell on top of both of them, all three panting and shuddering until the waves of their passion began to recede.

"So," Alea finally said after her breathing settled and her heartbeat returned to a more stable pace. "How long have the two of you been together?"

"We came together just for you, Alea," Rjant responded, kissing the back of her neck and working his way down her spine to the small of her back. "No pun intended."

Chapter Five

Alea never cared much for green gelatin, but here she was, staring at a plate of what was supposed to be her meal, praying it wasn't the innards of some alien creature she'd never heard of. Alea pushed the little, green cubes around her plate, with her spork, while listening and deciphering bits of the alien conversation going on around her. She looked up and watched Rjant, who was sitting to her right, scoop a purple mound of the stuff into his mouth. Alea looked back to her plate and furled her brow. The cubes were no longer green but yellow. Her attention shifted back to Rjant and the red glob he was shoving into his mouth. Thinking she might be losing her mind, Alea gawked at the food on her plate again. The yellow cubes were now orange. She pursed her lips, determined not to look away from her plate this time, but a hefty guffaw from the other side of the *hash pit*--the name given to the dining hall by the crew--caught her attention and she glanced up. Alea snapped her head back toward her plate quickly and found that the gelatin cubes were now red.

"God damn it!" She pounded her fist on the table top and then stabbed at one of the little blocks with her spork. It flew off of her plate and into Rjant's lap. "What the hell is this stuff? It keeps changing colors!"

All conversation at the table stopped and five Tertian heads turned to stare at her, but because she bellowed her frustration in English, Tren and Rjant were the only two who understood her words.

Rjant watched the food chunk slither down his thigh and onto the floor before shifting his head to look back at Alea. Her irritated expression was comical and he roared out a laugh. Tren smirked and interpreted Alea's words in Tertian, for the benefit of the others, and everyone else at the table laughed, as well.

"It's not funny." Alea frowned, folding her arms across her chest. "I'm hungry and this slop isn't fit for a dog."

Rjant's mocking smile softened at Alea's obvious frustration. "It's called nariwob, Alea, nari for short." He took Alea's spork from her and scooped a block of the now purple food into the curve of the utensil. "It's a technologically advanced, synthetic food that stores well for long galactic journeys. Its flavor and texture change with the color."

He held the spork to her lips. "Here, taste it."

"I'm not going to turn that color, am I?" She looked at him apprehensively.

It was Tren's turn to laugh. Once again he interpreted what Alea said and she endured another round of laughter.

Alea snarled, her glare shifting from Tren to Rjant and to the rest of the Tertani around the table. One of them was Calem, the voice from the intercom, who now had a face to match. The other two were Jesser and Lemac.

Lemac, who was from Terta Minor and a good friend to Rjant, volunteered for this journey. Earlier he'd told Alea his She'mana was very excited to meet her. When Alea asked why, he replied that some things were better left to surprise.

"I'm so glad you find me funny." Alea tightened her crossed arms and turned her head aside, trying to ignore their amusement at her expense.

"They think you're delightful Alea, and so do I." Tren nodded toward the utensil that Rjant was still holding. "Now eat. I think you'll find at least some of the flavors palatable."

"I guess I don't have much of a choice." Alea looked at the spork, which now held a blue cube. She took it from Rjant, slipped it in her mouth and held her breath. Everyone at the table was watching her, and she wondered briefly if they would get her drift if she flipped her middle finger at them.

Finally she relaxed, exhaled and tasted the nari. It had a fruity flavor and was juicy. It tasted good. Alea nodded her approval and received several smiles in return. The conversations resumed and Alea explored the various tastes that the nari offered.

Purple tasted like dirt and she decided to avoid that one. The orange reminded her of beef stew and Alea ate as much of it as she could before the nari changed colors again. She almost choked on a green one, which lit her throat and nose on fire, and caused her eyes to water like a faucet.

"The green is a bit spicy. Be careful with that one," Rjant cautioned, handing her a cup of taw.

"You could've warned me sooner," Alea coughed out.

"Tocol." Tren was holding up an arm and motioning to a sentry sitting across the room. The warrior acknowledged Tren's summons and moved towards their table.

"Yes, Commander." He nodded and presented the Delta to Tren.

"You haven't dined with us in quite awhile."

"I..." Tocol hesitated. "I wasn't sure if I was welcome, Commander."

"You should know by now, Chief, that I'm fair-minded. I can't hold you responsible for the sentries' behavior on Venuvia, only your insubordination, and I trust that it will not happen again."

"No, sir."

"Good," Tren said. "Now, let me present our Tina, Alea."

Tocol tipped his head toward Alea at a respectful angle. "A pleasure, Tina."

"Sit and join us, Tocol," Rjant added, motioning to an empty seat.

Alea was briefly affronted by the very intimate reference to her virginal state, but concluded quickly that the word was as much a title as it was a label. She was more interested in the way this sentry looked and studied Tocol as he moved around the table.

He was wearing the Tertian uniform--black pants and plum-colored jerkin style vest. There were three concentric, silver triangles embroidered on his epaulets signifying his status. Tocol, Alea assumed, was third in command, under Tren, who had five triangles and Rjant, who had four.

It was Tocol's features that caught Alea's interest however. He was tall and sinewy like the other sentrymen on the *Stardancer*, but his flesh was gray, though it was not an unhealthy color. It was deep in hue and oddly natural looking. His face was symmetrical and model perfect. He had pristine angles at his jaw line and a perfectly masculine nose. His full lips and long, curved lashes were a soft, butter yellow that contrasted pleasantly with the color of his skin. He had shaggy yellow-blonde hair layered around his head, with burgundy highlights running through it. Strands fell over his brow and part way over his eyelids. The length was cropped just past his ears and to the nape of his neck. His eyes were burgundy also, but they were rimmed in gray, not gold like Tren's and Rjant's, or the other crew members Alea had seen so far. He was quite handsome and sexy, in an alien sort of way. And quite colorful too.

"*Ayn, Tina, Alea. Tuclure ont Tertani*--No, Tina Alea. I am not Tertani," Tocol responded to her staring. "But I am dedicated to the Tertian cause."

He snapped his head as he sat down, tossing aside the locks of hair that fell over his eyes.

"Tocol is one of my best sentries, Alea," Tren said filling several rhytons with grata and passing them around the table. "I would trust him with my life."

Alea nodded and drew her attention away from Tocol, examining the intricately carved surface on the horn-shaped cup that Tren placed before her. She'd seen similar ones at the Renaissance fairs on Earth and always wished she could buy one, but they were so expensive.

"Grata is a favored cordial, but drink it slowly, Alea. It carries a strong punch."

"Actually, I was admiring the horn." Picking up the rhyton, Alea sniffed the liquid inside.

"These are plain. We have a shelf full of rhytons at home that are much more elaborately decorated."

"Really? I've always wanted one."

"Well," Rjant responded. "Now you'll have more than you know what to do with."

"What's the music like on your Earth, Tina Alea?" Tocol

asked after taking a large swallow of his drink.

"Diversified, I guess." Alea took a sip of her grata. She grimaced as she tested its flavor. The brew tasted like one-hundred and eighty proof bourbon, but it was smooth and savory going down. She could get used to enjoying a drink like this one, and since rule number one--no men *ever*--was obviously being broken, what harm could a little liquor do at this point? Alea took another sip.

Tocol reached inside of his vest pocket and pulled out a multi-faceted silver orb, no bigger than a golf ball. He held it out towards Alea.

"What is that?" she asked.

Cupping the object between the palms of his hands, Tocol closed his eyes. Within a few seconds he lifted his top hand. The ball levitated about a half of an inch above his palm and started to slowly spin. Tiny specks of light danced around it, reminding Alea of a strobe suspended over a dance floor. As she watched it rotate, a slight hum began to flow from it and then grew louder. It was music, alien music, but it wasn't unearthly peculiar, a soft rock-n-roll sounding tune that Alea could imagine being played over a radio on Earth somewhere.

"That's awesome," Alea responded, thinking about the electronics companies that would love to get their hands on it. "What kind of music is that?"

"Classic Gorbonta." Tocol told her. "This melody is over three hundred phases old."

"I didn't think to bring a lyradeck with me, did you, Tren?" Rjant asked.

"No, I didn't," Tren answered.

"Here, Tina Alea." Tocol closed his palm over the lyradeck and the music stopped. He held it out to her. "Take this one."

"I couldn't." Alea glanced at Tren and Rjant. She didn't know if it was proper to accept the gift or perhaps insulting to refuse it.

"It's a small token, Alea," Tren said. "The device is very inexpensive and you might need something to entertain yourself when Rjant and I are on duty together."

"Besides, I have another one my quarters." Tocol reached across the table and placed the lyradeck into Alea's hand.

"Thank you," she said. "How does it work?"

Tocol took her hands and folded them around the lyradeck. "Close your eyes and imagine a song you would like to hear."

Alea's eyes fell shut and she concentrated, thinking about a tune that epitomized many of the emotions she struggled with all of her life. It was her favorite song.

"Now uncover it."

Alea flattened her palm and the lyradeck began to float and spin. The hash pit fell silent as piano music flowed from it and echoed through the hall. The song *Clocks* by the Earth group *Coldplay* began playing.

Lights go out and I can't be saved. Tides that I tried to swim against. You've put me down upon my knees….

Rjant's expression sobered as he listened and his eyes met Tren's.

…Trouble that can't be named, tigers waiting to be tamed… Confusion never stops, closing walls and ticking clocks….

Everyone in the hash pit also seemed to be listening with appreciation of the new sound, though no one except Rjant and Tren understood the words. Alea, who had learned about some of the troubles in the CalyTron galaxy, could see by their expressions that they were both touched deeply, perhaps finding their own meaning in the song.

…Come out upon my seas, curse missed opportunities. Am I part of the cure, or am I part of the disease….

Wow, Alea thought. Besides Rjant and Tren, the lyradeck was best thing she had seen so far. And if music was a way to soothe her savage Sh'em, Alea had most certainly found a weapon. She allowed the song to finish before closing her hand over the lyradeck and then she picked up her rhyton and took a large gulp of grata.

Chapter Six

Alea awoke the next morning with a spinning head and a mouth so dry she could barely free her tongue from the roof of her mouth. She attempted to stretch and found that she was in her usual place, cocooned between Tren and Rjant. The three of them were on the large bed in their quarters. The last thing she recalled from the evening before was staring into her empty rhyton and listening to Calem talking about radicals and Krellians or something.

The rest was a blur.

Grunting, Alea tried to clear her mind. She felt her body and realized she was still in her running clothes. Her sneakers were off, but she still had her socks on. She peered at Tren who was in front of her and then back at Rjant, who was molded against her back. They were both wearing soft, loose-fitting pants that tied at the waist with drawstrings. Alea nuzzled against the soft, dark hair on Tren's chest and closed her eyes, drifting back to a semi-stupor.

Her next cognitive thought was that there was no word in the Tertian language for homophobia.

Rjant's cheek rested against the back of her head. His right arm was thrown over both her and Tren and his right leg was wedged between her thighs. His foot was between Tren's ankles. Tren's cheek was against the top of Rjant's head with his chin resting on Alea's head. Though his left arm was wrapped only around Alea's waist, his left leg was thrown over both her hip and Rjant's.

Geez! She could be crushed if they both forgot she was there and decided to move inward at the same time. Alea then wondered if they would continue to hug each other like that if she shimmied out from between them. That was not an option however because she was wedged in tightly and unable to move. She had a feeling that the way they were positioned was likely a male Tertian tactic to either protect their female or prevent her from fleeing.

Having sex with them was going to prove interesting.

Alea shifted a bit and they both pressed their groins against her.

Morning hard-ons--or piss hard-ons. Alea had a vague recollection of one of them, she didn't know which, showing her how to use the commode in the hygiene chamber. Had she thrown up? The realization that she had gotten drunk hit her hard and Alea had an uneasy sense she'd done something foolish. Her head spun again and she groaned.

"Did you sleep well, Tina?" Tren asked with a sleepy drag in his voice. He propped up on his elbow, rubbed his face and yawned.

Rjant released his hold on her, rolled to his back and stretched his arms and legs before sitting up. "Good dawning, Alea. Are you feeling better?"

Reaching for a pitcher on the side table, he poured her a cup of taw, and watched her drink down the liquid in five large gulps.

"I don't know... no." Her voice sounded like a toad's. "My head feels funny. What happened last night?"

"Nothing to fret about, Alea. Many of us have fallen out of our chairs after over-indulging in grata."

"I fell out of my chair?" Alea sat up looking a bit sheepish. The room started spinning and she grabbed Tren's shoulder to steady herself. "In front of everyone?"

"You're such a disgrace, Alea." Rjant chuckled, pushed her back down to the mattress and moved part way on top of her.

"Such unbecoming behavior for a Tina," Tren teased, running his hand along her inner thigh. "I think we should take her back and dump her for a better model, Rjant."

"Mmm. I agree. I think this one's defective." Rjant kissed her lips and then skimmed his mouth along her throat and lower to her breast. "Such a naughty little Tina."

"What are you talking about?" Alea arched and stretched, warming to their touches.

Tren's hand reached the area between her legs and he

fingered the outline of her pussy. "We nearly lost ourselves last dimming after carrying you here."

"Why?" Alea whispered, rocking her pelvis against his hand, too engaged in their fondling to really care. She closed her eyes and moaned as her arousal began to build.

"When you put your mouth on my trousers and tried to suck my cock through them...."

Rjant found her nipple through the cloth of her top and drew it into his mouth. He released it and flashed an amorous smile. "And when you bit my nipple and pleaded with us to fuck you...."

Alea's eyes flew open. "I did not do that!"

Did she? She couldn't remember a damn thing.

"It's a good thing your future Sh'em have such discipline, my lusty Tina, or the Triconjugal Ceremony would've taken place in this very chamber."

"Oh God!" Alea turned to her side and drew up her legs, curling into a ball. She brought her hands to her face and rubbed her temples. Being sexually aggressive with them wasn't what bothered Alea. She had a ferocious desire to have sex with them. It was the fact that she apparently lost her control and couldn't remember doing it. When she finally did lose her virginity, Alea wanted to be in full command of her faculties, not wake up the next day wondering what happened. Tren and Rjant could have taken advantage of her mindless state and she probably would've let them, but they didn't.

She was thankful for their Tertian integrity.

A chiming signal coming from the intercom on the wall interrupted them.

"Speak," Tren said.

"Commander? I hope I'm not disturbing you."

Tren rolled his eyes at Rjant. It was always a disturbance when the Sh'em were interrupted while trying to please their woman. "Speak, Calem."

"There's a cosmic storm approaching. We've been unable to chart a route around it."

"How big is it?" Rjant asked.

"It covers three quarters of a sector and our readings

indicate it is moderately violent."

"I'll be right there." Rjant rolled out of bed and stood. He would've much preferred staying in bed with Alea this dawning, but he had the next shift on the bridge.

Duty before pleasure.

Without thinking he pulled the tie at his waist and started to push off his pants.

What are you doing, Rjant?

Rjant abruptly stopped when he realized he was undressing in front of Alea. *I forgot myself. She's become so much a part of us.*

He looked at Alea. She was watching him. Her eyes were on his groin but slowly they drifted upward until her sleepy gaze met his.

Alea's mouth curved into a sensual smile. "Don't stop on my account."

Shifting her gaze downward again she admired the hint of golden, pubic hair peeking out from the top of his waistband. Her mouth watered as she thought about what nestled in that thicket just below. The little lecher demon in her head, that she knew existed somewhere in her brain, broke free and her thoughts turned devious. She wondered how resistant they would be if she attempted to seduce her future Sh'em, and since she was going to have sex with them anyway, Alea set her mind to find out. After all, they'd tortured her for two years, now it was her turn.

Rjant sucked in a breath at the delectable expression on her face and took a step forward, reaching the edge of the bed. The temptation to rip her clothes off and take their Tina here and now was almost unbearable, when it was so clear in his mind that she was ready for them. But they would not take her before they were married.

He almost recanted that thought when Alea reached out, hooked her fingers around the waistband of his pants and gave it a gentle tug. One of Rjant's hands flew to her wrist while the other held up his pants. At the same time Tren's arm came around and he grasped Alea's forearm, pulling her hand away.

"Enough, Tina. Be a good girl."

"Just one little peek?"

"No!" Rjant and Tren bellowed together.

Alea sighed with disappointment.

"You know what I think?" she said, walking her fingers up Rjant's thigh. "I think your Tertian scruples suck."

"You won't think much about our scruples after the ceremony, Tina." Tren grasped her hips and stroked his cock in the crease of her ass. "When we are free to take you as we please."

"Promises, promises," Alea taunted. She slid her hand between Rjant's legs, cupped his balls and squeezed them through the cloth of his trousers.

"Nice," she said and slid her hand upwards smoothing her palm along the bulging length of Rjant's shaft and then fitting her hand around it, wrapping it within the material. She began stroking up and down. Alea didn't know if she was doing it right but Rjant seemed to be enjoying it.

Ka! This Edification is going to kill me before it's over. Rjant threw back his head and groaned.

Hmm. Tren mentally agreed, closing his eyes to relish the building sensation from rubbing himself with Alea's bottom. *And you're leaving me alone with her? I'm not sure I can trust myself.*

Just be glad she's having a rushover from drinking too much. I don't think she's going to have much energy this dawning.

She seems to have plenty of energy right now.

Alea's hand suddenly fell away from Rjant and he looked down. *I think you've spoken too soon.*

He laughed out loud as Alea released a heavy snore. She was asleep, succumbing to the after affects of the grata.

So much for being sexed by her.

Tren peered at Alea and she snored again. *I'll have the dawning meal sent here along with a rushover remedy. She might have the spasms when she awakens.*

Rjant disappeared into the hygiene chamber and returned a half-dial later, with damp hair and a towel wrapped around his waist. Tren was picking at a breakfast platter and Alea was still asleep. *I'd better get to the bridge and see what's happening with the storm.* He dressed and then grabbed a chunk of nari from the platter on his way out the door.

Tren finished eating and took a shower. When he emerged from the hygiene chamber Alea was sitting up in bed. Her hair was a disheveled mass around her head, her clothes were twisted on her body and there were sleep creases along the side of her face. Tren smiled, thinking she never looked lovelier. He would enjoy waking up next to her each dawning.

"You could have a shower, Alea, or eat first if you like." Tren opened the door on a storage compartment in the wall, removed a bundle of clothing and a couple of towels. He placed them on the bed and sat down next to her.

"Achoo! Ow!" Alea rubbed her temple trying to ease the headache now stomping around in her brain.

"Achoo, achoo, achoo!" She sneezed again and rubbed her nose. "I must be catching cold."

"It's a rushover, Tina."

"A what?"

"From the grata."

"The headache or the sneezing?"

"Both."

"How long does it last? Achoo! Oh…" Each time Alea sneezed, her head pounded harder.

"A few dials, sometimes less."

"I didn't think I drank that much." She grimaced as she pictured a rhyton of grata.

"You poured enough grata down your throat to take down two warriors. In fact, while you were standing on the chair with Tocol…."

"I was standing on the chair?"

"With Tocol." Tren chuckled. "It was quite entertaining."

"Oh…" Alea dropped her face in her hands and sneezed into them. "Why didn't you stop me from drinking?"

"We did, but it was already too late."

Alea didn't know if she wanted an answer to her next question, but still she had to ask. "What was I doing on the chair?"

"Reciting poetry, singing off key. You both were, and then you fell off the chair."

"I'm so sorry if I humiliated you and Rjant."

"Why would we be humiliated?" He held out a small tube full of yellow powder. "Here, snort this."

"Up my nose? A-a-achoo! Ow!" Wincing at the pain, Alea squeezed her head between her hands. It felt like some foreign creature was trying to claw through her skull. "What is it?"

"It's a rushover cure."

"Oh, thank God!" Alea snatched the tube from Tren, stuck the nozzle up her nose and inhaled. Within seconds, her head stopped pounding and the room stopped swaying. She sneezed one more time for good measure and then that was over, too.

Alea sat in silent reflection for several moments. In less than twenty-four hours she had become brazen, gotten drunk and was now inhaling drugs.

Beth would be so proud.

"You're probably going to keep me locked up in here for the rest of the trip."

"Why would we do that?"

"To save you from further embarrassment."

"Your behavior was sedate compared to a typical Tertani female."

"Are you telling me that a Tertani woman would stand on a chair and make a fool of herself?"

"She would stand on the table with her feet in the meal if riled enough, and then sit down and eat it."

"You make your women sound like animals."

"Males of my race have been domesticated for over ten thousand phases, but as little as a thousand phases back our females were still quite primitive, living in the Tertian badlands and running in packs. We had to hunt them to mate, still do.

They are more civilized and educated now, living with their Sh'ems for longer periods before yielding to the urge to run off. By disposition Tertani females are still a bit untamed and do have a nose for trouble."

"Is that the reason for the Trigon? Your women are so wild it takes two males to tame them?"

Tren crooked an eyebrow at her and smirked. "Hardly, Tina. One Sh'em could handle his She'mana if the need be. It's genetically necessary, part of our biological evolution."

"Biological? How?"

"Tertani females give twenty-three chromosomes to our offspring, but each Trigon male gives only eleven and a half, which combine with each other before fertilizing the egg. Epochs ago Tertani males were barbaric and extremely violent, the females far less so. We believe that over time the female gene dominance is what led to our taming, but strange as it might be, our males went domestic before our females did."

Alea was caught off guard. Not because of the evolutionary and biological things Tren was telling her. It was the reproductive stuff that gave her pause. Up until now this had been about sex. She never considered pregnancy as a consequence or who the father of her child might be. With what Tren was telling her, *both* he and Rjant would be the fathers of any children she conceived. "That is very weird, Tren."

"Not to us."

"On Earth, both men and women contribute twenty-three chromosomes to create a baby. One father and one mother."

"I know that, and I also know that you are biologically capable of bearing us children."

Alea warmed to the idea. She always wanted to have children, but resigned herself to believing it would never happen. Looking at Tren, Alea suddenly saw him as being more than an object of desire. He would be the father--he and Rjant would both be the fathers of her children. The idea of it was both exhilarating and overwhelming to Alea, and she was assailed by such an intense flood of female, motherly yearning that she threw her arms around Tren and kissed him soundly on the lips.

As nature would have it though, her libido kicked in and Alea pressed her body to his, her kiss becoming passionate as she slipped her tongue inside Tren's mouth. She slid her hands down the back of his pants, grabbing his ass.

"Alea." Tren pulled away from her mouth and tugged her hands out. "Don't."

Alea relented, resting her hands on Tren's shoulders and started kissing his neck. She moved lower, pausing to draw his masculine nipple into her mouth, before licking a path along his stomach and then to his lower belly. Her tongue dipped below the waist of his pants and her fingers searched for the drawstring, aching to remove the cloth that separated her from ecstasy.

Tren released a strained laugh. His hands came up to her face and he tilted her head back. "You cannot even imagine how enticing you are right now, Alea. But do not tempt me." He kissed her lightly on her mouth and pushed her onto the mattress, hovering over her. His head dipped to plant kisses on her stomach, while his hand slid beneath her shorts.

He found what he was searching for.

Alea had another layer on beneath the outer garment, just as Tren suspected--her panties. His fingers curled around the waistband of her shorts and he started to strip them off of her.

Alea gasped and grabbed his wrists. "I thought you said...."

"You're still covered, Tina." Tren said, sliding the shorts along her legs and down to her feet until they were completely removed from her body. His lips curved up into an admiring smile as he scanned the lacy, black garment his Tina wore.

"Very sexy, Alea," he said, parting her legs. His head dove between her thighs and he lapped at the outline of her labia, tracing his tongue along the soft swellings of her female lips, enjoying the contours of her feminine core through the layer of the very thin panties. He found the hollow leading to her womb and circled his tongue around it few times before thrusting at it.

"Oh." Alea released a quivery breath and threaded her fingers through Tren's long, silky hair. Her legs fell further apart and Tren drew her lace covered clit between his lips and sucked on it. Alea rocked her pelvis against his face.

Tren was wild to touch his tongue to her bare flesh, and he was so close. Just one tug away. But with true Tertian honor, he resisted. "You smell so sweet, Tina. I could stay here all dawning and never tire of you."

"Please," she begged. "Don't stop."

"Cum," he said in a low husky whisper. "Let me smell how much you ache for me."

"Yes," Alea cried as she frantically pumped against his mouth, her orgasm building with vicious surmounting, but just before she burst Tren backed off and flipped her to her belly. He hooked his hands beneath her thighs, drew her hips up so that her ass was in the air. Spreading her legs open with his knees, he wedged his own hips in between and thumped her against his groin. Alea cried out, his hardened cock perfectly aligned with her pussy and stimulating her engorged clit. He repeated the movement again and again and again, pushing against her until finally, Alea was writhing on him, and her orgasm broke free. Tren grabbed Alea's hips to still her, pressing their genitalia together, rotating and growling out his own peak in return.

When their spasms finally subsided Alea fell face down on the mattress, awestruck by how intense a climax could be without actual penetration.

"Uh…" Alea said, her daze finally clearing. She was having trouble finding her words. "Shower… yes… please."

"It looks like I'll need one as well." Tren rose to stand on the floor. He held out a hand to help Alea to her feet, chuckling when her knees buckled and she nearly fell. Alea tossed her head back, a slow, sensuous smile creeping along her lips. "Would you like to join me?"

"Fair warning, Tina." Tren leaned down and planted a kissed on her mouth. "The more you taunt your Sh'em, the more aggressive we become. And we will remember how much you tormented us when it comes time to breach you."

He bent to the floor and gathered the clothes and towels that had fallen from the bed and dumped them into Alea's arms. Turnin her toward the hygiene chamber, Tren smacked her bottom. "Go now, before I decide to give you another tumble."

Alea swaggered into the bathing room, purposely swaying her hips. She knew he was still watching. She'd never understood how women could be such cock-teases, that is, until now, and this game of seduction with Rjant and Tren was proving to be a lot of fun.

Once inside the hygiene chamber, Alea dropped her bundle onto a ledge and paused to consider Tren's threat.

Did he mean to scare her?

It didn't work. If anything, his words enticed her even more. Immediately, Alea began cooking up ways to further excite her future Sh'em.

Alea hit the button on the wall and taw began dropping from the large, oval spout in the ceiling. She removed the rest of her clothing and stepped beneath it.

The shower was wonderful. Taw was like earth water, flowing and dripping when it collided with her skin, but it didn't fall in streams from the overhead faucet. It came out in small round balls about the size of a dime, bursting as it struck. The funny thing about the taw was that Alea couldn't tell if it was warm or cold. It just felt comfortable.

Alea cupped her hands and watched the pinkish liquid filling her palms. She tossed it in the air, but instead of splattering in a disarrayed pattern like water, the taw coalesced in tiny balls again. Alea giggled, feeling like a carefree child frolicking in a sprinkler. But she wasn't a child, and soon she was thinking about Tren again, sitting in the outer room, ripe for the picking. With that thought in mind, Alea stepped from the shower and draped the towel around her body.

Tren was at the table studying the screen of a paper thin computer device, when Alea stepped in front of him. He looked up at her and swallowed hard as his eyes began roaming along her curved form. His breathing quickened at the sight of her nearly nude body, her damp, auburn hair raked back and her flesh alluringly wet and glistening from her shower. An image of licking every taw drop from her skin formed in his mind. Tren's loins began to ache. She looked sexy... too sexy.

"What are you up to, Tina?" He eyed her with suspicion.

Alea smiled provocatively and dropped the towel.

Tren flew out of the chair, causing it to topple. His nostrils flared and his entire body went riotous. He curled his fingers into a ball, gritted his teeth and abruptly left their quarters.

Rjant sat in the captain's seat on the bridge. His nostrils flared and his entire body started to tremble. He curled his fingers around the ends of the armrests and he gritted his teeth. *Starfires, Tren. Are you trying to get us killed? I'm trying to navigate through a storm here. Do I have to shut out your channeling so I can concentrate?*

_He looked at the viewing window in time to see a meteor rushing toward them. "Fire," he commanded and watched the cosmic boulder disintegrate as the Stardancer's laser hit it directly on.

What's happening, brethren? I nearly lost it when you were lapping at her pussy, but_you're a blazing inferno right now.

I had to leave.

Why?

She's naked.

Rjant chuckled inwardly. It was going to be a long journey home.

Chapter Seven

Alea could hardly contain her excitement. She was in the observatory looking out at the universe. A few hours ago the Stardancer passed Terta minor, Rjant's home world, and now Tertia was coming into view. Both planets were nearly identical. Tertia was a bit larger, but neither looked anything like Earth. Both spheres were pink, probably from their taw colored oceans. The land looked like nothing but dark terrain from space, partially visible through its rose-colored clouds, but from the pictures she'd seen, the soil was an amber tint, nurturing various hues of plum foliage, trees and grasslands, with a variety of multi-colored flowers and other plants as well. It looked exotically beautiful. Alea couldn't wait to step foot on it.

But they weren't going there right away. Earlier, Rjant explained that they needed to register their arrival at the nearby way station and everyone on board had to be scanned to assure the Intergalactic System for Disease and Sickness Control that they were disease free.

Tocol stood next to her, off duty at the moment. Ever since their dance on the chair, Alea and the Krellian had become good friends. He helped with her Tertian, and Alea was speaking the language often now, feeling more comfortable with it. The symbols were giving her a bit more trouble, but she was starting to read simple sentences. Tocol occupied much of her time when both Rjant and Tren were on duty together, as they were at the moment, and sometimes he served as her future Sh'em's body guard, as well. Not that Tren or Rjant would ever admit they needed protection--from her.

Alea's endeavor to bait her Trigon males had become a major past time of hers. Oh, they still gave her luscious orgasms, but she went a step further, daring them to touch her bare flesh or trying to sink her hands down their pants when they were busy pleasuring her. They were stellar in their conviction to wait however, and there were times she thought they were made of stone. At other times they seemed so close to breaking that Alea was sure they would surrender, but it didn't happen. Instead, they would call on Tocol to take her to the amusement carrels whenever Alea become overly randy, telling her they needed time to settle down, whatever that meant, but it certainly fed into her carnal imagination. Tocol actually slept on the sofa in their quarters one night after Alea pulled one of her stunts. She had set the lyradeck to playing a couple of the most sensual songs she could think of and danced for Tren and Rjant, using her best sexually enticing moves. They were definitely turned on by it, if the fiery sparkle in their eyes, dilated pupils and their strong aromatic blend of pheromones were any indication. But when she started to strip off her clothes, they ended the show, and called Tocol to the rescue.

"Sleep there." Tren ordered Tocol, pointing to the sofa. He knew Alea would behave with someone else present in their quarters.

"Sir?" Tocol was confused, but settled himself on the sofa as commanded.

"It's an order. Don't question it."

"Of course, Commander."

Alea suspected if her Trigon males went to sleep elsewhere the rest of the crew might become aware they were having trouble handling their her. Tocol would be discreet, saving Rjant and Tren from a shit load of razzing by the crew.

Despite all of it, they never got angry with her. On Earth, most men would have either called her vulgar names or taken her up on her offerings. But not Tren or Rjant. They took her behavior in stride and were sometimes even amused.

Alea was at ease with Tocol by then, enough to explain why he'd been summoned to sleep in their quarters. He laughed about it, telling her that she might be from Earth, but she definitely had Tertani female instincts. Alea was flattered by the comment. She wanted to fit in--wanted to feel normal when, on Earth, she felt like a freak for having such left-handed desires.

"How are your hands, Tocol?" Alea asked as she gazed out the window.

"Just fine, Tina Alea. I only wish I found out sooner what an aggressive little bitch you are."

Alea chuckled. She didn't mind him calling her that. It was stated with affection and he was also right. When it came to playing *hot hands*, she could be quite sadistic.

Though Tocol taught her a few of the Tertian games that everyone on the Stardancer played to amuse themselves, *hot hands*, an old Earth game that Alea taught them, became a favorite among the crew. It was a game of reflex, speed and endurance, which was much to the liking of the sentries on board the ship.

The game involved two opponents standing or sitting and facing each other. The one doing the slapping held his palms up and the other player placed his palms on top. The object was to slap the top of an opponent's hands before he is able to pull them away, but enough slaps could also cause a nice stinging that culminated into hot flesh, which felt about as bad as a nasty brush burn, and might eventually lead a player into backing down. Each *slapper* was given three sixty-second rounds. Whoever achieved the most hits won the kitty. On Earth, money was typically used to make bets, but the sentries on the Stardancer used their credit discs. The *credics* were quarter-sized chips activated by the owner's thumb print and, as with the lyradeck, a specified amount of currency could be thought-programmed into it and transferred to the winner's chip through a built-in sensor. Credics were also the monetary means of buying and selling throughout the CalyTron Galaxy.

Tren gave Alea a chip of her own, but she only got the chance to use it with Tocol. The other sentries on board would only play her for fun, refusing to bet with their Commanders' Tina. She also suspected the sentries went easy on her as well, afraid they might hurt her.

Much to Alea's appreciation, Tocol was just the opposite. The game was only fun when everyone put forth their best effort to win, and Alea certainly held back nothing. She was good at the game. Her hand slapping technique was perfect, and last night Alea counted at least seventy five strikes. Tocol only managed a few good strikes on her hands, about twenty, enough to make her flesh red and hot but still, she was winning. Tocol refused to give in, however and kept challenging her. When his creamy gray flesh started turning purple, Alea felt guilty and refused to play him anymore. Since she was the one who ceded, she lost her wager. Tocol took her money with a grin, and she respected him for that. It was the way the game was played. If you quit in the middle of a round, you lost, forfeiting the pot.

"There, Tina Alea," Tocol said, pointing at the window. The way station, Angard was coming into view. The free-floating station reminded Alea of the CN tower in Toronto. It was an enormous oval shape with shimmering lights radiating from the multiple lookout levels. Two soaring needle-like projections protruded from it, one at the bottom and one above. The entire structure was revolving like a slow spinning top. Glowing dots were moving toward and away from Angard, and as the Stardancer drew closer, Alea discovered that the dots were spaceships arriving and departing.

"It's incredible. Earth has been trying to build a space station for years but things keep going wrong."

She watched as the Stardancer maneuvered closer to the landing area. Tren was at the controls on the bridge and the thought of him taking power over the massive vessel, commanding it, made Alea hot.

The engines hummed and surged as the ship slowed its forward progress. There was a slight shudder and Tocol told her they just engaged with the dock.

Alea heard the swishing sound of the observatory door sliding open and turned around. Rjant was standing there. He was dressed in his formal Tertian attire, black pants tucked into knee-high boots, long-sleeved plum jerkin with black epaulets and his rank pinned to his shoulders. His talon arc was sheathed at his back, slipped into the baldric, which was strapped across his chest and buckled at his waist, emphasizing his broad chest and masculine thighs. He was tantalizingly handsome and Alea sighed at the rugged sight of him.

She'd always loved a man in uniform.

"Sir." Tocol presented the delta and bowed his head.

"At ease, Tocol." Rjant patted one of Tocol's shoulders. "You'll be on leave soon."

Tocol nodded, his stiff, military stance visibly relaxing. "It's good to be home, Rjant. I do have some final duties to attend to however."

"Thank you for your help this journey." Rjant's eyes drifted to Alea and a slow, passionate smile crept along his lips. He and Tren would no longer have to endure her tantalizing torment. They would soon be able to taste her fully.

"My pleasure." Tocol turned a quick smile toward Alea. "And congratulations on your upcoming Triconjugal ceremony."

Alea took hold of his hands. "Thanks for the company, Tocol. Will I see you again soon?"

He nodded. "I'll be at the feast."

"Not the ceremony?"

Tocol shook his head from side to side. "I am neither Tertani nor am I a mated male. Now if you'll excuse me."

He then headed for the door and left the observation deck.

"What did he mean by that?" Alea turned to ask Rjant.

"Only males of the Trigon, mated males, can partake as Prowlers."

Alea lifted her brows. "Prowlers?"

Grasping Alea's waist, Rjant smoothed his hands along her hips and moved back up again, skimming his hands along her ribs. He wrapped his arms around her and drew her close. If Alea were Tertani she would know all of their rituals and customs, but the hunt was a complicated thing to explain. The Triconjugal hunt was an important part of the Trigon Rituals. It evolved long ago in Tertian history. The hunt was instinctual, a predatory behavior based on sexual urges and the need to mate. And it was the Tertani female's nature to run from it--Tinas were often very frightened by it--and they were quite cunning about eluding capture. Even so, when the pursuing Sh'em, called Prowlers, did manage to outwit and corner their woman, the female's extraordinary agility and running speed often allowed her to escape. Because of this, it was the Prowlers' duty to assist each other in tracking their females through transdelta mind linking bestowed on them during meditation prior to the hunt. Once the Trigon males captured their females, they fornicated, often in a wicked act of breeding, as the hunt got them quite riled. But it also relieved their frenzy before witnessing at the Triconjugal Ceremony--the breaching of the Tina.

"Well?" Alea tipped her head to look up at him.

Rjant dropped his head back and examined the ceiling. How could he tell Alea all of this without upsetting her? Though it was not uncommon for Tinas to become frantic, Rjant did not want his Tina fretting. It might lead to hysteria during the hunt, and he and Tren would have trouble mating with her. Though they might've done so in the ancient times of their savage history, no modern Sh'em ever took their She'mana's body by force.

Drawing in a deep breath, Rjant looked at Alea. He threaded one hand to the back of her hair, gave her head a gentle tug backwards and kissed her briefly on the mouth. "The other She'mana will explain it to you."

Alea wrenched free and stepped back from him. "But...."

Rjant placed his finger across her lips to silence her. "Alea, I cannot explain the nature of the female during the Triconjugal hunt, and I will not explain the nature of the male. It is what it is and leave it at that."

"Huh?" Alea scrunched her face in confusion. "That doesn't make any sense."

"It will. Now, are you ready? Tren is waiting for us."

Alea threw up her hands in surrender. "Fine, whatever. Let's go." She snapped her head to shake off her irritation, and stomped away from Rjant at her fullest walking pace.

Rjant's eyes narrowed, tracking her movements as she left the room, and a low growl rumbled in his throat. Something primal was stirring in him as Alea rushed off. The faster she went the greater was his instinctive need to chase her. He followed her down the hall, prowling behind her at a quick pace, the prowler's urge already starting to besiege him.

Tren was waiting at the Stardancer's hatchway when he caught sight of his Tina coming down the corridor. Just as he figured there was an annoyance in her step and she looked as though she'd just had her feathers ruffled. Tren knew what it was about, and did not want her troubled about the hunt either.

His loins began to ache, as his eyes roamed her form. She was wearing the traditional hunt clothing and it hugged her curves like a second skin.

He groaned. Soon they would be thrusting inside of her. Tren resisted the sudden, primeval compulsion to stalk toward her and trap her beneath his body.

Completely ignoring Tren, Alea tried to pass him by, but his arm snaked out and hooked her around her waist, preventing her from leaving the ship.

"Going somewhere, Tina?"

"Are *you* going to tell me about this hunt?"

"No."

Alea looked down and her clothing. She wasn't so naïve that she couldn't deduce the reason behind what she wore. The stretchy, but durable material that molded her body was definitely made for heavy exercise like climbing or running. The three-quarter sleeve top was a wrap around style that tied in a knot behind her back. The calf length pants fit her like leggings, allowing her a great deal of movement, and the thick, knee-high boots with non-slip, flat soles were designed for gripping surfaces. But it was the plum and amber patterns threaded through the material, that matched the Tertian terrain and looked like camouflage, that clued Alea to the fact that she was the one who would be hunted.

The idea of it was titillating, but it also made Alea feel a bit wary. She had a feeling that there was more to the Triconjugal hunt than just a mere chasing of the Tina by her Trigon males.

Rjant approached from behind. Alea's chin went up a notch as her gaze shifted between the two of them. They exchanged a look and there was something so feral and somatically male in their expressions that it sent a shiver up Alea's spine--part arousal and part apprehension.

Her breathing accelerated and she gulped as their masculine aroma assailed her, soothed her. They smiled at each other and then at her. It was enough to pull Alea from her swooning. She was immediately annoyed by their silent uttering, and that they could calm her senses so quickly, with just their scents and their smiles.

Stepping out from her usual place between them, Alea walked through the hatch and trod down the ramp that connected the ship to the platform. She looked around the terminal, scrutinizing the activity around her, expecting to see androids, laser lights and ultra-tech automations, but what caught her attention was the two seven foot tall, bumpy-skinned aliens with fleshy, floppy, rabbit-like ears greeting one another. They both turned together and looked at her, and their three foot long ears stiffened, darting straight up into the air.

Alea stopped dead in her tracks.

Reality check... aliens... oh God. I'm Alice and I've just dropped through the rabbit hole.

Pretending nonchalance, Alea nodded her head to them. She wasn't about to let a little thing like mutant humanoids disturb her. After all, she'd gotten used to Tocol, and his appearance seemed normal after awhile, although he was much better looking than these two oversized, lumpy hares. With that thought in check she straightened her shoulders and headed down one of the corridors.

"Do you have any idea where you're going, Tina?" Tren said. He and Rjant paced beside her.

"Sure I do." Alea stopped, her eyes darting around and looking for Tertian symbols that would indicate the direction to the scanning chamber, but she recognized nothing.

"This way." She said confidently, but not really sure at all and started off again.

Rjant grasped Alea's forearm. "You are going the wrong way, Alea."

"Tertani female pride. Never stop and ask for directions." Tren chuckled.

"Earthly female pride too." Alea grinned back, unabashedly. "And just for your information, rule number one, women are always right. Rule number two, if we are wrong, shut up and say 'yes, dear.'"

"Yes, dear," Tren said through a smirk. "Now, shall we go?"

"Hmm. You're a fast learner. I like that." Alea swept her hand outward. "Now, lead on then, sentryman."

Rjant turned Alea in the opposite direction.

The scanning chamber was packed, mostly with Tertani sentries, but there were a few odd looking creatures milling about, including Alea's mutant, ninja bunnies. As they made their way through the crowd, the sea of aliens parted, allowing a path directly to the scanners.

Tren grinned. "Must be my charismatic charm."

"I highly doubt it. It's my good looks." Rjant waggled his eyebrows.

Alea rolled her eyes. "It's more likely that you both scare the piss out of them being first and second Commanders of the entire planet."

"Hmm." Rjant pounded a fist on his chest. "We are quite fearsome, aren't we?"

Alea just shook her head.

"Welcome home, Commanders." The healthtek standing by one of the scanning rooms acknowledged them.

"Glad to be home, Tamary." Tren motioned for Alea and Rjant to enter the room.

Alea gave the woman the once over. The patch on her one piece, tan jump suit indicated she worked for the ISDS. Her hair was light brown and she had brown eyes. She looked so... normal.

"So, how are things on Dormoth, uh..." The woman

double-checked Alea's name from the list she was holding, looked up again and smiled. "…Tina Alea? I haven't been home for over two phases."

So that was it. The inhabitants of this planet Dormoth must look much like Earthlings.

"Oh, I'm not from Dormoth," Alea started to say. "I'm from…."

Rjant clamped a hand over her mouth and leaned in. "That's privileged information, Tina."

Tamary raised an eyebrow but kept silent. Positioning herself behind a podium, she began tapping calibrations into a flashing grid.

"Let's get this done," Tren said impatiently, stepping inside a compartment that looked like a small shower stall. Rjant led Alea to a bench against the wall and sat down. He leaned back and casually propped the back of his head in his hands, stretching out his long legs.

"So, I take it by the way I'm dressed that the ceremony is going to take place as soon as we reach Tertia?" Alea asked Rjant, taking a seat beside him.

"After enduring four sept-dawnings of your tormenting would you have us wait any longer, Tina?" Tren responded.

"Hold still." Tamary said to Tren. She touched one of the tiles and it lit up. A red beam emerged from a dot in the stall's ceiling and began spiraling around Tren's body until he was completely encased within a coil of light.

"I suppose not." Alea answered Tren's question timidly. A rack of nerves suddenly formed in the pit of her stomach.

Pre-wedding jitters.

Alea inhaled a shaky breath.

She was getting married!

"Step out," Tamary ordered. "Who's next?"

"I'll go." Alea traded places with Tren, standing in the scanner stall. "So everyone has to do this?"

"Everyone except the creepy, nocturnal inhabitants on the planet Neopis," Tren answered. "They can't become infected."

"Are they immune?"

"In a way. They're gynandromorphs, both male and female."

Rjant laughed and slapped a knee. "I once told one to go fuck itself and it said, 'Sure, why not.'"

Alea gave him a confused look. "I don't understand?"

"They self-impregnate." Tren snickered.

"Oh…" Alea brought her hand to her mouth and giggled. She heard a hum as the scanner re-activated and she tracked the beam coiling around her. A slight tingling sensation moved through her body.

"Is our Tina healthy, Tamary?" Rjant asked.

"Clean and fertile." Tamary continued to scan her readouts without looking up. "And she's definitely a virgin."

Alea's mouth dropped open and she turned as red as the beam surrounding her.

"Are you sure?" Tren's mouth curled up on one side at the sight of Alea's reddening face. She wouldn't be blushing for long. Soon she would be purring like a satiated, wild feline.

"Oh, quite sure," Tamary said as she scrutinized the read-out screen, pointing to a specific area. "See this fleshy membrane here? It's definitely covering her…."

"Do you mind?" Alea glared at them.

Tren ignored her, amused at how flustered she was becoming. "What about her breasts. Are her glands sufficient enough to nourish…."

"Oh, for the love of God! Did I ask for a sperm count when you were standing in here?"

You can be ruthless sometimes, Tren. Rjant turned his head away, hiding his mirth from Alea.

Tren rubbed his chin between his finger and thumb, his eyes darting back and forth across the screen, his expression pensive. "What about her womb is it…?"

"Tren!"

Tren turned his head to look at Alea. "Did you say something, Tina?"

"Are you having fun yet?" Alea crossed her arms over her chest and sucked in an irritated breath. She didn't notice that the beam disappeared moments ago.

Tren walked to the scanning stall and beamed a bright, full smile. "Why yes, dear."

Rjant burst out laughing.

Chapter Eight

With all three of them properly scanned and cleared to leave Angard, they boarded the Stardancer with the rest of the crew and continued on to Tertia. A brief ride in a hover pod brought them to a borough called Canyon City. Alea anticipated massive buildings with towering skyscrapers, given how advanced the Tertani were, but she was pleasantly surprised to find a quaint, little village. A tranquil taw river meandered through it and children were romping about. There was a moderately sized marketplace with cafes and shops and amusement centers. The homes were one or two story, white stone dwellings accented with a lovely array of fresh smelling gardens, and dotting the mossy, plum hillside like a scene from a Norman Rockwell painting--with a bit of an alien surrealistic twist, given the unearthly colors of the foliage and the hover vehicles that occasionally zoomed by.

Tren pointed out a few of the larger homes explaining that the higher ranking sentries lived in those. He also told her that their dwelling, which was called the compound, was the largest and also more elaborate because he and Rjant were of the highest status. It housed four Trigons, nine children, two widows, six unmated sentries and a bevy of servants. Tren assured Alea that the servants were paid workers and not thralls after she gave him a lecture on American slave history and cultural prejudices, such as Hitler's regime and the Sarajevo genocides. He agreed that such machinations were indeed horrible and that those things were outlawed from the Tertian planets long ago.

"I've sent Lemac ahead to gather our chosen Prowlers," Rjant said.

The hover pod reached its destination and the door slid open. Tren and Alea exited and Rjant followed departing last. His gaze shifted down the temple's stone path to the slinking form that was heading toward them.

Alea's eyes widened as the figure drew closer and she was able to get a better look.

"Welcome home, sirs." Gorsch nodded. "My wife has prepared your residence to receive the Tina Alea."

Forgetting her Tertian and speaking English instead, Alea leaned in toward Rjant. "What is that thing?"

She clamped her hands behind her back to keep from pointing at it.

At the sound of her words the creature turned and slithered up to her. "I beg your pardon, madam. I am not a *what*, but a *who*."

Horton Hears a Who. Okay. Alea bit her lip to suppress a laugh, recalling all of the bizarre shaped beings from her favorite Dr. Seuss books. The creature was ridiculous looking.

Rjant placed a firm hand on her shoulder. "He understands you, Tina."

"Correct." Gorsch responded in English, extending his knobby pointer finger into the air. The thick, yellow nail on the appendage was so long and curled it would have made a manicurist nauseous. "My wife and I thought it would give you comfort to speak your own tongue from time to time, so we studied it."

Alea merely blinked at him.

"You're staring, Alea," Rjant whispered in her ear.

Realizing that she might be insulting the *thing*, Alea found her composure and flattened her hand to her chest. "I'm so sorry. I have never met anyone quite like you. I... I was a bit surprised."

"Quiet fine, madam. I do understand." The creature bowed, his body sliding into an even deeper s-shape. Where his waist would be, his trunk curved left and at the level of his chest, his trunk curved to the right. He looked a bit lopsided.

How did he keep from falling over?

"The steward Gorsch, at your service." He swept his skinny arm across his body, and then stood fully upright, his torso straightening into a long, skinny tube.

Good God. He had to be over ten feet tall.

"I perfectly understand your reaction, madam," he continued, flashing a smile from a mouth that had to contain at least fifty teeth and spread from pointy ear to pointy ear. "Your planet is primitive and has yet to have the opportunity to experience other intelligent species."

Other species was a good way to describe him.

"My form does not move as yours. It is a remnant of our uncivilized phases when we hunted on all fours, and before we walked on two limbs." He bowed again, dropped to his belly and sped down the path like a scrambling gecko.

"Oh my goodness!" Alea exclaimed as she brought her fingertips to her lips in shock. "That was so weird."

_Tren removed her hand from her mouth and held it between his own. She looked at him, still a bit stunned. "I hope I didn't make him feel bad."

"Relax, Tina." Tren patted her hand and smirked. "I agree with you. He is quite peculiar, but he's harmless."

They continued their short walk and were soon at the temple doors. Pausing, Alea inspected the large, circular edifice, arching her back and craning her neck to get a better look at the domed roof, capping the entire structure. A sea of blue lights were glittering all over it, but rather than appearing like an over decorated house on Christmas day it cast a more rapturous glow, pouring out an energy so powerful that Alea could nearly feel its spiritual surge.

"So what happens now?" Taking a deep breath, Alea attempted to ease her tingling nerves. She was starting to feel a bit overwhelmed.

"The Mahatma Tribunal and the Prowlers await us inside," Tren said. "There will be a blessing of our Trigon by the Tribunal, the Prowlers will link with both of us and with each other."

"Why do you have to link?"

Rjant's eyes sparkled with anticipation. He cupped her face in his hands and brought his face to within inches from hers. "So they can help us hunt you."

"But I'm right here."

"For now." Tren pressed his body along her back and

gave her a gentle nip on the shoulder.

He was trembling.

Alea's heart starting pounding and she gulped, their essence flooding her nostrils, stronger than ever before. A tantalizing yearning crept between her legs, but in the depths of her rational brain there was restive uncertainty. Tren and Rjant seemed different somehow. She'd noticed a change in them ever since docking on Angard--in the way they looked at her, more feral, more savage, like--*oh God*--hungry prowlers.

Are you ready, brethren? Tren's eyes shifted to meet Rjant's gaze.

Maybe we should explain the Rituals to her more thoroughly.

No. I want her to react as naturally as a Tertani Tina. If we prepare her it would not be the same.

Releasing Alea, Tren turned toward the temple. He placed his hands on the ancient, hinged double doors and gave them a hefty shove. With a loud banging, they crashed open. Rjant moved beside him in the open entrance and they withdrew their Talon arcs, holding them with two hands and lifting them over their heads. They both roared out a mighty cry.

Their sudden outburst startled Alea and she jumped back. Ferocious masculine howling returned their call, spewing from somewhere deep inside the temple.

Alea's defenses went up and her flight or fight reaction took hold.

Run. The little voice inside her head beckoned.

Rjant and Tren both roared again, threw down their talons, and started ripping off their clothes, until they were down to nothing but loin cloths that barely covered their assets. Alea gasped and backed away as they turned toward her, two brutally muscular savages, eyeing her with a carnal intent that was terrifyingly obvious. Alca felt as though they were stripping her with their leers alone.

"Come here, Tina!" Tren bellowed, his voice deep and commanding. Rjant said nothing. He just lunged at her. He grabbed one of her wrists and within seconds, Tren's hand closed around the other one. Alea shrieked as they dragged her inside, their pace so quick that she could barely stay on her feet.

"What the fuck are you doing?"

"It's tradition, Alea." A twinge of guilt etched along Rjant's brain, but the primal urge was too overwhelming and soon he could think of nothing but mating with his woman.

Inside the temple the male shouting echoed so loud that Alea thought her eardrums would burst. She spotted Lemac standing with five other warriors she did not know. They were ranting and shaking their talons. All of them were wearing loin cloths.

It was a regular Tarzan convention.

Where was a vine when she needed it? This was one place she definitely wanted to swing out of.

Alea was brought to the other side of the temple, to stand before a row of men, heavily robed in hooded garments, and sitting in a line of thrones befitting kings. Most of them were rather elderly, but a few of them seemed quite young.

The Mahatma Tribunal.

Twelve imperious wise men, called to the position by mystical summoning, celibate males who dedicated their lives to dictate the Tertian laws and rituals.

Twelve pairs of pompous eyes staring at Alea.

Rjant and Tren released her and presented the delta. The room went silent, as one of the Tribunal elders stood and raised a bejeweled, wooden talon arc, smooth on one end, honed to a point on the other. Holding it with two hands, he raised it over his head, in the same manner as Tren and Rjant had done outside the temple.

The elder approached Alea, lowered the talon and poked the blunt end of it under her chin, tipping her head back. He examined her face. One of his hands came up and he lifted a tuft of her hair, rolling it between his fingers.

"Beautiful," he said and bent forward to sniff it.

Alea balled her hands into fists and pressed them to her thighs, wondering what would happen if she belted the old crony. *What right did he have to touch her like that?*

Alea was getting pissed. This was totally not what she expected. What kind of wedding ceremony was this, anyway? They should have warned her. Alea shot an angry glare first at Tren and then Rjant. They ignored her and stared straight ahead.

What the elder did next was most bizarre and Alea nearly did punch him.

He set aside the talon and then yanked her lips apart to check her teeth!

Was she supposed to whinny now and scratch her hoof on the floor?

She swore to herself that if he tried to look down her shirt, she was going to bite him. But he backed away and slowly walked around her. Alea could actually sense his eyes grazing up and down her body. Totally and utterly irritated, she bit her lip and shuffled on her feet.

And then Alea did the strangest and most uncharacteristic thing.

As he came back around to the front of her, she bared her teeth and hissed at the man! It was no little hiss either. Her head actually lurched forward and a *SSSSSSSS* spit from her mouth!

Alea didn't know what made her do it, she just felt like it.

The warriors in the room snickered and the elder threw off his hood grabbed his belly and released a hearty guffaw. He was joined by the rest of the Tribunal.

Tren and Rjant continued to stare straight ahead, and it was a damn good thing too, because if they dared to laugh, Alea was going to stomp on their damn feet! No wonder Tinas ran away from their mates. This was despicable!

I'm dying here, Tren.

Don't you dare laugh. Alea will never forgive us.

It's hard to believe the Tribunal still engages in the old practices. They're so obsolete.

"The divinities have chosen well!" The elder settled his amusement and clapped his hands together. "Shall we proceed?"

"Please do, Pontiff Jer." Tren stepped forward and Rjant followed. They were both relieved the elder was finished with his inspection. It was hard to tell how much more Alea would have tolerated before becoming completely unfurled.

They both faced Alea. Her furious glare was arousing to them. Tren's cock hardened instantly and Rjant's was not far behind. Alea narrowed her eyes, her nostrils flaring as she inhaled their scents, ignoring the bulges in their groins. She wanted to rip their throats out.

The six Prowlers moved to form a semi-circle, sitting cross-legged behind her. The Tribunal did the same to her front and just behind Rjant and Tren. They all lifted their hands to form the delta and began chanting a Triconjugal mantra, blessing the trio before them.

Tren and Rjant raised their closest arms and their fingers made contact to form a single delta between them. They lifted their free hands toward her. Alea stared at them for a moment before realizing what they wanted her to do. She hesitated, her temper still simmering, her sensible mind debating with her desire.

Desire won out.

She wanted them.

Alea raised her arms and her fingers and thumbs met theirs, forming a delta with each of them--binding herself to them.

"By the grace of the divinities do you humbly accept the gift of this tripling?" the Pontiff began.

"With open faith," Tren and Rjant murmured in unison.

"Are you willing to freely give your patience, your loyalty and your understanding to the Tina Alea who stands before you?"

"Always," they said, again together.

"Lay down your lives to protect her?"

"Without hesitation."

"Accept all offspring she gives you?"

"With joy."

"From this day forward, I give my decree that Tren ot Dmor and Rjant ot Pel'r will be hereby known as Tren and Rjant ot Alea, Together you will be called the Sh'em ot Alea."

Tren turned Alea to face the Prowlers. He and Rjant each placed a hand on her shoulders.

"Witnesses, I now present the Trigon ot Alea," the Pontiff proclaimed.

Alea's nose was tickling. The mist in her eyes pooled and threatened to spill free. What beautiful words to give her. And they had taken *her* name, not the other way around. Why would anyone want to run from that?

She no sooner completed the thought when high pitched shrieks flooded the room. From somewhere in the recesses of the dimly lit temple, three women, dressed identically to Alea bounded across the floor, two of them leaping over the heads of the seated Prowlers with the most perfect hurdle jumps she had ever seen. They headed straight for her. A third woman flew from the side, wielding a dagger toward Rjant and Tren, and before Alea could react the women had a hold of her. The Prowlers jumped to their feet and bellowed out angry shouts, but none of them, not even Alea's new Sh'em moved to help her, as she was dragged out of the temple in the same manner that she was dragged in. They ran with her around the columned portico that circled the temple, and then over a hill at the temple's backside.

"Come on! Come on! Hurry!"

"Stop!" Alea shouted. At first, she was too stunned by the commotion to resist, but now coming to her senses, she dug in her heels and broke free from their clutches, refusing to go any further. "What are you doing?"

"Stealing you away from them."

"Why?"

"You have to run."

They expected her to run?

"Why?" Alea surprised herself. She never thought she would ever question the need to run.

The woman's sky blue, gold rimmed Tcrtian eyes locked with Alea's. She stared at Alea looking quite dumbfounded that she would even question such a thing. "It's what we do."

"Why?" Alea was beginning to feel like a small child in

broken record mode.

Why is the sky blue, mommy... where do babies come from... will I grow hair down there too?

"You ask a lot of questions." The woman started pacing back and forth, looking very edgy. "We don't have time for this."

"Leave her be, Syrat. This is all new to her." The second woman standing there, the one who wielded the dagger to keep the men at bay, held out her hand. "Hi, I'm Karen."

"Uh, nice to meet you... I think." Alea took her hand and shook it. Karen was a blonde with hazel eyes, about Alea's size, maybe a tad shorter. She looked as normal as Tamary, and Alea assumed that Karen was from Dormoth.

"We're protecting you from being ravaged, Tina," the other Tertian female piped in. She looked every bit as anxious as Syrat. "Now let's go!"

She tried to grab at Alea's arm, but Alea recoiled dodging the woman's hand.

Well, Alea thought. *This is half-assed backwards.*

"But I've already consented to marry them. I *am* already married to them."

"Don't be a fool, Tina! They want to rut on your body and we saved you from that. You should be a little more grateful."

"Oh, for goodness sake, Reasa." Karen threw her hands in the air. "How can you expect her to understand this? I didn't."

"They're linking!" Syrat said, halting her pacing to scan the crest of the hill. Her breathing was rapid and shallow. "I can feel it. They'll be here soon."

Alea looked at Karen. "Is she always this hyper?"

"No." Karen chuckled. "Only when the urge to run seizes her. Most of the time she's actually quite subdued. In fact, she's a highly educated scientist for the ISDS, concentrating on a cure for Brits Scorn."

"Don't you like to run, Alea?" Reasa asked.

"I love to run."

"Had to figure that. No Trigon males have ever shown up with an off world female who didn't."

Alea strolled over to a small boulder, sat down on it and crossed her arms over her chest. She didn't understand any of this and therefore was not going anywhere until she did. "But for what reason would I run now?"

Reasa and Syrat looked at her with shocked expressions and wide eyes. Alea chuckled, finding it very amusing that they would be so panicked.

"She's sitting, Syrat!" Reasa shrieked. "You can't sit!"

"Maybe we should carry her." Syrat rubbed her forehead in frustration.

"I'm not moving. Not until you explain."

Syrat's shoulders slumped in defeat, and she blew out a resigned breath.

"Oh fine!" she said scanning the hillside once more before sitting on the mossy, plum ground. "It will probably take at least a half a dial of meditating before their minds are linked anyway. Though I did want to get a good head start."

Karen sat on the ground beside Syrat, crossed her ankles and wrapped her arms around her bent knees. Her tightly pressed lips were turned up slightly at the corners revealing that she was every bit as amused as Alea was.

Reasa however, could not contain her edginess and continued to pace back and forth. "Get on with it then, Syrat, but be quick about it."

Syrat released a heavy sigh. "All Tertani females run from their mates from time to time. It's an innate drive."

Alea opened her mouth to speak, but Syrat held out a hand to silence her. "Don't ask me why. I don't know. It's just the way it is."

"Long, long ago." Reasa stopped pacing to speak. "Tertani females packed together, and yes, the males hunted them to mate. The men were feral and angry and violent so the women ran from them."

"It's why the Edification was so necessary, Alea," Karen added. "Despite how ferocious the males were, it lured the female, easing some of her fears. By many degrees that nature remains a part of the Tertani people."

"And Tinas still always run," Syrat explained. "So the

Prowlers link their minds. During the hunt, they can spread out to track her, keeping the new Sh'em informed as to her whereabouts. As soon as she is captured and breached, the link dissolves."

"Between all of them?"

"No, it will still exist between Sh'em of the same Trigon."

"Damn. I hate when I can't hear what they're saying to each other."

"Don't worry, Alea, you'll develop a sixth sense about what's going on in their minds, just like you would a single mate," Karen said.

"I suppose, but still… damn."

"It's all a part of the mating game, Alea. Just go with it."

"If they want to trap and have sex with me so badly, why don't they just do that transdelta linking thingy and put me to sleep?"

"They probably will, but only when they're close enough to you."

"If you're too far away, as soon as they break the link, you would wake up and run off," Reasa added and started pacing again.

"Okay, I can buy into this." Alea stood and Syrat actually looked relieved that Alea was on her feet. "And I can certainly understand why a virgin would flee, but all of you are mated, so why do you run?"

Syrat rose to her feet and Karen followed.

"To keep the Prowlers away from you. Our Sh'em instinctively chase us when we run," Syrat told her.

Karen waggled her eyebrows. "It makes the men very horny."

"If we don't run," Syrat continued, "they will ignore us and stalk after you, and believe me, you don't want to find yourself surrounded by all of those brawny warriors. It's rather a frightening thought. Don't you think?"

"Would make me panic." Reasa shuddered. "It was bad enough having my own Sh'em stalking me when I was a Tina."

"Well, they don't scare me," Alea stated firmly.

Reasa suddenly froze. Her nostrils flared and she sniffed

the air. "They're coming. I can smell my Sh'em, and they are very aroused."

Karen and Syrat started sniffing the air as well. Alea laughed out loud because they looked so silly.

But then, the aroma of Alea's own Sh'em tickled at her nose.

The heads of all four women snapped toward the top of the hill.

They were there, quietly creeping over the crest on their bellies, halting when they spied their prey and then drawing upright to their full masculine lengths. They started down the hill at a steady, sauntering pace, eight virile savages stalking toward their females with carnal intent, evidenced by their scents and lust hungry-eyes and erections that swelled beneath their loincloths.

Alea's heart started thumping and her breathing grew rapid. She felt like a deer trapped in the headlights of an oncoming car, aroused and intrigued and entranced.

The sight was overwhelming.

The other She'mana must have been just as captivated, because none of them were moving.

Tren's hand skimmed over his groin as his gaze stroked Alea's body. Rjant kept on swaggering toward her, eyeing her with an equal amorous delight.

And then, Rjant and Tren drew their wooden talons, lifting them high in the air. Rjant roared first, and thrust his pelvis with a sexual sway. Tren leapt forward with Rjant at his side and the rest of the Prowlers followed. Chests heaving, they howled their savage bed-lust cries, and started rushing toward the women.

"Oh shit!" Alea shrieked and took off like a scared, little bunny leaving Karen, Syrat and Reasa in the wake of her dust, darting to the forest beyond.

Chapter Nine

Alea was sitting in a tree.

She was reasonably sure she was concealed, her clothing suitably blending with the plum-colored leaves and the fact that the Prowlers had run right beneath without detecting her. The other She'mana did finally run as well, Alea knew, since they too, passed beneath her only moments before their Sh'em did.

Syrat must have circled around, for now Alea was watching her. She looked like a lioness as she crept on all fours, her head held low and her back in a hunch. She crouched behind a large boulder, sniffing the air.

All Syrat needed was a tail sticking out of her ass to complete the picture. Apparently content that she evaded her Sh'em, Syrat suddenly stood and with a two-footed vault, she sprang atop the rock, brought her hand to her forehead to shield her eyes and scanned the surrounding area. Her attention fixated in Alea's direction. Smiling smugly, Syrat strolled to the tree and tilted her face upward.

"I told you Tinas always run," she said with a hushed tone, her head darting around to be sure she was not heard.

"Yeah, well." Alea pushed from her perch, hung from the branch for a moment, her feet dangling about four feet from the ground. "It was an impulsive reaction."

She let go and dropped down, landing elegantly on her feet and thinking she had to have been a cat in her former life, considering how fast she scrambled up the tree earlier.

"So, now what?" Alea brushed her palms together a few times and looked around.

"I'll show you how to survive out here since you will be the last one captured."

"What makes you so sure of that?"

Syrat crooked an eyebrow at her. "Your Sh'em aren't familiar with your behaviors, therefore you're at an advantage to evade them. Ours however are much more aware of what we will do. Therefore, we will likely be caught first."

"Maybe I'll just let them catch me."

Syrat threw back her head and released a hearty guffaw. "I'd like to see you try."

"What's that supposed to mean?"

"Never mind." Taking Alea by the upper arm, Syrat led her down a roughly worn path. She stopped at a short, rounded bush bursting with bright red flowers. Releasing Alea she parted the branches and then motioned Alea to take a look.

Alea bent to get a better view, and Syrat stuck her hand into the foliage, felt around a bit and pulled out something that resembled a large, misshapen mushroom. "This grows at the base of the plant's stem."

She tore the mushroom in half and put one piece in her mouth. The other she handed to Alea. "It's nutritious and filling. You could survive on this alone for many dawnings."

Alea placed the chunk in her mouth and tasted it. "It's not too bad. But what about water?"

"Water?"

"Taw." Alea corrected her word.

"Oh, well…" Syrat started to point down the trail, but her body suddenly stiffened and her head whipped to one side. She tipped her head as if listening for something and she sniffed the air.

"Your Sh'em are close by?" Alea asked, scanning the foliage surrounding them. She didn't smell or hear a thing.

"Let's go." Syrat motioned for Alea to follow her, cautiously looking around, and they started up the trail, "They're close."

Alea's heart thumped as she tread behind Syrat, her head darting from tree to tree, searching for signs of the Prowlers, as well. She wasn't exactly afraid anymore. The hunt was feeling more like a game--sort of like hide and go seek--though some amount of anxiety was still lurking inside of her.

Several yards down the path, Syrat paused and pointed to another plant. It was a dwarfed tree that stood about six feet high. Its amber colored bark and branches twisted like an arthritic appendage, and its leaves were like ribbons of lavender silk. Syrat reached up and plucked a pear-shaped fruit from one of the branches. She held it up for Alea to inspect.

"Looks good, doesn't it?"

Alea shrugged. "Sure, I guess."

"Well, it's not. Don't eat these. Your belly will swell like a ball of gas, and you'll be sick for at least three dawnings." Syrat tossed the fruit over her shoulder and continued down the trail, until they reached a small clearing. "There's a taw lake just beyond...."

Syrat fell silent and swallowed hard.

A twig snapped somewhere within the forest, and then another.

"Take this." Syrat removed a belt from around her waist and wrapped it around Alea, buckling it into place. Alea fingered the sheath on the belt that held a ten inch dagger.

"What am I supposed to do with the knife?" She gave Syrat a confused look.

"You'll need it to gut your kill."

Alea's face twisted with distaste at the idea of killing something for food. She liked meat, especially steak, but slaughtering was a job that belonged to other people.

"What about fire?" Alea patted her hands down the length of her clothing, a gestural search for matches. "How am I supposed to cook it?"

"You don't. Just gut it and eat it."

"E-y-yeck!" Alea nearly gagged at the thought. "Isn't that unhealthy?"

"No."

"I think I'll just stick with those fungus plants."

"Suit yourself, but you'll probably tire of them." Syrat's head jerked around and she tossed a nervous glance over her shoulder. "I have to go!"

Leaping away from Alea, Syrat began darting across the clearing. There was a crashing sound from the forest and two male bodies burst through the foliage from two different directions. Alea shrieked as one of them brushed by her, ignoring her completely. Syrat squealed as she was suddenly grabbed from behind by Reo, one of her Sh'em. Merse, her other Sh'em stood in front.

Before Alea knew what was happening, Syrat's clothing was shed from her body and she was down on all fours. Both of her Sh'em freed their stiff cocks and they dropped to their knees. Reo leaned forward and lapped at Syrat's pussy, running his tongue along her slit. With two hands, Merse grabbed locks of Syrat's hair and brought her head forward, stuffing his shaft into her mouth.

Syrat sucked him wildly.

Alea couldn't help but watch, mesmerized by the erotic scene playing out before her eyes. And they didn't even seem to care that she was there.

Reo's head came up and he straightened to a tall kneel, bringing Syrat with him, pressing her back against his chest. He impaled her from behind and began pumping into her. Merse shifted between her thighs then both of Syrat's mates were ramming into her with such force that Syrat was being lifted from the ground.

Alea was awestruck that one female body could take so much masculine flesh at one time.

Apparently it could, for Syrat was crooning her bliss while her two horny mates groaned in response.

Merse glanced back at Alea, his shiny, dark hair flying in an untamed mass about his head, as he ferociously pummeled into his wife. His royal blue, gold-rimmed eyes locked with Alea's. "Come around, *yitrup*."

He called her *innocent one*.

"I want to see your face."

Alea felt herself blush and looked away, but slowly she lifted her eyes again, drawn to the carnal ménage.

Merse still watched her.

Her feet began to move, as she sidestepped around the periphery of the clearing until she was face to face with Merse. He lifted his chin and flashed a lecherous smile.

Rjant, Tren, are you both close by?

Merse?
Yes, it's me.
Where are you?
In the clearing at the end of the nortdum path.
What are you doing?
I'm fucking Syrat.
Rjant received a telepathic groan from Merse.
And why do we need to know this?
I am watching Alea watch me fuck Syrat.
Is she frightened?
I believe she looks aroused.

Rjant's groin tightened in anticipation. He glanced at Tren, who was circling around to the other path that would take him to the opposite side of the clearing. Tren's lips curled with victorious satisfaction. They were closing in.

They would trap her.

Merse continued to fixate on Alea, while maintaining his cocking rhythm inside of Syrat, amused by her fascinated expression. Most Tinas fled screaming when they witnessed the Prowlers' aggressive mating. He was surprised that this was one did not. Now, if he could just hold her attention until her Sh'em arrived.

Reo, fully aware and integrated with the linking, deepened his thrusts, intent on keeping Syrat's pleasure heightened. Syrat had been their She'mana long enough to know when he and Merse were transmitting thoughts. She would warn the Tina of their telepathic plot, and the Tina would then likely flee.

"Watch us, *Tina*. Watch a true Tertian mating." Merse shifted onto his haunches, bringing Syrat forward to his chest. Reo leaned back slightly and pulled his hips back, giving Alea a full view of the sexual playground.

Her eyes widened in disbelief.

What were they doing? Syrat's anus was clearly visible and untouched.

But they couldn't both possibly be in her at the same time!

One... two... three.... Alea counted. *Impossible.*

She counted again, but there was no mistake about it.

Alea saw three openings, and Syrat had two vaginas!

Two!

The need for two males is biological, Alea. Tren's words floated into her brain.

If they wanted children.

Rjant and Tren had to know that she wasn't built like that. Their fingers and mouths explored her enough on the Stardancer to at least have a tactile idea of her anatomy.

But what if they didn't? What if they tried to both...They would never fit!

Alea started to panic.

You won't think much about our scruples after the ceremony, Tina.

Well, Syrat might have a canyon-sized vagina but Alea most certainly didn't. There was no way on God's green Earth or Tertia's amber soil that Alea was going to let them do that to her.

They would rip her apart!

Fair warning, Tina. The more you taunt your Sh'em, the more aggressive we become.

She made an immediate decision that her Sh'em would be the first in Tertian history to *never* catch their female.

Alea started backing away, but someone grabbed her wrist and she screeched.

"Let's get out of here." It was only Karen, thank goodness. "I saw Rjant coming down the path and I'm sure Tren is nearby."

Pulling Alea away from the scene, Karen led her through the brush. They passed a small taw lake, probably the one that Syrat mentioned, and continued until they reached a crag of rocks. She guided Alea into a crevice between them, ducking to enter a small, but well-hidden cave.

"Well, that was something." Karen sat down on the cave's floor. "I've never seen a Tertian tripling before."

"I can't do that!" Alea cried.

Karen stared at her. "Why not?"

"I only have one vagina!"

"Well, so do I, silly." Karen stood, crouching to keep from hitting her head on the cave's low ceiling. She placed a comforting hand on Alea's shoulder. "You'll be fine. I was."

Alea shook her head from side to side. "I don't care. The women on Dormoth might be used to that sort of thing, but I...."

"Dormoth?" Karen interrupted. "Didn't Lemac tell you? I'm from Earth, just like you."

Alea went silent. She'd forgotten that Lemac's She'mana was anxious to meet her. "You are?"

"Come and sit down. I think we have a little time."

Alea sat on the ground, attempting to catch her breath and calm her nerves. Karen joined her.

"I've been in the galaxy for three years, living on Terta Minor with my Sh'em, Lemac and Dgor. They and Rjant are good friends. I was so thrilled when they told me that their Tina was from my home world. I get so homesick sometimes."

Karen leaned forward and propped her forearms onto her crossed legs, lacing her fingers together. "Tell me some news."

Alea blinked at her for a few moments, letting the fact that Karen was also an earthling sink in, and was suddenly comforted by it. "Well," Alea finally started talking. "There's a new president and another war in the Middle East."

"I guess some things never change," Karen responded dryly.

Alea studied Karen's face. "Hey, wait a minute. I know you. You're that jogger that disappeared from Central Park. You're Karen Whitaker!"

"That would be me."

"Your parents were crazy with worry. It was all over the news. They had a two million dollar reward for information leading to...."

Alea snapped her mouth shut at the saddened expression that swept across Karen's face. "I'm sorry that was insensitive of me."

Karen inhaled a deep breath and then exhaled. "It's okay. I miss my family terribly, but my Sh'em said it's too dangerous to visit, that Earth's location must be kept a secret."

"Well I think it's awful that you were taken away from your loved ones. At least I had no one to leave behind."

"Oh no, Alea. I belong here."

Alea furled her brow. "Are you happy?"

"Very! I love my Sh'em. We have a son together." Karen cast her gaze downward and a contented smile graced her lips. Her voice grew quieter. "Tell me Alea, did the cravings for two men drive you insane?"

"How do you know about that?"

Karen looked up. "Why else would you have been chosen by Trigon males? I suffered from the same urges. It was maddening. I thought there was something wrong with me."

"So did I." Alea eyes darted to the cave's opening as she thought about Syrat and her mates. "But still, I'm not sure I can do that."

"Oh don't worry about it. Syrat has been with her Sh'em for ten years. They have six children together. Your Sh'em will understand. They'll be as gentle with you as they possibly can."

Alea gave her an *I'm not so sure about that* glance, remembering how she tormented them on the Stardancer.

Karen stood, crouching low and headed for the mouth of the cave. "I have to go now."

"Why?" Standing as well, Alea crouched along with her.

"My Sh'em are looking for me. If they find me with you they will inform your Sh'em."

Embracing Alea, Karen gave her a quick, but awkward hug considering their bent positions, before disappearing through the cave's opening. Alea sat back down and leaned against the rocky wall. She rubbed her forehead. The She'mana all assumed she would eventually be captured by Tren and Rjant, yet they were doing everything in their power to hide her.

This was all so weird.

Maybe she should swallow her fears and go find her Sh'em herself--just get it over with. A picture of the mating between the Trigon ot Syrat floated into her brain again, and Alea started to shake.

No way. Not *ever.*

She looked toward the cave's opening. The light was fading and night was beginning to fall. Alea sniffed the air. Nothing but its fresh warmth reached her senses. She yawned and started to relax. Within minutes Alea was sound asleep.

Chapter Ten

Alea crawled from her hiding space keeping low to the ground and sniffing the air. Amused that she was mimicking Syrat, Alea twisted her head around to see if a tail *had* grown from her ass. She had to admit that there was merit in the behavior, because if her Sh'em were close by, she would smell them. To her relief, Alea was greeted by the warmth and brightness of an early morning sun, and nothing else.

Had they given up? And why was she feeling disappointed by that thought?

Alea shook away the feeling. She needed a plan, but first things first. She was hungry and thirsty. Standing upright, Alea looked around. The exotic coloring of the Tertian terrain and purplish hue of the dawning light was a vivid reminder that Alea was far from Earth. How would she survive out here alone? Could the other She'mana help her? Alea fingered the hilt of the dagger in the sheath. Though she had yet to see any wild life, Alea wondered how she would know if any creatures she encountered were dangerous. It would be the only thing that made her capable of killing anything. Alea leaned back against the rocks behind her, and scrutinized the path that she and Karen traveled on the day before. It appeared deserted, but of course that didn't mean that it was. Nevertheless the lake was in that direction, so Alea headed down the path. She got no further than several yards when Lemac, who was hiding behind a bush, jumped out in front of her.

Startled, Alea released a shrilling screech. "Don't touch me!"

His lips turned up in an eerily calm smile. "We won't touch you, Tina."

We? She started backing away from him, afraid to interpret what he meant by that, when a pair of hands grabbed her shoulders from behind. Alea stiffened, sprang forward and spun around.

Another Prowler.

"Dgor?"

He nodded.

Turning once more to face Lemac, Alea waited to see what they would do, but they just stood there. It suddenly occurred to her that they might be channeling to Tren and Rjant.

Fear took hold of her.

What should she do?

Well, she wasn't about to wait around and let herself be trapped. Alea drew the knife, and when they didn't react, she brushed by Lemac and continued on her way. They followed her at close range, keeping time with her pace. It was then that Alea caught a glimpse of Merse as he moved between the trees, stalking alongside her, off the edge of the path. Alea bit her lip, worry creasing her brow. They had to know these woods better than she did. How could she lose them? Alea came to a crossroads and abruptly stopped. Reo was blocking one of the trails. He stood there, talon arc in one hand, arms crossed over his chest and feet splayed apart. He eyed her, but said nothing. Alea shot him a defiant look and headed up the open path, feeling much like a wayward sheep being corralled to the barn.

Where the hell were the other She'mana now that she really needed them?

Probably lying comatose after having their brains fucked out by their Sh'em.

Keep your eyes peeled and your nose open, Alea. She reminded herself, taking a whiff of the air, but there was no sign of either Rjant or Tren.

Alea turned round and round, narrowing her eyes and searching through the dense foliage surrounding her. It seemed she was no longer being trailed. The Prowlers either disappeared, or were just hiding. She tipped her head to listen, but heard nothing except a mild breeze as it rustled through the forest and the bird-like whistling sounds of some unseen creature.

Realizing that she still held the knife in her hand, Alea sheathed the weapon. It was ridiculous to think she would actually stab someone, but maybe it served as a good threat. Maybe that's why they refrained from pouncing on her.

Maybe.

But where were they now?

It was ominously quiet as she reached the lake, but Alea had a strange feeling that she was being watched. What difference did it make? She wouldn't be able to fight them all off anyway. She imagined herself as superwoman, cape and all, tossing the Prowlers into the lake, one after the other, as they tried to nab her. How comical their stupefied expressions would be as she demonstrated her superhuman strength.

That'll teach them to mess with *Earth bitch girl!*

Alea giggled at her own stupid thoughts and knelt beside the lake. Scooping some taw into her cupped hands she took several drinks. Once her thirst was satisfied, Alea splashed her face and then dragged her fingers through her tangled hair, combing until it was relatively free of snarls. She really could use a rubber band. In fact she could use a big pile of rubber bands. They made great weapons. All she had to do was take aim beneath their loincloths and with one snap to their nuts, the Prowlers would be howling and scampering like wounded dogs.

Alea inhaled and sighed, inhaled again and froze. A familiar fragrance wafted to her nose. Her head snapped up.

Rjant was sitting on a boulder across the small lake. One foot flattened to the ground, the other propped on top of the rock, a muscular arm resting on his knee. His gold and bronze hair was tucked behind an ear on one side. On the other side, the wavy mane fell across his face, partially covering it, fanning occasionally under the drift of the slightly moving air. His expression was so intense and alluring that a tantalizing fire went up Alea's spine, inflamed by the sight of his hand shifting beneath his loincloth. He slid his palm along his cock, rocking his pelvis in rhythm with his strokes, as he probed her with his gripping gaze. Alea's nipples hardened and her vagina tightened. Her heart beat harder and she clenched her fists, remembering how badly she wanted to touch him.

Her attention shifted to the form that stood just behind him.

Tren leaned against a tree, arms folded, one leg crossed over the other in a near casual posture. His riveting glare was unblinking--turquoise pools of untamed lust--his eyes bore into her like a famished predator. And she couldn't miss the rock hard bulge throbbing beneath his loincloth. Slowly her gaze wandered upward, watching every firm muscle in his abdomen and chest rippling under the caress of her admiring eyes. His silky mane was tied in a queue and draped over one of his shoulders. His masculine mouth was full and enticing, and Alea licked her lips as she focused on his face, remembering how badly she wanted to taste him.

There was a sensual gleam in both of their eyes, as they watched her… waiting… craving.

Heat shot through Alea and danced along her flesh. Her pussy was soaking wet. Unconsciously her hand skimmed up her body, her fingers molding around a breast.

Desire… need… fear.

She shuddered.

Tren stepped forward and Rjant was moving. They were circling the lake in opposite directions, stalking closer. Unrestrained bestial masculinity prowling toward her, paralyzing Alea, capturing her with their sexual power, and she felt helpless.

Run.

Alea ran, dashing down the nearest path--an unknown path--as fast as she could, with her Sh'em just on her heels. It was terrifying and exhilarating, though she knew she could not outrun them. But still she had to try.

She burst into an open field of nothing but flat terrain and started sprinting across it. In perfect speed, her long legs carried her with alternating precision and ease--her heartbeat, her breathing in rhythmic accord as she pounded the soil beneath her feet. She thought about the words of her coach and his comment about another dimension.

If he could see her now.

Quickly she scanned ahead, mapping out her course, and came to the sudden realization that there was nowhere to go. A rocky barrier lay just ahead, spanning the entire horizon like a massive step in the Tertian terrain, and there appeared to be no way around it.

Without another option Alea ran toward it surveying the cliff as she drew closer. It looked to be about fifty feet high, with many jags and crevices that would provide plenty of holds.

But without any safety lines, if she lost her grip....

Alea could only hope that Tertian medicine was advanced enough to put her back together should she fall.

She could scale it, though it would be moderately difficult. Back on Earth she did this whenever she got the chance--at the climbing center in the mall--and she was pretty darn good at it.

Only fell a couple of times.

Maybe the real thing wouldn't be so different.

Alea took a deep breath and began to climb, carefully testing the protrusions and concaves, as she pushed upward. It was more difficult than she thought it would be, but she was managing. At this point she wouldn't worry about what she would find at the top, though it would really suck if there was a steep ravine or another cliff beyond it. Without warning her right foot slipped and she stiffened, cleaving her fingers to the stony surface.

Her heart thumped and she held her breath. *Easy, find your footing. Don't look down.*

She looked down.

Stupid, stupid, stupid!

Alea never thought that twenty-five short feet could look so far away. Closing her eyes, she tried with desperation to tamp down her alarm.

Her Sh'em were down there, she'd caught a quick glimpse of them. They were glaring up at her with disbelief written all over their gorgeous faces. Alea would have laughed if she wasn't so frightened.

Concentrate.

Alea skimmed the wall with her wayward foot and exhaled in sharp relief when it found a solid surface. Pushing with her feet and reaching with her hands she continued her vertical ascent. Her legs and arms were burning with the exertion, but still she pushed upward.

Rjant's mouth dropped open with awe and admiration. Being an avid climber himself, when time allowed, he was quite appreciative of his Tina's skill. His eyes searched the rocky face, seeking Alea's next hold. He nodded in approval as she chose exactly the way he would have. "She's fantastic, brethren."

"She is going break her fucking neck!" Tren watched in horror as Alea scaled the wall, his heart lurching forward when she lost a foothold, causing a multitude of tiny pebbles to come tumbling down upon them. Though he'd tried the climbing sport a few times, Tren preferred the abandoned freedom of racing his hover cycle across the open plains with the wind whipping through his hair. He preferred that his feet remain close to the ground.

Rjant grinned at his brethren as he found a firm grip on the face of the cliff. He started scrambling after Alea. Tren had no intention of following. Scanning the base of the cliff, he located the landmarks of the concealed passage that led to the top and moved toward it.

Alea looked up. Five more feet and she would be curling her fingers around the brim. This time she did not look down, but focused on reaching the top, and within moments she was there. She'd actually done it! Alea beamed proudly at her accomplishment, but her excitement was short-lived when two hands clamped around her wrists and jerked her the rest of the way over the edge. She let out a scream of surprise, as Tren rolled to his back, pulling Alea on top of him. She fought him, catching only glimpses of the savage, carnal look on his face as he tumbled her across the plush Tertian carpet beneath them. With one final twist Alea was trapped beneath his body. He stilled her thrashing head between his hands and lowered his mouth to kiss her. In that brief, still moment she caught a glimpse of Rjant vaulting over the cliff's edge. He leapt, but not at her. It was Tren he went after, and with a wild howl, he yanked Tren off of her and they were fighting. They drew their wooden talons, clashing and striking, consumed by a primal, subconscious need to demonstrate their prowess.

Alea struggled to her feet, watching as Tren swung his arc, striking horizontally, catching Rjant against his rib cage. Rjant roared as he staggered sideways, but in the same instant drove his talon upward. It caught Tren's sparring arm, slamming against his wrist. His talon arc flew from his hand, spun through the air like a wayward boomerang, and speared itself into the ground several yards away. Tren growled like a ferocious beast and threw a backhanded strike to Rjant's jaw. Rjant retaliated with his own wild roar, burying his fist into Tren's stomach, and then they were rolling on the ground again. Alea started to scream, as Rjant's hands clasped around Tren's face and he smashed the back of Tren's head against the ground. Tren snarled, clamping a hand onto Rjant's face, his other hand at Rjant's throat and with one, swift and mighty push Tren threw Rjant off of him, and Rjant landed flat on his back.

They were going to kill each other and Alea didn't know why, or what to do about it. She buried her face in her hands, not wanting to witness the outcome. This was not the way the other Trigon males reacted to finding their She'mana, so why were Tren and Rjant behaving this way?

The first mating.

They were claiming the Tina, engaged in the most ancient and barbaric form of the Tertian Flaunting, a savage, brutal battle, two alpha males fighting for the rights to their female, proving their worth.

Alea spread her fingers to peek at what was happening.

They were crouched low and facing each other, arms outspread and fingers clawed, chests heaving, brows sweating, feral eyes locked. Their individual scents flooded the air and then mingled. They were equally dominant.

One could not defeat the other.

Alea yelped drawing their attention to her. In unanimous relenting, they both drew up to their full heights and with quick, long strides began stalking in her direction.

Alea started to tremble and panic assailed her. She was terrified they would shred her apart. There was no way they would be able to calmly make love to her after what she'd just seen.

Her head darted to and fro searching for escape. Without thinking she drew her blade, glaring into their predatory eyes.

"Get away from me!"

She's hysterical. Rjant eyed her warily, plotting a way to disarm her.

We have to calm her or she won't mate. Tren silently responded back, waiting for an opening to pounce on her without getting any of them stabbed.

Do you need our help? Lemac entered their thoughts.

No. I think your presence will only make it worse. Stay back until you are summoned.

"Don't you think you're over-reacting, Alea?" Tren took a step toward her, his body glistening with sweat, his chest heaving from his exertion.

She took a step back.

"I never over-react," she answered in a firm voice though every nerve in her body vibrated tautly, like guitar strings that had just been plucked.

Rjant moved forward, wiping the sweat from his forehead. "Then what do you call that?" He waved his hand in the direction of the blade she held.

"I call it a knife." Her chin went up a notch.

"You don't really mean to stab us, do you, *wife?*" Tren used the Earth word for She'mana, and for a brief moment, Alea warmed to it. But fear overcame her once more when Rjant reached, took her wrist and uncurled her fingers from around the hilt of the dagger. He removed it from her grasp with relative ease and then tossed it aside.

Alea's shoulders sagged at her lack of defenses, both physical and emotional. She was vulnerable and at their mercy, made most apparent when Tren and Rjant lifted their hands to form the transdelta link to enter the core of her mind. Alea had only a moment to shake her head in the negative before her eyes drifted shut.

Within a fragment of a second she was lying supine in their arms and they were caressing and kissing her body. Supernal mixed with tangible as Rjant slid her pants down her legs, and as he did so, he planted kisses along one of her legs, from the top of her thigh, down to the top of her foot. Her boots were apparently gone already. She had no awareness of when they were removed. Her eyes began to flutter open to the realization that her top was off too, and Tren was cradling her over his thighs and suckling her breasts. Alea groaned, dropping her head back, as Rjant's face dipped between her legs and he started licking her pussy.

With foggy awareness, murmuring chants drifted to her ears. Alea opened her eyes and scanned around. Much to her dismay she saw that they were surrounded by the Prowlers, who were sitting cross-legged in a circle around them, eyes closed and reciting their mantras through the deltas they formed with their hands.

"What are they doing here?" she gasped out, her body going rigid. Being watched was never one of her fantasies.

"They are here to witness and to beseech the divinities to bless our joining," Tren whispered in her ear.

Alea was mortified. She didn't want others around when she lost her virginity. It was too… too personal. She sprang to her feet so quickly that Rjant fell face down into the empty space she left behind.

Alea darted from the circle, a final but feeble attempt at best, for when a Prowler's hand shot out to clasp her ankle, Alea knew she could easily dodge it. But her mind reacted to her heart's desires and her reflexes did not respond. Alea was affirmatively glad, because deep, deep down she really didn't want to flee.

Her body hit the ground with a heavy thud and the air was expelled from her lungs. A Prowler was instantly on top of her, his limbs and his trunk pinning her down, his semi-erection pressing into her butt. It was a bit humiliating, considering she was totally naked, and she was thankful for the loincloth that separated their flesh from making contact.

"We serve a third purpose, Tina. To make sure you don't escape once you are captured," the Prowler whispered, his deep, bass voice tickling her ear.

"You can get off her now, Merse." Tren knelt down as Merse rolled off of Alea and returned to his place among the other Prowlers. Alea pushed to a sitting position, drawing up her legs and crossing her arms over her chest in an attempt to hide her private areas. The first thing she noticed was that Tren was nude, her eyes magnetically drawn to the hardened shaft between his legs and the swollen gonads that hung below it. Embarrassed, she glanced away only to find herself eye level with Rjant's erection as he crouched before her. Alea blushed profusely, realizing it was the first time she had ever been this up close and personal with the uncovered, male appendage. Of course she'd seen pictures, but this was much, much different. These were real, and not just for her viewing pleasure either. Her Sh'em meant to use them on her.

Rjant crooked a finger under her chin and tilted her head to see her face. "Do you really still want to leave us, Tina?"

"I don't want them watching," she whispered.

Tren smoothed his hand along her back. "We could send them away, Alea, but I assure you they are not watching."

Alea turned to look at him. There was a concerned expression on his face.

"They ask the divinities for the blessing of our joining," Rjant said. "Don't you want our joining to be blessed?"

Alea shifted her gaze to Rjant. His expression was tight and there was a line of worry crossing his handsome brow, as well.

They were disturbed that she wanted the Prowlers sent away.

Realization struck her. The first mating was a sacred event for the Tertani people, one that was not taken lightly or with disregard. The blessing was momentously important to their spirituality and their beliefs.

Still partially aroused, Alea dropped her head and studied Rjant's manhood, and then shifted to look at Tren's. Her head tipped up see Tren's face and then she turned to look back at Rjant.

Two years….

They courted her and grew to care for her. And they *did* care for her. She could read it in their expressions, see it in their actions. She could feel it deep within her soul.

When they could've taken her, instead they waited-- patiently they waited for this moment that they could rightfully make her their own. With sudden awareness, Alea knew that she had waited patiently for them too. She openly accepted and willingly trusted them.

She *loved* them and wanted to make love to them with no uncertainty. If that meant the Prowlers being present, then so it shall be.

Firmly ignoring her hammering, frightened heart, Alea silently held out a hand to each of her Sh'em and they helped her to her feet, leading her back to the center of the Prowler's circle.

Chapter Eleven

Tren pulled Alea against him, pressing his erection against her backside, and sliding his arms around her. He scooped her breasts within his hands and worked at them, lifting and kneading them, gently plucking and pinching her nipples. Alea shuddered at the sweet sensation, and then suddenly tensed, her eyes darting to the circle of Prowlers around them. They chanted their prayers from where they sat, and just as Tren assured her, it seemed they weren't watching. Their eyes were closed and their expressions were solemn. They appeared oblivious to the tripling, absorbed only by their prayers.

"Alea." The sound of Rjant's voice swayed her attention from the Prowlers and she shifted her eyes to meet his gaze. He smiled softly and placed his hand on her hips, stepping toward her, pressing a gentle kiss to her lips.

Alea relaxed, focusing on Rjant's face and the warmth of Tren's hands as he caressed her, putting the Prowlers to the back of her mind. She was going to make love to her Sh'em now and that was all that mattered. Alea swallowed hard. The thought incited a combination of both nervous excitement and apprehension, and she started to tremble.

Rjant's hands grazed along the front of her thighs and then one hand swept up to touch her between the legs. Alea sucked in her breath and held it as Rjant dropped to his knees in front of her. He grazed his knuckles along the curls of hair, skimming her clit and causing a cadence of shockwaves to ripple through her. He leaned in, bringing his face so close that his warm breath feathered against her. Alea released her breath in a heavy quiver and she squirmed with anticipation. Rjant's tongue darted out and he licked along the crease between her labia, before parting her lips with his fingers to sip on her clitoris. Her balance started to waver, but Tren held her hips, steadying her from behind. He was grinding his cock against her bottom while nibbling her neck and shoulders. Slowly he started to lower her down, bringing her to rest on one of his thighs, as he sat back on his haunches.

Rjant followed their descent, with his mouth still firmly latched to her pussy. He bent her knees and spread her legs, kneeling between them, and continued to lap at her, long slow licks, quick sucks to her clit, his teeth teasing her inner swellings, his tongue exploring every crevice of her vulva, sexing her with his mouth.

Alea's breath quickened and she threaded her fingers through Rjant's hair and stilled his head. She rotated her pelvis, fucking his mouth. Her body quaked, responding to the stimulation between her legs and to the sensual feel of Tren kissing her throat, and then moving lower, skimming his lips across the swell of her breasts. He drew a stiffened nipple into his mouth, flicking it with his tongue, nipping lightly at the delicate flesh with his teeth, and then shifting to attend to the other one. A cry of protest left her lips when he moved away, but was quickly replaced by her breathy gasps when his mouth joined Rjant's between her thighs.

"Oh…" Alea crooned, opening her legs impossibly wider, her knees nearly touching the ground beneath her, giving them both enough room. She tipped her pelvis toward their faces, her fingers digging into the mossy surface at her sides. Tren's tongue dabbed repeatedly at her clit, while Rjant's tongue dipped in and out of her vagina--two, soft, warm tongues slurping at her pussy.

Their masculine scents were emanating stronger than ever before, enrapturing her, capturing her, and Alea thrashed her head from side to side, overwhelmed with the carnal tide flooding her.

Tren's side-lying position brought his groin in close proximity to Alea's head, and she stopped her writhing abruptly as his stiffened cock came deliciously close to her face, brushed against her cheek. She stared at the appendage, thick and long, jutting upward against his abdomen, and she reached for it, tracing the pulsating vein that ran along its underside with one of her fingers. She fit her hand around the shaft, surprised by the dry, hot, silky feel of it as it throbbed beneath her palm. Slowly she stroked her hand down its length, and then stopped to fondle his balls. They were tight and swollen, and Alea marveled at how large and heavy they felt. Tren groaned, and Rjant, catching the wave of pleasure their Tina was giving Tren, groaned in tempo. Alea's tongue darted out to taste the tip, and Tren's hips jerked slightly in response. In an almost instinctual manner, Alea began swirling her tongue around the crown, losing herself in the heady feeling of finally being able to fully stimulate her Sh'em. Tren angled his pelvis, sliding his rod forward, and Alea molded her lips around it, her tongue flattened and gliding along the shaft as he moved in and out of her mouth. His momentum increased and Alea felt him stiffen more as he stroked deeper inside, closer to the opening of her throat.

She was surprised she could take so much of him.

Her other hand moved down her body to comb her fingers first through Tren's hair and then Rjant's, as they continued to stimulate her pussy. Tren licked her clitoris with his tongue, while Rjant replaced his mouth with an index finger, slipping it slightly into the hollow between her legs. He circled his finger around inside, dipping deeper and then pulling back. Alea bucked at the alien sensation, but her feminine muscles clamped around it, and she sighed with a quivering breath. She had never even done this to herself before, and the feeling of being penetrated, even if it was just a modest invasion, sent delectable shivers up her spine. Her vagina responded, growing wet with arousal, and she was ready for more.

Tren and Rjant both inhaled deeply, savoring Alea's excitement, smiling with satisfaction at the heated moisture and fragrance of her growing need.

Slowly Rjant stretched up the length of her, pausing to suck at her breast, and then turning her head away from Tren, he fastened his lips with hers. He kissed her hungrily, plying her tongue with his own, mimicking what his finger was doing as it slipped in and out of her. Alea moaned as he kissed her and he moaned back, her mouth an enticing treasure to him, full and soft and inviting--a mouth he could kiss until the end of all time and never grow tired of doing it.

Rjant rolled Alea to her side so she was facing him, his hardened shaft resting against her lower belly, and he slid his finger further inside of her, up to the second knuckle. He could feel the flesh of her hymen and didn't dare press any further.

Ka, Tren! She is so tight! Rjant clenched his teeth, shuddering wildly, and Tren knew his brethren was straining for control. He was feeling quite randy himself, but was also aware they were capable of hurting her.

Take ease, Rjant. Tren began reversing his position, nipping at the back of Alea's thigh and her bottom, drawing torrid shivers from her as he worked his way along her back. His hand came to rest on her waist, his thickened rod nested in the crevice of her behind and he bit lightly at her shoulder, before moving to the side of her neck and then to her earlobe. Bracing one hand beneath her chin, he broke her contact with Rjant and she willingly turned her head toward him. Tren lowered his lips to cover her mouth, gently caressing her supple, warm flesh, holding her unaware of his young brethren's building need to plunder her innocent body.

His heart thumped hard against his breast bone and something deep inside of him stirred. It amazed him how much he enjoyed kissing her. Alea roused emotions in him he thought were long-dead, softening his battle-hardened soul. He knew without pause that he would cherish this first mating with her--*cherish her*--until his mind could no longer think, until the breath left his body forever.

Tren deepened his kiss, threading his fingers through her thick, luxurious hair, holding her head steady so he could ravish her mouth thoroughly, his tongue gliding with hers, tasting her sweetness, feeling as though he couldn't get enough--he would never get enough of her.

Kissing Alea was lovemaking all on its own.

Rjant pressed his thumb to Alea's feminine swelling, circling, rotating her bud, exactly in the way he knew she liked, while his finger continued to move in and out of her. He was stroking deeper, faster, his hips moving back and forth against her stomach in time with his hand. His breathing grew harsh and he was losing himself.

Stroke easy, brethren, Tren warned, tamping down the primal Tertani urge to take their She'mana roughly.

"Join me," Rjant grunted out loud. *I don't know how much longer I can wait.*

Tren smoothed his hand along the curve of Alea's bottom and down the back of her thigh. Lifting and bending her leg, he placed it to rest over Rjant's hip. He pressed his thumb against her anal opening, entering just a tiny bit, while pushing his index finger inside her hollow, sliding it inward to meet Rjant's finger.

Her labia were swollen. She was hot and wet and willing... and damn....

He was so fucking horny.

Alea sucked in her breath, assaulted by a delicious sexual surge she didn't even know her body was capable of. There were two fingers inside her, not quite as thick as a single cock but filling her nonetheless. And the titillating sensation of the ever-so-slight trespass to her bottom by Tren's thumb sent ripples of pleasure through her pelvic area. Her breath quickened, as her arousal began a riotous rise.

"Oh, don't stop..." she pleaded, moving her hips, clenching her vagina, seeking more. Her Sh'em continued to finger fuck her, sometimes in unison and sometimes alternating, circling around, widening her opening and pressing further inside, giving her a sample of what they might do to her once they penetrated her with their cocks. With each deepening stroke, Alea could feel the pressure, could feel them coming closer to that part of her she fiercely protected, but was now freely surrendering.

She whimpered, as Rjant circled her clit just a little harder, flicked it a little faster. Alea rocked her pelvis, pushing and yearning for deeper penetration, squeezing tightly, her climax building, her breath breaking into heavy pants, her body rushing toward ecstasy and she was almost there.

"Oh!" she sucked in a hard gulp of air and then gasped it out, her arousal beginning to culminate.

There was an effectual pause between Rjant and Tren as their gazes locked in silent communication--unspoken understanding.

And the chants of the forgotten Prowlers grew louder around them.

Alea's Sh'em both looked down at her, Tren leaning over her from behind and Rjant in the front, watching as rapture began to consume her beautiful face and Alea keened, teetering on the edge, and finally falling over. Tren nodded. With one deep thrust they burrowed their fingers inward as far as they would go, and Alea screamed out her pleasure-pain, caught in the middle of her exploding orgasm and the shearing bite of her shredding virginal vault.

It was exquisitely, painfully, wonderful, and she didn't think she would've wanted to be taken in any other way. A tear rolled from the corner of her eye, liquid heat oozed between her legs, and her feminine spasms exploded. They held their fingers rigid within her as she clenched and rotated her hips, whirling in a mindless haze, riding out the rest of her climax. "No more pain, She'mana, only pleasure," Tren whispered in her ear, his voice ragged, his body frenzied with his arousal. He hoped they would be able to keep their promise.

She'mana.

It was the first time they called her that, Alea realized, as clarity began returning to her thoughts. She was nearly, fully their woman now and wanted to give them all that she could and hoped they would take her in every possible way.

Alea felt the tip of Rjant's penis nudging between her legs. A new set of nerves set in, swiftly quelled by the fullness and carnal rush of his cock entering her wct, newly opened channel, re-igniting an aching need. She exhaled slowly with rousing approval as the head of Tren's shaft poised just behind her. She desperately wanted him to fill her in another way, but knew this was not the time. They were Tertani men, not of the Earth kind, and by what was natural to them, they would both have need to breach her vagina.

She just didn't know how they would do it, how she could possibly accommodate the inevitable, though she was no longer afraid.

Her fiercely building desire craved for them to try.

Tren braced her from behind and Rjant was half over her, stroking, pushing in and pulling out in an exquisite pace, in perfect alignment so that his pubic bone rubbed and stimulated her clitoris. He withdrew and instantly, without breaking rhythm Tren was inside her. A shock wave bolted through Alea's body, caused by the incredible sensation of the change in angle brought on by their shift, the back side of her vagina being stimulated by the head of Tren's cock and her clit by Rjant's stroking penis as he slid it along her labia.

They switched again and Alea cried out, the front of her vagina now being teased by the curve of Rjant's cock and she lost her breath, overcome at being ravaged, in dire need of receiving more.

They touched her everywhere. Their hands, their mouths--fingers dug into the flesh of her ass. A mouth was nipping her nipples. Tongues were licking, kissing, tasting. Bodies were pressed and hips were pumping. Rjant was plunging and then it was Tren, and Alea was mindless with her building lust, not knowing where one of them ended and the other began, which was jamming her with his cock--or was it both?

She didn't know.

She didn't care.

Alea was crying and moaning and moving her hips in time with their even thrusts.

Reaching, building, grinding. Her legs were somewhere--probably detached--but she'd worry about the aches tomorrow.

She was thankful for her unusual flexibility.

Teeth were on her throat, someone was mussing her hair, plucking her nipples, squeezing her breasts and she tried to touch them back but she couldn't. A finger pushed into her ass and she nearly lost it. And all Alea could do was clutch for dear life, her fingers digging into a tightly wrapped arm, a shoulder, a hip, wherever she could brace herself. She rocked between them, being duly fucked and fucking back, hanging on for the ride.

The harder they pumped the wilder she became, relenting her apprehensions and years of self-restraint.

Tren's hair had come loose and was flying around their bodies, tickling her flesh in delicious torment, and in a moment of untamed abandonment, Alea reached back and grabbed a clump of it, pulling his head down. She latched onto his mouth and then bit his lip, releasing him when he growled, satisfied that he liked it when his hands clasped her hips and he plunged into her harder, before withdrawing and giving Rjant his turn. She raked her fingers through Rjant's hair and grasped it tightly, yanking his head toward her, she nipped at his throat. Her hand slid down and she pinched his masculine nipple and twisted it.

"She'mana! Alea… damn!" he muttered, tossing back his head, his breath growing harsher and his pelvis slamming harder. He drove more deeply inside her.

Alea's clitoris was swelling--throbbing, her body shuddering and her vulva soaking, contracting, milking their cocks. Every muscle tensed and she droned out her climatic song, her moans of ecstasy growing louder.

"Give, She'mana. Do it," Tren rasped out. "We can't stop now."

He was inside her and stroking, long, deep penetrations that had her gasping. And then Rjant had her, his voice rumbling deep in his throat as he pumped, his rod swelling and ready to erupt.

Tren again… and then Rjant.

Their hips moved in frenzied drives, alternating, shifting, trading places within her in an unbroken rhythm that had her panting and then screaming, and she was cumming.

Tren was cumming.

Rjant was cumming.

Tren grasped her hips and rotated his pelvis, throwing his

head back and groaning with ecstatic pleasure and then Rjant, from the front of her, thrust upward and drove deep inside. Alea was dying, exploding, shattering, as they slammed her hard, their ejaculations bursting in rapid surges and a howling of pleasure, and Alea was screaming out her orgasm in a shriek so loud she could have wakened the dead.

Alea collapsed to the slowing pace of their alternating thrusts, her euphoria receding to a satiated daze. The words, *I love you, She'mana* floated to her ears--a doubling of both her husbands' voices, and she began to drift into a blissful sleep, cocooned between them.

The chants of the Prowlers hummed somewhere in her muddled brain, growing fainter, retreating, with blessings offered. Transdelta linking now broken, they left the new Trigon, completed in their joining.

Chapter Twelve

"It's part of the Rituals, She'mana." Rjant was looking at Alea as though this was nothing more than casual thing.

"I don't care!" Alea emerged from the lake and stomped over to her boots, shoving her wet feet into them. Her boots were all that remained of her garments. Her clothes had mysteriously disappeared. "I will not walk back to the village naked."

"Just be glad we allowed you to wash first," Tren added. "By the old ways, the female was brought through village painted in her own virginal blood."

"That's disgusting!" she spat, standing with hands on hips and feet splayed apart, naked as a jaybird except for her footwear.

Rjant's eyes sparkled at the sight of her. She looked positively, erotically sensual. "Well that's quite a sexy look, She'mana." He smiled at her amorously and then stalked toward her.

Alea jumped in reverse, avoiding his outstretched arms. "Did the Prowlers' She'manas have to do it?"

"Of course."

Her eyes darted to their loincloths. "I'll tell you what. Give me what you're wearing and you can walk back naked."

Tren's eyes widened. "We couldn't do that, Alea. It would be indecent."

"Oh, for the love of…" Alea threw her hands up in the air recalling some parental advice that the Miltons once gave her.

Pick your battles.

Well, Alea wasn't about to relent on this one. This was one battle she intended to pick. There was no way in hell she was parading around naked for the entire village to see. In a bluster, she walked to the nearest bush and began

breaking off branches to cover herself, a string of curses
spewing from her mouth.

"I wouldn't cover up with that," Rjant warned, quickly
moving toward her.

"And why not?" Alea shot him a defiant look.

"The leaves are covered with a powdered substance that
will irritate your skin. You'll have a bothersome rash for
weeks." He pulled the branches free from her grasp, tossing
them aside. "Besides that, the bush is loaded with rami
beetles. They have a fetish for crevices, if you get my
drift."

Alea grimaced and then shuddered at the thought of
strange, tiny creatures taking refuge in her crannies.

"We could take her back by way of the ancient custom."
Tren flashed a wry smile in Rjant's direction and then
turned to scan Alea's body. "I think we could manage to
restrain her."

"What ancient way?" Alea asked, suddenly curious.
"Restrain?"

"Tie your wrists and ankles to our talon arcs and carry
you home by force," Tren said.

"Naked," Rjant added, crossing his arms over his chest
and leaning against a boulder.

Alea's eyes widened. "You wouldn't dare!"

"Won't we?" Rjant grinned. His eyes held a devilish
guise. "Or do you prefer to walk home of your own
accord?"

"Which is it, wife?" Tren ambled over to where Rjant
stood, leaning on the boulder next to him.

"For crying out loud! Do you two always take each
other's sides?" If this is what she had to put up with for the
rest of her life....

"We are linked, She'mana." Tren turned his palms up
toward her, as if it were a viable excuse. "Of the same
mi...."

"Yeah, yeah, yeah." Alea cut him off, rolling her eyes.
She blew out a frustrated gust of air. "I'd rather stay here in
the woods and eat bugs than do what you're suggesting."

"I suppose you could live out here in the wilderness,

She'mana," Tren said rubbing his jaw. "Though I warn you we will come to mate with you from time to time."

He wrinkled his forehead into a pensive pause. He glanced toward Rjant. "I just hope she doesn't get eaten by a drubic."

A what? Rjant crooked an eyebrow, giving Tren a sidelong glance.

"A what?" Alea asked out loud.

"They're enormous and heinous and vicious."

They are? Rjant drew his brows together, pondering Tren's motives.

"They are?" Alea's eyes widened, reading Rjant's expression as worry.

"They have long, sharp fangs and scissor-like claws."

They do? Rjant pressed his lips together to keep from laughing. He mustered a serious façade as realization dawned.

"They do?" Alea's eyes darted around, searching the forest for signs of the gruesome beast.

"And they're always hungry."

Rjant snorted as Alea's face whitened.

Fretful about confronting a drubic, she didn't notice the glint of humor in their expressions.

Alea's mental scales tipped in favor of nudity.

She sucked in a breath and said, "Well then, fine. Let's go."

Ten minutes later, after hiking a short distance, she wanted to kill them for scaring the bejabbers out of her when Rjant lifted a sack from a storage compartment in one of the two hover cycles waiting for them in a clearing. He removed a bundle of clothing for her to wear and handed her a grooming set containing a brush, mirror and some hair ties.

Alea gave Tren an irate look. "There's no such thing as a drubic, is there?"

"No." Tren chortled. "I made that up."

"And you went right along with him." She threw darts with her glare in Rjant's direction.

Rjant shrugged sheepishly. "It was just a joke,

She'mana."

"I suppose the rami beetles and itch powder were made-up too?"

"No, that was true." Tren chuckled. "You can thank Rjant for saving your lovely hide."

Alea's hand unconsciously lifted to her chest as she scratched an imaginary itch. "Well I can hardly believe that the ancient Tertani men tied their women to their talons and carried them back to the village nude."

"Well yes, actually they did."

"Oh." Alea muttered, breathing a sigh of relief, grateful her Sh'em were modern Tertani males. She smoothed her hands over her trousers, pausing to admire the clothing she wore. The cloth was called *rebned*, she was told, imported from the Fourth Ward. It was a soft and comfortable material that felt like cotton against her skin, but shimmered with a brushed, metallic glow in deep purple or rich blue, depending on how the light struck it. The shirt was a bell-sleeved pullover that ended just at her waist. The trousers were form fitting around her waist and hips with flared legs that tapered at the ankles. They reminded her of harem pants. The undergarment she wore was a one-piece, lacy, lavender teddy, similar to one she had on Earth. In fact, if Alea recalled correctly she was wearing hers on at least one occasion when her Sh'em paid a nighttime visit to her. Alea smiled, suspecting that it's where they got the idea for the design.

"How did you know what size clothes to bring me?" Alea asked. "Everything fits so perfectly."

"We've had our hands all over you for two years, Alea. It wasn't too difficult to figure out your size." Rjant skimmed his hands along the indent of her waist and then stepped back, slightly away from her to appraise the outfit, smiling approvingly.

Alea conjured a picture of Tren and Rjant describing her size to a seamstress, Tren holding his hands out to give her waist size, Rjant hold his hands cupped to describe how large her breasts were. She laughed out loud, unable to imagine any earthly male with skill enough to be that accurate.

"Since you weren't here to style a gown for the Triconjugal celebration, my mother took the liberty of having one designed for you." Tren leaned over her from behind, placing his hands lightly on her shoulder. "I hope you don't mind."

"Mother?" Alea's heartbeat nearly arrested. "You have parents?"

Rjant raised his eyebrows. "Of course we have parents, Alea. Did you think we crawled out from under a rock?"

He paused looking at Tren. "At least I didn't. Tren, I'm not so sure."

Tren made a hand gesture at Rjant that Alea assumed was meant to be obscene. Rjant snorted.

"That's not what I meant." She rubbed her forehead and paced away from them. She never considered their parents, or any family members for that matter. What if they didn't accept her? *Oh my God!* What if they hated her?

"Relax, Alea, they're going to love you." Rjant assured her. Moving behind her, he slipped his arms around her waist.

"Will *all* your parents be there?" She gulped.

"Of course, as will my five brothers and sisters." Tren motioned in the direction of the cycles. "Shall we go?"

Alea bit her lip and closed her eyes. Her stomach took a hefty dive. She had six parents to worry about--four fathers, two mothers and then siblings to boot.

"Uh, why don't we eat first?" She pulled away from Rjant, lifted the sack from the compartment in the hover cycle and started rummaging through it. "Surely you brought a snack, and I'm starving."

"You're stalling." Tren pried the bag from her hands and stuffed it back into the storage area. "There will be plenty of food at the celebration."

"How many brothers and sisters do you have, Rjant?" Alea turned to her other Sh'em.

"Eight."

Eight? Holy cow.

"Well then." Alea plopped down on the ground and

stretched out, crossing her ankles. She patted the dirt beside her. "Come and sit down. Tell me about them."

Rjant and Tren stared down at her. Neither of them moved.

Shall I pick her up and throw on one of the hover cycles, Tren?

Alea's attention shifted between them and she pressed her lips into a thin line before puffing out a nervous breath of air.

Damn. It looked like there would be no dodging of the new in-laws.

Standing, she brushed herself off, making an exaggerated ordeal of it, shifting her clothes, straightening them and brushing off once more. She rolled her sleeves half way up her arm and then unrolled them, taking and excessive amount of time to smooth them out. Then, she strolled over to the hover cycle, opened the sack again and pulled out the brush.

Tren caught her wrist. "You look fine, She'mana."

Alea's shoulders sagged in defeat. She dropped the brush back into the bag and climbed onto one of the hover cycles. Tren shoved a shiny black helmet onto her head and hooked a strap under her chin, before seating himself in front of her, and stuffing his head into his own helmet.

"So, why don't we take the scenic route and you can show me the sights?"

Rjant laughed as he mounted the other cycle, donned his own helmet and adjusted the strap. He leaned over and swept a hand to the back of Alea's neck, pulling her head across the small gap between the two cycles, the front of their helmets thwacking together. He snorted and tipped his head sideways, planting a quick kiss on her mouth. "Maybe some other time, She'mana."

"Eek!" Alea's arms flew around Tren's waist as he revved the engine, a whirring sound instead of a cracking rumble, and the cycle sped off. Alea's body jerked backwards with the quick acceleration. Rjant's cycle was immediately alongside and they were hastening across the plain. Alea threw back her head laughing heartily at the rushing sensation, and then she snapped her mouth shut, concerned the open cavity might snatch up an unwanted bug.

Much to Alea's surprise, the air whipping around them was warm, not cold, as it would have been had they been speeding along on a motorcycle in the Earth's atmosphere. She wondered if the weather was always this abiding. Gripping Tren tighter, Alea turned her head to look over at Rjant's cycle and watched as his craft intimately aligned to theirs, the hover ring that surrounded the bottom closing the gap to mere inches away. She lifted her head to Rjant's, unable to see his eyes because of the helmet shield that covered them, but he was grinning at her and crooking his fingers, beckoning her over to him. Alea alit with a sense of daring and adventure. Having seen it done in the movies many times, she thought it would be a very cool thing to try.

Tren's brain caught the flow of Rjant's thinking and shot him a silent warning to cease his foolish idea. Alea shifted behind him and he stiffened with fear. She stood, causing the cycle to tip slightly to one side.

Alea stared at tiny gap. The hover rims were nearly touching. All she had to do was step over and she would be there.

Nothing to it.

With the wind slapping her face and her heart pounding erratically, Alea took a deep breath and lifted her foot, thrill flushing through her at what she was about to do.

"Sit down, Alea!" But it was too late. Tren couldn't slow his craft. Rjant would speed ahead if he did so, and Alea would be leaping into empty air. Instead he concentrated on maintaining his pace, deciding that trying to grab her was out of the question as well. If he released a hold on the steering handles the cycle might jerk and tumble her over the side.

"Don't do it, Alea!" Tren pleaded with her one more time, his head twisting back spontaneously, his eyes flicking behind him to see what she was doing. His distraction toward Alea was only fleeting, but long enough for him to miss the approaching elevation in the terrain. Not dangerous by any means, but distending upward enough to cause his cycle to suddenly lift as it passed over the swell in the surface. His attention snapped forward belatedly, and he was unable to compensate. The gap between the cycles widened to at least four feet, just as Alea was stepping off.

"Oh fuck!" Alea's breath hitched, her eye catching the wide open space of ground as they sped over it.

And she was falling forward.

She was going to miss Rjant's cycle!

With an impulsive adjustment, Alea pushed off of the hover rim as hard as she could using her one, still planted foot.

Tren gritted his teeth, attempting to quickly maneuver closer, cursing under his breath. There was a slight jerking motion on his bike and Alea was gone. He slammed the brakes, screeching to a halt, the rear of his cycle swerving one-hundred and eighty degrees so that he was completely turned around. He closed his eyes in relief as Rjant's craft sped past with Alea clinging to the seat, her knees firmly atop the hover ring.

And she was laughing!

Rjant's hover cycle came to a stop just thirty feet beyond. He removed his helmet while dismounting, leaning down to help Alea to her feet. She was still chuckling, senses on high alert as her heart pumped an overdose of adrenaline through her. Pulling her own helmet from her head, Alea turned in Tren's direction and immediately clamped her mouth shut.

There was no mistaking his expression. He was furious.

Tren yanked off his helmet, propelling it to the ground with such force it bounced three times and rolled several feet before coming to a rest. He stalked toward them his glare on Rjant. "Is your brain out of rocket fuel?"

He snapped his angry eyes to Alea. "Did the single brain cell in your head elude your sensibilities, Alea?"

Tren pressed a pointed finger into Rjant's chest, wanting dearly to smack the smug expression from his face. "And you, goading her!"

Turning his back on them he paced away, dragging his fingers through his hair. He was actually trembling. "If I wanted to marry a Tertani female I would have done so!"

I remind you we had no choice in the matter, brethren. Rjant calmly walked away from the cycle and settled himself to the ground. He leaned back on his hands, stretching his legs out in front of him, crossing one ankle over the other. *Besides you're as pleased as I am that she is so untamed.* He would not reveal that he was as unnerved by Alea's near mishap as Tren, tamping down the thought that he had almost gotten her hurt.

Tren narrowed his eyes on Rjant and then began treading back and forth. Alea could swear a trench was forming beneath his feet.

"You're overreacting, brethren. She was perfectly safe," Rjant said, following the movement of Tren's fuming gait.

"She could have been maimed!" Tren bellowed, spilling a flood of curses into Rjant's mind.

Tren stomped over to Alea, grabbing her upper arms and leaning in. Alea's head recoiled in reaction. "You could have been killed!"

And he was not overreacting! Alea's actions terrified him. Had she been a Tertani female, perhaps he would have trusted her skill--perhaps not--probably not. Nevertheless, Alea was from Earth and though he knew she was agile, he had no idea how capable she was.

It won't be long, Rjant mused, desire already heating his blood, his cock stiffening between his legs. He knew Tren's anger would subside. Wild behavior was natural in Tertani females and Tertani males were always aroused by it. Although their She'mana was of outer-galaxy blood, she reacted no differently than should be expected if she were of their race.

Tren scowled at Rjant, attempting to battle what nature inherently stirred. He wanted to be angry not excited by this. His fierce need to protect Alea from harm coupled with his fear of losing her was what caused him to react so strongly. Spinning on his heels, Tren paced several feet away before turning to face her again.

Alea stared at him, frozen with his fury, watching his muscles ripple under the strain of his temper. She felt small, like a child taking a severe scolding from her father, his looming anger making him large and threatening, but oddly she wasn't afraid. He was right. It was a stupid thing to do. She deserved his reprimanding.

"What if you already carry a child, Alea?" His expression grew tight, his voice lowered to a scolding bass tone, accusingly, his eyes searching her face as his chest heaved heavy breaths. "Would you risk harming our babe?"

Pregnant... already? Alea's hand unconsciously lifted to her lower belly and she dropped her head in shame. But her eyes didn't survey the dirt for very along, however. They flicked upward slightly and much to Alea's amusement there was a rock hard bulge poking between Tren's legs.

Well what do you know about that?

Apparently her unruliness was making him horny. She wondered what he would do if she took off running, but decided against it. Her legs were still aching from the previous day's hunt.

With her head still nodding Alea continued to stare at his crotch. *Hmm.* There really was no sense in wasting such a marvelous thing.

Tren continued his ranting and pacing, not noticing that Alea was removing her boots. Rjant snickered at Tren's oblivion and watched Alea under hooded eyes as she pulled her top over her head and dropped it to the ground. He couldn't believe Tren was unaware that Alea was undressing, especially when he was having difficulty closing off his thoughts to his brethren.

Alea's eyes flicked to Rjant and her lips curved into a lascivious grin as she dropped her pants. Rjant's eyes flooded with a blaze of lust and it was then, finally, that Tren stopped, fixating on Rjant first and then snapping his head around to look at Alea.

She stood in nothing but her lace teddy, one hand dipping beneath the material at her juncture, fingers moving as she played with her pussy, her other hand teasing the nipple on one of her breasts. Their gazes locked briefly, and then

Alea's eyes roamed all over his body. She licked her lips, and Tren lost all libidinous control.

Alea shrieked when he flew at her, grabbing her roughly around the waist and lifting her off of the ground. Tren flung her over the seat of Rjant's hover cycle so that she was straddling it, facing forward. He lifted her hips and straightened her legs, and then pushed his palm between her shoulder blades forcing her chest down onto the seat, leaving her ass sticking up into the air.

"Stay," he ordered, freeing his cock from beneath his loincloth and pulling aside the crotch of her teddy. He recalled how he thumped her in this position when they were on the Stardancer and how dictates of the Edification would allow him nothing more.

Not this time.

"Do you want this?" He shoved the crown of his penis between her labia.

"Ow! Yes-s-s," she hissed.

Tren frowned.

"Are you sore, She'mana?" he asked, suddenly reluctant to continue.

"Just a tad," Alea answered through clenched teeth.

"Tell me to stop."

"No."

"A stubborn woman." He pushed in a bit more.

"Ow!"

"I warned you not to taunt your Sh'em," Tren responded, slapping her on the bottom and pushing further inside of her hollow.

"Ow! Ow!"

"You're dry."

Alea grunted.

Tren hesitated, looking down at her. She was red and swollen from their rutting on her the dawning before. He closed his eyes and tossed his head to one side.

He couldn't do it.

Tren pulled out, backing away and Alea exhaled the breath she was holding. Her body visibly relaxed. She started to rise but he pushed her down again. "I said 'stay.'"

And she obeyed.

Tren bent forward, bringing his mouth to her vulva. From her clitoris to her hollow, he licked her with one, slow stroke, and Alea sighed, his moist, warm tongue soothing the rawness between her legs. He swirled his tongue around inside and moved to her inner lips, licking them and then blowing a cooling stream of air along the swelled fleshed. He continued to lap at her and cool her with his breath until she began to moan and writhe, begging for penetration, her vagina wet and wanting.

He rose behind her and with relevant ease slid in his cock, burying himself deep inside, both of them gasping at the rush of pleasure that flooded through them. Tren shuddered and began to move, pumping his hips rapidly against her, his orgasm swiftly building. Alea crooned, arching her back further, rising on the sensation of Tren filling her completely and his balls slapping against her clit, stimulating her with each forward thrust.

"Faster," she mumbled and Tren obliged.

Rjant sat back in the grass, breathing hard. It was sweet agony to watch. His mind enjoyed the erotic scene playing out before him, though his cock had other ideas, stiffening and tenting his loincloth. He waited patiently, drinking in the passion between his brethren and their She'mana, Tren's lusty thoughts washing through him, intensifying his need, and bringing him into the middle of their lovemaking, though he sat nearly ten feet away.

Alea's juncture was glistening and dripping with her arousal, the flesh of her vagina molding around Tren's cock, her hips undulating in response to his slamming pelvis. Tren's ass cheeks squeezed together each time he thrust within her, his shaft disappearing and reappearing as he stroked in and out, his heavy balls swinging and smacking her pussy. Rjant knew that feeling, and groaned with the thought of it, knew it would make her cum. His hand slid beneath his loincloth to cup and squeeze his own balls, and he panted in cadence with Tren, inhaling the scent of their sex, his eyes moving upward to focus on Alea's face.

She held her mouth in a sensual gape. Her breaths were short and rapid. She fixed her eyes on him, locking him with her gaze, and he could see the daze pass through them, as her orgasm set its siege and she began crying out.

An untamed lust suddenly seized Rjant and he trembled with agonizing need. Unable to wait any longer, he pounced toward the pair, seating himself astride the cycle's seat just in front of Alea's head. It was not her hollow he aimed for, it was her mouth he sought.

He reached to the back of Alea's head, grasping her mane, wrapping it around his hand. Her body lifted slightly, and he tipped her head back, savoring the sweep of passion flooding across her face. Rjant's hands shifted. He reached toward the straps of her teddy pushing them down from her shoulders and then sliding his hands down the front of it, he cupped her breasts. Alea groaned at the mixed sensation of Rjant's warm hands gently kneading her breasts and the force of Tren's hard thrusts ravaging her pussy from behind.

Reaching beneath his loincloth, Rjant pulled his cock free and rubbed the head lightly against her cheek, swiping it across her lips and to the other side of her face. Tren clutched her hips tighter, steadying her, grinding his pelvis against her. His body grew rigid, his voice rumbled with pleasure, and he spilled his seed inside her womb, holding her tight against him as his body shuddered. Alea's carnal flight peaked with a fury and then languidly descended as Tren pulled back, slowly sliding in and out of her several times before grinding against her once more.

Alea's hazy eyes flickered upward to Rjant's face and then slowly drifted downward until she was eyeing his swollen rod. Tren settled back onto the seat, pulling Alea down onto his lap, his semi-erect cock still embedded inside of her. Rjant's hips followed her head upward as he stood. Her hands swept around him grabbing his ass, drawing his pelvis to her face and she opened her mouth. Rjant took liberty between her lips, slipping his shaft between them. Alea exhaled sharply, drawing him deeper and Rjant wondered how far he could venture. He pushed farther, past her tongue, and when she offered no resistance, he slid his cock into her throat--to the hilt.

"Starfires!" Rjant choked out and then grunted, stilling himself as Alea's head bobbed back and forth, taking every last inch of him. She would have chuckled if she could have, surprise shining in her eyes at her new-found skill, pleased that she was able to give this to him.

Tren groaned as thoughts of Rjant's lust filled his brain, and his cock thickened and lengthened inside of her once more. His fingers slithered along her hips, one hand finding her pussy and he stroked her clit with the tip of his finger. Alea jerked, still over-sensitive from her recent peak and he pressed his fingers against her vulva, heightening the still lingering sensation. Her vagina squeezed around him and she gyrated her hips, riding him in rhythm as she continued stimulating Rjant with her mouth. Tren didn't move. There was no need. Alea's steady movements and Rjant's inflamed thoughts were enough to help him find release again.

A sound something akin to a yelp expelled from Rjant's mouth. His nuts tightened and he threw his head back. Alea's fingers dug into his ass, urging him, permitting him to take his pleasure in her mouth, her throat. His hand moved down, to catch her breast, lazily playing with the rounded mound--*a nice handful*, he thought and his cock gushed.

Alea held her breath, swallowing Rjant's warm juices, quivering as Tren's fingers rubbed her pussy. Rjant pulled free of her mouth, and she pressed her cheek against his warm, satiated groin, as Tren pressed his chest against her from behind. She rocked back and forth on his lap, squeezing his growing erection with her feminine muscle, taking delight in the steamy, languorous rise escalating inside of her. She crooned as it built, slowly at first, but then gaining power and then speed as she pumped her hips faster, harder. Her nipples jutting, begging to be touched and then Rjant's mouth and hands were on them, massaging, sucking and licking, heightening her sensual pleasure.

And it came without warning.

"O-h-h!" She huffed, and blew apart, her orgasm slamming through her in a forceful explosion between her thighs and sending a massive frisson rushing along her flesh.

Tren stiffened and he groaned, a mere wisp of breath against her ear, throbbing as he spurted into her vagina.

Alea collapsed, thankful for the support of her Sh'ems' bodies, keeping her from tumbling from the cycle's seat and cracking her head on the ground.

Not that she would have felt it. All that sat in her brain at the moment was a pile of mush and a single, barely coherent, "Wow."

Chapter Thirteen

"So this is the alien woman who captured my young son's heart."

And hello to you, too, mother-in-law who looks young enough to be my older sister.

Alea stood perfectly still as Rjant's mother, Pel'r, walked 'round and 'round her.

Cradle robber. Cradle robber. Cradle robber, echoed in Alea's brain. Could this be what his mother was thinking? Rjant's age was frequently caught up in Alea's thoughts, but every time she looked at him, her heart did a little flip and she saw a wonderful, handsome *man.* There was nothing boyish about him. Besides, it was he who came after her, not the other way around.

Would she have refused him had she known his real age?

Damn, that was a tough question. If he was an Earth male, of course, absolutely, but he most certainly wasn't from Earth.

"The gown looks lovely on you, Alea," Dmor, Tren's mother said, pulling Alea away from her thoughts. She studied the woman's features, before turning her gaze to Pel'r. There was no mistaking whose parents they were. Both Tren and Rjant bore a strong resemblance to their mothers. *Must be the extra maternal genes they inherited.*

"Thank you," Alea finally responded. "It was very thoughtful of you."

It was hardly a gown, at least not of the sort she was used to, the top being nothing more than a strapless bikini bra and the bottom, an ankle-length sarong, wrapped around her hips and tied in a knot to one side. The material was nice though, a soft peach color that felt like silk against her skin.

Her Sh'ems' mothers weren't dressed any more elaborately. Pel'r's garment was nearly identical to Alea's except it was pale green, and the only difference with Dmor's was that she wore a loose fitting, long sleeved, waist-length shirt instead of a teensy bra. Her *gown* was a lilac color. They both wore jeweled chains around each of their ankles that jingled like tiny wind chimes when they walked.

A chirping sound drew their attention to the door. "Enter," said Dmor and the door slid open. Theld, Gorsch's wife, who Alea had met earlier, slithered through the door. Alea gawked at the Junparian as it... er... *she* made her way across the room. No matter how many times she saw them, Alea didn't think she would ever get used to their odd forms or the weird way their bodies moved.

"I've brought the charms, mistresses," Theld said, holding an intricately carved box out toward them.

"Very good, Theld." Pel'r took it from her and placed it on a small table in the room. "Have the guests arrived?"

"Yes, mistress, and well into enjoying the festivities."

"Wonderful." Dmor flashed a bright smile. "Now where are our men?"

"We're here, mother," Tren said, coming through the garden entranceway. He was followed by Rjant and four other men--their fathers. All were bare-chested, wearing nothing but loincloths, longer than those worn by the Prowlers, with the hems falling to their knees. But they were slit up the sides nearly to their hips, giving the women a tantalizing view of muscular, male thigh as they moved across the room.

Alea caught herself thinking about what was beneath her Sh'ems' garments, wondering if anything else covered their nether regions, and her fingers ached to crawl beneath them to find out. Her nipples hardened and a tingling swept its way between her legs, pooling in her lower belly, as she recalled her earlier, sexual encounter with her husbands.

"Ka!" Pel'r exclaimed. "She's besotted!"

Realizing it was obvious where her attention was fixed, Alea immediately changed the direction of her gaping, lifting her head to look at her Sh'ems' faces.

It wasn't just the sex.

With Tren and Rjant, Alea felt utterly complete. She loved everything about them, separately and together.

But mostly together, Alea thought, releasing a slow, pleasurable sigh.

Rjant moved toward her and cupped his hand beneath her chin, as Tren caressed her arm. They both smiled, recognizing the hunger that lingered in her eyes, but there was a deeper emotion there that warmed them immensely.

Drawing her brows together pensively, Dmor tipped her head to one side, clearly understanding the sensuality in Alea's expression. And she was well-pleased. When her son first told her that his and Rjant's She'mana was an off-world woman, it worried her. Tertani men needed to join with passionate, adventurous women, lest they grow bored and unsatisfied. Dmor's worry was in vain. It was obvious the She'mana Alea was a fiery mate and would give her Sh'em many phases of pleasure.

And probably many headaches too, she chuckled inwardly at the thought.

"The divinities have chosen well, but of course I shouldn't have doubted that they would," Dmor exclaimed, pushing her way between Tren and Rjant. Bending forward, she placed a kiss, first on Alea's right cheek and then her left. She then planted a kiss on the tip of Alea's nose.

Alea's brows rose. *That was weird.*

"It's a gesture of affection shared between family members, She'mana." Tren leaned down and whispered in her ear after noting her perplexed expression.

Pel'r stepped forward, giving Alea the same trio of kisses as Dmor.

Was she supposed to kiss them back?

Rjant turned toward the four sires. "Fathers, may we present the She'mana, Alea."

Alea's eyes drifted to the four males who stood a short distance away. Tren's and Rjant's fathers were talking quietly among themselves, not paying much heed to their She'mana. Alea had yet to meet them, and the sight of the four large, Tertani warriors was a bit intimidating. She wondered what kind of scrutiny she would receive from them.

One of Tren's fathers, Ileg, approached her first, and Alea prepared to have her teeth examined. Dropping to on knee, Ileg bowed instead. "Welcome, She'mana Alea. You are honored to be in our presence."

"Thank... what?" Alea started to say before she caught the phrasing of his words.

Tren snorted and Alea noted the humor in Ileg's face as he looked up at her. *Oh, a wise guy, eh?*

_"Enough, Ileg. You'll scare the woman." Dmor reached for her Sh'em's hand and he stood.

"My son would never be joined to a woman who scares easily," Ileg remarked.

Tonor, Tren's other father, along with Grange and Dombac, who were Rjant's fathers, all came forward, each offering their welcome to Alea with a nod.

"It's time to celebrate this Trigon. Shall we depart?" Pel'r addressed the group and they mumbled in agreement.

"The hover conveyance you asked for, Dmor, is outside the compound," Tonor told her.

"Well, I think we're ready then. I'll just get the charm box."

"What are the charms for?" Alea asked.

"Symbols of our Trigon, She'mana. You'll see," Tren answered.

"Should I be worried?" Alea said, wondering what they had in store for her next.

Chuckling, Tren kissed her temple. "Not a bit."

Rjant took her hand and started for the door. Tren followed so closely behind Alea that she could feel the heat from his body radiating against her back. She stopped abruptly, laughing when Tren slammed up against her, causing her to stumble forward and crash into Rjant.

"What are you doing, She'mana?" Rjant peered over his shoulder, while reaching back with both hands to steady her at the hips.

"Making a sandwich?" Alea answered with a smirk.

Tren's hand slipped down the front of her and he fingered

her mound through the cloth of her skirt. "Will you ever learn that taunting your Sh'em can be a dangerous thing?"

Rjant spun around and his hands came up to her breasts, his mouth latching on to her throat. Alea moaned.

"Not if it gets me this," she rasped out.

"Excuse me children." Dmor stood in the doorway, tapping her foot, hands akimbo, but there was a glint of humor in her expression. "There will be plenty of time for that later."

"Of course mother," Tren answered.

Alea chuckled as she looked back at him. There was an adorable blush on his face at being caught in the act by his mother. Rjant merely sighed his disappointment at the interruption. He stepped back, linked his arm with Alea's and they left the compound.

The conveyance that hovered in front of the building was large enough to accommodate the group, a stretch limousine of sorts, with large windows and cushy seats inside. A lyradeck was playing soft music and there was a small sidebar holding refreshments. Alea felt like a princess in the lap of luxury, and was amazed that she could be so lucky.

Taking a seat in the back of the vehicle, she looked out the window and appraised the outside of the building. Although her Sh'em told her that their home would be more elaborate than the other dwellings she'd seen, because it was built on their military compound, Alea pictured that it would resemble a fortress--a cold looking structure reinforced by stones. It was nothing like that at all. The enormous residence was like a series of townhouses, each connected unit unique in its design and color trimmings. Most had private gardens, some had second floor balconies. There was a communal hall at the back used for group dining and entertainment, and an outdoor terrace where large numbers of people could gather. The residence housed the highest ranking families in the territory.

The unit she would share with Rjant and Tren was the largest, which she supposed was appropriate considering her Sh'ems' ranks. It had ten rooms including five bedrooms, a study, a den she likened to a living room, two elegant bathrooms, and a small kitchenette where they could dine in, if they so desired.

Twenty-five servants were employed by the household, and included cooks, maids, gardeners and maintenance personnel. None of them were Tertani natives. Most were alien refugees seeking sanctuary from embattled territories. The servants and their families resided within a small apartment complex that sat to the back of the Tertian residence.

"...so when the Trigon males chased the Tinas who discovered the planet Terta Minor...."

"What?" Alea, too absorbed in contemplating all that happened to her over the last few weeks, had only been half listening to the conversation buzzing around the compartment of the vehicle. "Your women discovered the planet?"

Tren smiled. "Is that so surprising? Once our females became more domesticated they also became more educated. They took it upon themselves to study the stars and eventually a team of women designed the mechanisms to travel amongst them."

"Yes," Tonor agreed. "And their sense of adventure made them almost feverish about space travel."

"Much to the agony of the Tertani males," Dombac added with a grin. "It gave our Tinas a wider expanse into which they could flee."

"My ancestral grandmother, twenty generations back, was the first to step foot on Terta Minor, She'mana." Rjant told her. "My family has thrived there ever since."

"Later we were discovered by the Allegiance and charted as two planets within the Third Ward. Our technological capabilities expanded from there." Pel'r grinned, almost mischievously. "Our Tinas were exuberant with the idea of so much space to explore and many left the planets."

Dombac groaned beside her. "Yes, and because of that our males, who were called to the Trigon, have suffered great misery while chasing down their mates, ever since."

Pel'r snorted. "I evaded my Sh'em well, did I not?" Her

eyes twinkled as she shifted her attention between Dombac and Grange.

Alea chuckled quietly as they both rubbed their foreheads *in-sync*.

"It is likely the reason our ancient, spiritual gifts such as the transdelta linking did not suffer extinction." Tren leaned closer to her. His breath wisped against her cheek and sent a tingle down her spine. "In fact it became even stronger. The bestowal was needed more than ever by then, as the Tinas fled to even farther regions and the males had to hunt them down."

"Well, thank goodness for that!" Alea blurted and then blushed when they all laughed at her comment. Embarrassed, she sank into the cushion and averted her eyes downward.

"We're almost there," Rjant announced.

Looking up again Alea's mouth fell open in surprise. They were riding atop plum-colored sands, parallel to a vast body of taw--an ocean--with large fluid waves tumbling at the shore-line in fizzling caps, like pink champagne being poured into a glass. Alea inhaled deeply and closed her eyes absorbing the liquid scent teasing her nose, trying to remember the last time she'd been to the shores.

Ocean City, Maryland--a vacation with the Miltons.

Sifting through her memories, Alea recalled how she strolled along the boardwalk, stopping to watch the artist carve sculptures in the sand, remembering the nearly forgotten kiss from a boy she met there. She smiled thinking about how she didn't get pleasure from it until her mind drifted to thoughts of both the boy and his twin brother who stood snickering behind him--those images making Alea realize she was different, her desire peaking for the first time on the boardwalk that day, as she fantasized about having both their lips on her.

"A crystal for your thoughts, She'mana," Tren whispered in her ear.

"I was just thinking about my first kiss," Alea told him and he crooked a brow.

"That wasn't the answer I was expecting."

"Was he as devilishly handsome as me?" Rjant flashed a wide grin.

Alea chuckled. "Not nearly."

"Ka! You pet my ego."

I'd like to pet more than your ego, Alea thought before her attention was drawn forward of the conveyance. Through the front window she caught sight of a massive illumination in the distance. It looked like a bonfire, but not quite. The light radiating from it bubbled erratically upward, similar to globs in a lava lamp, before bursting into sparks of shimmering fluorescent blue. There were people, milling all around it, and as they drew closer she could see the floral decorations and hear the music and see the party of people, some talking and some dancing. Clad in colorful sarongs and loincloths it reminded her of a Hawaiian luau. When the hover vehicle came to a stop, Alea realized the party was their destination.

The door slid open. Rjant's and Tren's parents exited first. Tren offered Alea his hand and helped her to the sand with Rjant hopping after them.

"A beach party?" Alea's attention shifted back and forth between them.

"A traditional Tertian celebration." Tren leaned down to plant a kiss on her cheek. "I hope it pleases you."

"Many Trigons prefer elaborate affairs to celebrate their joining," Rjant added. "But Tren and I agreed that this was more to our liking, and we thought yours, as well."

"I should be irritated that I didn't even get to plan my own wedding." Alea shot them both a serious look and they frowned at her.

Alea laughed in response. "It's perfect."

Rising on her tiptoes, she kissed Rjant and then turning, her mouth sought Tren's. "All of it."

"Thank us later." Tren squeezed her close to him and his shaft immediately hardened. He chuckled at his body's reaction. "Or now."

Tren pushed aside her sarong and stripped off her panties, pressing her back against his brethren, and Rjant leaned against the hull of the vehicle to give them both support. "Ka, Tren! Take her and then she's mine."

But he couldn't wait and his fingers came up to skim along the side of her ribcage and then catching her breasts in his hands, he gently squeezed them before exploring and plucking at the tips through the cloth of her top. Alea lifted her arms, reaching back to cup the back of Rjant's head and turned toward him, drawing his mouth down to hers. She kissed him deeply, slipping her tongue into his mouth, melding, stroking it against his tongue.

Rjant murmured into her mouth, drinking in the sweet taste of her as one of his hands released his penis from behind his loincloth.

Groaning, Tren too, yanked out his cock, and then lifted Alea's legs to wrap around his waist. He supported her legs while Rjant held her ass. Tren shoved himself up inside of her, stroked deeply, sliding in and out several times before lifting her off of his shaft and lowering her onto Rjant's waiting, throbbing cock and he too took his turn stroking inside of her.

"Oh my..." Alea barely croaked out the words as she released Rjant's mouth, turning to seize Tren's mouth with her lips. She came almost as soon as Tren re-entered her, and now, with Tren and Rjant repeatedly trading places, pumping into her, she was starting to cum again.

"Yes, harder," she begged throwing back her head, her body shuddering as she squeezed her vagina tighter, her juices soaking their cocks, easing their way inside of her. Her fingers dug into Tren's shoulders as she turned her head and bit at Rjant's jaw, and then his neck. Tren bent his head, pulling down her top with his teeth and suckled one of her breasts, while Rjant nibbled a path along her collar bone, up along her neck and then nipping lightly at her earlobe. The dual sensation of their hands, both their bodies taking their claim to her, was all she needed and her second orgasm broke free on a scream, muffled by Rjant's mouth covering her own. She eased her legs from around Tren's waist, letting her feet come to the ground.

And then they took her, in the way of Tertani males,

intent on making love to their She'mana.

With Rjant's hands on her hips, and Tren's on her waist, Alea could feel them both stroking inside her, their heavy, deep thrusts lifting her to her toes and then off of the ground, strong male grasps steadied her in place, hard cocks slick with her moisture, sliding in and out, her Sh'em, taking their pleasure, spilling their seed into her with intense force. She was stuffed full, amazed that it was possible at all, but unquestioning in their ability to do it.

It was an unearthly thing.

She was so glad her Sh'em had found her.

Pel'r peeked from around the front of the hovercraft, her eyes alight with mirth.

"What's taking them so long?" Dmor whispered from just behind her.

"They're making love," Pel'r answered with a low snicker, thankful the vehicle's door faced away from the party, as she watched their tripling.

"I make such pretty babies." Pel'r sighed. "My son is such a glorious male."

Rolling her eyes Dmor yanked on Pel'r's shoulder, forcing her to turn around. "Yes, Pel'r. All eight of your babies are beautiful." She pulled Pel'r away from the hovercraft. "And I'm sure with your overactive libido there will be a few more to boot."

Pel'r merely laughed, knowing it was probably true, as she followed Dmor to the celebration. "If they keep that up we will have grandbabes soon, Dmor."

"Who was that?" Alea asked quietly as she straightened her sarong and top.

"Sounded like my mother," Rjant answered.

Alea's mouth dropped open, as she turned to look at him. "Do you think she saw us?"

How mortifying! she thought.

"Probably." Rjant chuckled feebly and then he attempted to soothe Alea by saying, "She is not easily offended, She'mana."

It didn't work. Alea dropped her face to her hands, shaking her head. "How will I look her in the eye?" She hadn't missed Rjant's profuse blush.

"I don't think our tripling is a major secret, Alea," Tren answered, helping her straighten her clothing while Rjant smoothed out her mussed up hair. "Let's join the party."

Chapter Fourteen

Alea couldn't help herself. As soon as they left the side of
the hover vehicle and started heading toward the party, she
just had to remove her sandals. She wanted to feel the
warm sand between her toes. Rjant and Tren
wholeheartedly agreed, pulling their own sandals from their
feet, as well. Tren took the three pairs of sandals and tossed
them to the ground in front of the craft and then took one of
Alea's hands into his own. Rjant smiled and took her other
hand and they joined the celebration.

The new triple was greeted by the reception as they
approached, and congratulations were offered as they
moved through the gathering. Several Junparians were
scurrying about carrying trays of food and filling rhytons
with drink. Gorsch was among them, and he paused briefly
from his duties and nodded at them. There were at least
fifty guests, many that Alea recognized. Aside from her
new in-laws, she saw all of the Triconjugal Prowlers and
their She'mana, and a number of the warriors from the
Stardancer were there too, Calem and Tocol included. She
smiled brightly at Tocol, remembering that there was
another Earth game she wanted to teach him--thumb
wrestling. Tocol lifted his rhyton horn to her in response to
her expression as he moved toward them, his arm hooked
around the elbow of a lovely looking female. Her skin had
a bluish tint. Her white hair shimmered with silver
highlights, and Alea thought that with skin that hue, there
were colors she definitely couldn't wear. But then again,
wasn't it like that on Earth, with all the different fleshy skin
tones? Alea looked terrible in red, and avoided wearing the
color at all costs.

"You look radiant, Alea." Tocol kissed her cheek.

"Thank you." Alea blushed, remembering that she asked
him if he was going to attend the Triconjugal ceremony and

was suddenly glad that he hadn't. At the same time she wondered how she was going to unabashedly face the Prowlers who had participated, knowing that they witnessed her Sh'em making love to her for the first time.

It's just the culture, she reminded herself. *Totally acceptable.* Alea shook her shoulders and tried to present a nonchalant facade.

"I see you survived," Karen said to her as she approached. Alea felt her cheeks heat as her eyes averted downward. "Several times," she answered, pressing her lips to keep from smirking, despite her slight discomfiture. The term blushing bride suddenly seemed to make sense.

"She was worried the two of you weren't going to fit," Karen whispered to Tren and Rjant while chuckling at the same time.

Overhearing her comment, Tocol snorted.

Alea's head shot up and her eyes widened. "Oh my God, Karen! I can't believe you just told them that!"

Rjant stroked his palm down Alea's back, letting it come to rest in the small of her spine. "Get used to it, She'mana. There will be much razzing tonight." He turned his attention to speak with Tocol, as Tren signaled one of the servers for refreshments.

"Great," she mumbled under her breath.

"We're leaving for Terta Minor after the celebration," Karen commented.

Forgetting her embarrassment momentarily, Alea frowned. "Do you have to? We were just getting to know each other."

Karen shrugged. "My Sh'em and I have duties to return to. We were only given a few days vacation to come here for the rituals."

"You have duties?" Alea hadn't thought much about how she would occupy her time on Tertia. Her Sh'em also had duties and she couldn't spend all day in bed with them after all.

Hmm... or could she? Nah, a nice thought, but not practical.

"I'm the coordinator of children's health activities in

region Si's edu-commune."

"Really?" Alea asked with surprise. It occurred to her suddenly that she would need a job or a hobby or something. She couldn't just sit around all day and play with herself. Alea mentally chuckled. There would be no more of that now that she had her men.

"What is turning through your brain, She'mana?" Tren asked, handing a rhyton of grata to both her and Rjant. "By your expression I can see the rockets firing in your head."

"I need a job."

Rjant rolled his eyes. "Married only three dawnings and already she complains of needing more to do."

"You could always run and we could chase you," Tren whispered seductively in her ear and then nipped lightly at the sensitive flesh of her neck. A heated shiver pushed through her and for a moment, Alea thought that it might not be a bad idea. She certainly did like to run, and now she had an even better reason for doing it--to get chased, caught and pleasured.

A clacking sound drew Alea's attention to a stone, slab table. Her four fathers-in-law were banging their wooden talon arcs together, each with his Trigon brethren. The Prowlers joined them striking their own talon arcs in a clattering rhythm, drawing the attention of the rest of the guests and little by little the conversations amongst them quieted.

Alea noticed that her Sh'em, fathers-in-law and the Prowlers all still carried the traditional wooden talon arcs. The rest of the warriors present however, were armed with the modern, metal version of the weapon.

"If we still practiced the customs from the days of old, Alea," Rjant whispered, "this would be when we'd arrive, carrying you tied naked to our talon arcs."

"It would have been done just after our Triconjugal mating, a public declaration of our claim to you," Tren added.

Rjant chuckled. "I've heard stories of how some She'mana had to be trussed to the table to keep them in place."

"What?" Alea gave them both a suspicious look, as Rjant and Tren each took one of Alea's hands and led her forward, stopping in front of the slab table where their mothers and fathers stood.

"You are not tying me to this table!" Alea yelled and turned to run, but her Sh'em simultaneously grabbed her about the waist, stopping her. A string of curses fell from her mouth as she struggled against them. Tren laughed loudly, a bellow that nearly shattered her ear.

"We're not going to tie you up, Alea," Rjant spoke from her other side, the tone of his words matching his amused expression.

Although it's a thought, Rjant channeled to Tren.

"Oh..." Alea stilled immediately. "Sorry, but you could've explained all this to me."

"And miss all of your surprised and spontaneous reactions?" Tren smirked. "Not a chance."

"I didn't realize you had such a trash mouth, wife," Rjant said as he turned her back to the table. Alea grimaced. Thank goodness she'd spewed in English.

The twelve members of the Mahatma Tribunal had arrived and gathered just behind Alea's in-laws.

"Now then, if the She'mana Alea is done with her tantrum..." The Pontiff Jer stepped forward.

Alea eyed him indignantly. *Tantrum?* She was truly going to clock that man upside his head some day.

She watched as he opened the charm box on the table, and withdrew a small velvet-lined salver. There were two bracelets on the plate that looked like they were made of at least a hundred interlocking, tiny, crystal rings. "Do the Prowlers concur that this Trigon was consummated?"

"With absolution," Merse called out. "The Prowlers, all six, bear witness."

"And a virgin, as well," Lemac added.

Alea's eyes widened and her mouth fell open. Her cheeks heated instantly. She felt like digging a hole and burying her head in the sand, she was so embarrassed by their blatant references.

"I thought you said they weren't watching," Alea

mumbled to her Sh'em.

"Well, maybe just bit," Rjant whispered to her. "But their mantra to the divinities was of utmost importance."

Dgor's voice rose behind her. "And a feisty Tina she was too. Quite the runner!"

"Aroused her Sh'em to a frenzy!" Reo added, and Alea heard a few male chuckles in response. "It was the most lascivious of matings!"

"I reaped the benefit of that!" Syrat shouted from her place among the guests, and the women then joined the men, also chuckling.

Oh for the love of what should be sacred! Alea bit her lip as they made casual comments about the fact she had gotten laid.

And six men had watched her do it.

Vivid reminders of the hunt and her capture flooded her brain. She'd enjoyed the ritual, and had been quite wanton with her husbands. Truth be told, Alea was fascinated with watching Syrat being sexed by her mates, and after her initial discomfiture with the Prowlers presence when her Sh'em first made love to her, she actually didn't mind their presence. Alea knew deep down they weren't just praying. If she was to be totally honest with herself, she was completely aroused by being watched by six horny men. And because of their transdelta links to each other, they were probably *hearing* all of her Sh'ems' lusty thoughts and *feeling* every sensation that her Sh'em were feeling--a mental orgy. It was a heady feeling being the center of sexual attraction, something Alea thought she would forever deny herself when she was on Earth.

Okay, Alea thought. *I guess I can add voyeurism and exhibitionism to my growing list of vices.* If she ever got back to Earth, Beth would faint dead away at Alea's behavior.

The clanking of the talon arcs grew louder and faster, drawing Alea from her reverie. The Pontiff held out the salver toward Alea's Sh'em, and they each took a bracelet.

"Friends, family," the Pontiff then spoke, "By the grace of the Mahatma Divinities I offer these fetter charms as a symbol of the She'mana Alea's claiming."

Alea's eyebrows rose as Tren and Rjant crouched down at her feet. *Fetter charms? As in manacles... shackles... restraints?*

Alea stiffened, ready to bolt again, but Tren grabbed her thigh. "It's not what you think."

Before she could consider the implications further her Sh'em clamped a bracelet around each of her ankles and cheers went up--blatantly male whoops that made her feel like she had just been conquered. It was then that Alea noticed that her mothers-in-law were silent, though their slightly upturned mouths showed hints of delight. She had the sense that the same was happening with the female guests behind her. Alea had learned that by way of the ancient cultures, Tertani females were not supposed to be pleased when a Tina was caught, and in keeping with the old traditions, the women did not cheer.

Alea twisted her mouth as she looked down at the charms clasped around her ankles. "What the heck is this little detail you forgot to tell me about?" She shook her foot feeling like a dog kicking out his leg while being tickled in the ribs. The bracelet tinkled. It was the same sound made by the ankle charms that Pel'r and Dmor wore. In fact the design was exactly the same, as well.

Hmm... like wearing a wedding ring, Alea supposed.

Rjant picked up Alea's rhyton and handed it to her. He then took his own, lifting it into the air. Tren did the same and the rest of guests followed suit, and they all drank to the new triple. Behind her, drums began to beat and music similar to the sound of a xylophone began to play. Karen grabbed her hand, yanking Alea away from Rjant and Tren, and leading her toward the bonfire. The women were already beginning their dance. Releasing her grasp on Alea, Karen joined them, strutting within the group that circled the fire. Alea studied their steps and their arm movements, an eclectic mix that she could only describe as tribal gambol and the Earth dance called the *electric slide*.

I can do this, Alea decided after several moments of watching and she joined them, awkwardly copying the moves until her body found the rhythm. When she noticed her Sh'em eyeing her, Alea added her own flavor to the dancing lark making sinuous movements with her hips, seductively swaying and taunting Rjant and Tren with her body.

Karen smiled broadly and mimicked her, and the rest of the dancing women followed, drawing the attention of many males present at the party.

Our She'mana dances quite well, Tren channeled to Rjant watching her sexual dance with lust-filled eyes. *Of course we already knew that considering the demonstration she gave us on the Stardancer.*

My cock is near to bursting, Rjant mentally answered, his desire rising as Alea flashed a sultry smile. *And this time I intend to make her pay for tormenting us like she did.*

Tren looked over at Rjant and sent him a teasing chortle before laughing out loud. Rjant's hard-on was clearly evident beneath his loincloth. Rjant lowered his rhyton and held it front of his groin, but couldn't hide the smirk on his face.

And I see you are the epitome of self-control, brethren, Rjant channeled back as he noticed the obvious tenting in Tren's own loincloth. Tren deliberately refrained from covering himself, but instead flicked a look toward Rjant that clearly expressed he was quite proud of his stiff cock.

Their scents emanated and flooded to Alea's nose.

Well now, I've done my good deed for the day. She smiled smugly, though her pussy was growing wet with arousal. She knew they were linking--had grown quickly accustomed to their mannerisms when they were doing so. And she was pretty sure she could guess what they were thinking too, based on the aroma tickling her nostrils at the moment, but she could also tell by their facial comportments that a taunting exchange was happening between them.

Taking advantage of her husbands' mental bantering, and needing to catch her breath, Alea slipped away from celebration, finding a cozy place near the water, a bit further up the beach. She sat down in the sand, watching the waves roll in, as the sun started setting behind a deep, red Tertian horizon. She inhaled, absorbing the beautiful scene, listening to the faint sounds of the laughter and music coming from the celebration, knowing it wouldn't be long before her Sh'em realized she was missing and tracked her down. They were horny, and her disappearance and need to chase her would be enhanced. Her Sh'em would be hungry for her when they found her. Their delicious scents told Alea that.

Propping back on her elbows and drawing up her legs, Alea crossed one knee over the other. She bounced a foot up and down causing her ankle charm to chink with the movement, as though she were ringing the dinner bell. *Come and get me, boys. I've something for you to eat.*

It won't be long. Alea chuckled quietly.

Her attention was drawn to shrieks coming from the celebration, and she laughed out loud when she saw clothes flying into the air and naked bodies running into the taw ocean. Alea recognized Karen's form slung over Lemac's shoulder as he ran with her into the waves and tossed her into the taw.

"Apparently the Tertani people have a penchant for skinny dipping," Alea said out loud.

And then her nostrils flared. Tren and Rjant were right behind her, she could smell them, but pretended not to notice. Two hands shifted beneath her hair and skimmed along the back of her neck until they came around to cup her jaw. Alea closed her eyes--Rjant. She didn't have to see him to recognize the feel of him. Another pair of hands caressed her waist, slipping up her rib cage, moving toward her breasts and molding around them--Tren. He was kneeling and straddled over her thighs.

Rjant tipped her head back and his lips touched hers. She eagerly opened her mouth to him and he swept his tongue inside. A warm moist mouth closed over her covered breast, drawing on her nipple peaking through her top. Of their own accord Alea's legs parted and Tren's hand slid down her body, beneath her sarong and the panties she wore. He ran a single finger between her labia, coaxing her clit with an upward stroke until it was throbbing with need. Alea opened her eyes.

"Wait," she gasped out. Though this was one reason she wanted to lure them away from the party, she actually did have another. It was impossible to talk to them with all the guests constantly interrupting. Not that she minded. Everyone was there to celebrate with them and that was wonderful.

"Tell me about these ankle char... oh!" Tren slid a finger inside of her hollow.

"Not now, She'mana," Rjant gently scolded, his mouth teasing her ear.

"Ha!" Alea giggled, as Tren stuck his tongue in her belly button. "Yes, now."

Breaking contact with them, she squirmed a few feet away and sat back on her rump, swearing she could hear a low growl coming from the back of Rjant's throat as his lust-hazed eyes fell upon her. Tren looked as though he were in pain.

Now, how mean do I feel?--not! Alea knew that torment was a perfect route to great Tertian sex. The longer she tortured them, the lustier they would become. And oh how she loved to torture her Sh'em.

"There's an old Earth saying," Alea said, moving her foot into Rjant's lap, caressing his swollen cock with her toes. "Curiosity killed the cat."

"You are without a doubt killing us, woman," Rjant groaned and Tren agreed.

Alea lifted both her feet and placed one on each of Rjant's shoulders, spreading her legs slightly, giving him a tantalizing view of her pussy. His eyes dropped and his chest heaved faster as his respiration quickened. Her fingers dipped between her legs and Alea to hold of his hand, guiding the tips of his fingers along her crotch. Both of her Sh'em swallowed hard.

"But satisfaction brought it back," she continued, her eyes alight with mirth blending with a raging yearning to be ravaged by her men.

"We'll show you satisfaction, wife," Tren said. "Straight

into the far wards if you keep this up."

"Oh, I don't think there will be a problem keeping it… er… them up." Alea laughed, her eyes snapping to his bulging cock.

"Tell me about these." She shook her foot, causing her bracelet to jingle, and quoting the Earth tabloid Alea added. "Inquiring minds want to know."

With a resigned sigh, Tren moved up alongside her. "Alright then, Alea. What do you want to know?"

His hand came to her belly, and he gently rubbed it with his palm.

"Why am I wearing these... what's the history behind them?"

Rjant lifted one of her feet and began kissing the flesh atop her foot. He tugged at the bracelet with his teeth before moving his lips along her calf.

"When a female was mated, the chains were placed around her ankles. One by each of her Sh'em," he told her.

"The chiming sound made it easier for the Sh'em to track their She'mana when the urge to run assailed her," Tren added. He unfastened her top, exposing her breasts. The slight breeze caused her nipples to harden and Tren lowered his head to draw one into his mouth.

Alea closed her eyes with pleasure at their touch and reclined to her back. Her hand shifted beneath Tren's loincloth and she found his cock. It was thick and hard. She stroked it a few times and then moved to play with his balls.

"Why didn't your women just cut them off with a stone or something?"

"That's the beauty of the metal, Alea. It is light in weight, but highly resilient to being damaged. Even the sharpest of stones would barely mar its surface." Rjant's head was beneath her sarong now, his mouth teasing the crease at her juncture. She shuddered when he released a hot, open-mouthed breath that seared through the cloth of her panties. Her pelvis jerked as her clit craved to feel his tongue.

"It's the same material used in our modern talon arcs, though our weapons are made of a deeper gray type," Tren rasped out as Alea continued to play with him. He climbed over her, straddling her shoulders. Alea's fingers untied his loincloth and she pulled it from his hips. His heavy cock bobbed freely above her face. Her tongue slipped through her lips and she licked the head of it. Tren dropped his head back, closing his eyes. His mouth parted and he expelled a low growl.

"I'm surprised you don't just put a tracking device in them... oh-h-h." Alea's pussy twitched as Rjant pulled the leg opening to her panties aside and began stroking a finger inside of her.

"There would be no fun in that, She'mana. The hunt is half the pleasure of the capture," he told her.

"Well, the charm anklets are beautiful." Alea wrapped her palm around Tren's shaft and using it like a handle, pulled it toward her mouth. She paused and looked up at him.

Tren looked down at her, his eyes passion-clouded. His breath grew heavy at the sight of his manhood perched near his wife's lips. "You're beautiful, woman."

His hips started pumping when Alea drew his cock into her mouth and sucked on him.

"And the bracelets match your hair so well, She'mana," Rjant added as he pulled her panties down the length of her legs removing them, his eyes fixed on her pussy. He licked his lips and his head dropped between her thighs.

"Perfectly," he whispered and started licking her pussy.

The sun dropped down below the horizon to the passion sounds of the Trigon ot Alea as they made love in the sand.

Chapter Fifteen

Alea dug her toes into the moist, plum-colored sand, thinking about her life on Tertia, musing on her favorite memories and watching as another taw wave rolled in and swirled around her.

Had three months gone by already?

She was happy and content, and had made new friends, one of them being Syrat, who lived with her own Sh'em in the compound at Canyon City. Alea participated with Syrat in the Triconjugal hunt for the mating of Bjead, Larimon and Bligh, and ever since then, Alea and Syrat had become quite close.

Taking Karen up on her advice, Alea started looking for something productive to do. Syrat even took her to the lab, where she worked for the ISDS, and gave her a tour of the place, telling Alea that there were many jobs she could perform there. But the only ones that Alea took interest in required educating. Tren suggested that she could attend an Edu-commune for higher learning, but Alea really didn't want to return to college. In the end, she settled on teaching swimming lessons three times a week to the children, something she did on Earth at the local YMCA to earn a little extra cash. She was satisfied with her decision. Alea always enjoyed working with children very much. Today was her day off though, and Alea was now enjoying some solitude at the beach, while Rjant and Tren were training with the sentrics.

Her eyes slid to the cycle hovering nearby and she smirked. Each of her Sh'em had taken turns trying to teach her to drive the thing, both eventually throwing up their hands in frustration babbling something about *women drivers* and *women never listen*. It was Pel'r that finally got the task done, and much to her Sh'ems' amazement Alea was quite good at maneuvering the hover cycle. In fact, she was so good at it that Tren forbade her to drive for three entire days when he caught her playing *chicken* with Rjant in one of the open fields. He even went as far as to banish Rjant from the cycle saying that she and Rjant would cause him to die from heart rupture if they continued to engage in such untamed behavior. Rjant merely laughed at him and when Alea responded in like, Tren threw her over his knee, yanked down her pants and spanked her bare bottom. It wasn't meant as punishment, as he was being quite light-hearted about it. What it did result in was arousing Alea to the point where she was begging for more.

Please sir, might I have another? she crooned through her tear-filled laughter. *Oh yes, again... more please.*

The three of them ended up entangled in what turned out to be almost a full day of mind blowing sex. They missed all of the meals in the main hall and Tren missed a meeting with his sentries. Alea was supposed to go shopping with Syrat, who finally ended up going on her own, after growing tired of waiting for her. Rjant was scheduled to be in the field to train novices with the talon arc. As a result from his absence, two of the trainees burned their hands on the lasers from their talons. The intercom kept buzzing and the door chimes kept ringing, but the triple ignored everyone's attempt to reach them. At one point Tocol was sent and threatened to break down the door if they failed to answer. Their acquaintances were worried that something might be wrong. Well, based on their compromising entanglement they had no desire to be seen, so in unison they answered Tocol, telling him to go away. They weren't disturbed after that, but by the time they emerged from their quarters, the looks on the faces of Tren's parents and the rest of residents in-house told them they were in deep doo doo. It was on that day Alea found out about the *zapping*. She learned that it was a form of punishment used on insubordinate sentries and entailed giving the warrior a jolting shock that supposedly was very painful. Alea was appalled and had a conniption about the corporal punishment and it took Dmor to calm her down, while her Sh'em stood by with dumbfounded expressions, not quite understanding why she was so upset about it. Later they endured a round of lecturing from Alea as she attempted to explain cruel and inhumane ideals to them. In the end, nothing was settled and they all agreed to disagree on the subject.

Not that there was any intention of punishing Alea and her Sh'em in such a manner. The three of them were admittedly being neglectful and irresponsible by having sex all day long, instead of attending to their responsibilities. But Tocol and a few other residents did tease her about it at dinner one night, telling her that She'mana who distracted their Sh'em from their duties in such a manner should be zapped for two full dials. Alea responded with a spiteful glare, receiving an abundance of laughter in return.

It was the Pontiff Jer who handed down their actual punishment. They were given commode duty in the public hygiene chambers, ordered to scrub all of the toilets on the compound, every day for three full weeks. Alea didn't think it was all that bad, *really*. What was rather annoying was that the whole damn place knew exactly why they were being punished and certainly let Alea, Tren and Rjant know that they knew at every crossing. Alea thought her Sh'em were more embarrassed about it than she was.

Well, at least the servants were happy to be rid of the chore for awhile.

"I aim to please," Alea told one of the servant women one day, a smile planted on her face. And the servant actually encouraged Alea to do the deed with her Sh'em again, only this time to disappear for more than a day, expressing how she liked the little bit of free time the shenanigans of the Trigon of Alea had given her. Alea laughed at that, telling the woman that chances for it to happen again were probably in her favor, but that they were not likely to misbehave for awhile.

Rjant and Tren hated cleaning the toilets.

As Alea sat on the beach she continued to think about the life she was sharing with her Sh'em. Inhaling deeply she let out a murmur of contentment and then tipped her face upward, soaking in the rays of the warm, Tertian sun.

Despite her being at odds with some of the customs and laws, she liked the life that fate had tossed her way.

Two hands slipped around her neck and something was clasped around it. "Happy birthing day, She'mana"

Alea smiled brightly as she felt Rjant lean into her from behind. "How did you know it was my birthday?"

"Do you need to ask, wife?" She opened her eyes and saw Tren kneeling down in front of her.

No. She didn't have to ask how they knew.

"This is beautiful," Alea said as she fingered the lavaliere that Rjant placed around her neck. It was made of finely weaved, filigree links that converged to cradle a citrine-colored gem. Tren held out his gift to her, and she touched the small crystal block.

"It looks like an ice cube," she said. "What is it?"

He smiled at her without offense, knowing there was still much about his world that she had yet to experience. "It's a holojectory, Alea."

"A holo who?" she asked.

"Let me show you." Tren activated the device and the cube opened and flattened like a piece of paper. Videos started playing, the first, a record of the rites given in the chapel and the celebration on the beach.

"How did you get this stuff recorded?" Alea looked at him, her eyes wide, a delighted expression on her face.

"There was an image maker at both rituals."

"You didn't tell me."

"I wanted it to be a surprise."

Her face suddenly fell and she looked at him with a furl in her brow. "You didn't record the hunt, did you?"

Some things were just way too personal.

Rjant snorted behind her. "Of course not, She'mana."

Alea released a relieved breath and her expression brightened again. "I love both my gifts. Thank you."

There was truly an advantage to having two husbands, in more ways than one. Double gifts was definitely one of the bonuses.

"I don't know when your birthdays are." Alea frowned, shifting her attention between the two of them. "Did I miss them?"

She bit her lip. *How awful if she had.*

"My birthing day is in four sept-dawnings, Alea," Rjant answered. "And Tren's isn't for five more lunar cycles."

"Well that's good." Alea stood. "I'll have to think of something wonderful for the both of you."

She brushed the sand from her legs and bottom, readjusting the leopard patterned, thong bikini bottom that was clinging just a bit too far into the crack of her butt. Back on Earth, Alea wouldn't have been caught dead in a thong, but now, she wore it as comfortably as she did her own skin. A seamstress in Canyon City's marketplace designed the revealing bikini after Alea described the design to her. When Rjant and Tren had first seen it, they were overwhelmingly pleased. In fact, it almost led to another two weeks of punishment.

"I think I'll go for a run." She bent and gave Tren a quick kiss on the mouth and then turned to give Rjant the same before darting down the beach, her ankle charms jingling in time with her stride.

Rjant and Tren eyed her amorously.

She really does have a nice ass, don't you think, Tren?

Indubitably. Tren wholeheartedly agreed. *Shall we chase her?*

Do we have a choice? Rjant's cock was already thickening at the thought.

I'd like to see either of us try not to. Tren gave a mental chuckle and began stalking after his She'mana. Rjant was close at his heels.

Alea knew they were behind her, or would be shortly. She sniffed the air as she ran, searching for their scents. She'd grown to thoroughly enjoy this game of cat and mouse, and intended to take full advantage of her husbands' natural instincts.

Ahead of her, a formation of craggy, plum colored rocks traversed from the forest and across the sands, tapering down to plunge into the water. It was blocking her way, and she quickly scanned the formation, looking for a way to cross it. Tren would have her hide if she tried to scale it.

Besides, her manner of dress was definitely not conducive to a strenuous climb. A sprinkling of light between the rocks caught her eyes and she smirked victoriously. There was an opening there and she could jog her way through it. Sniffing the air once more, the familiar, sensual aroma caught in her nostrils, telling her that Tren and Rjant were nearby.

She slowed her pace when she came to the rocks and eased her way through the narrow passage, careful to avoid scraping her skin. On the other side she spied a form in the distance stalking toward her.

Rjant? Now how the heck did he... never mind. She sensed Tren's presence not far behind her and she stopped, looking over her shoulder. There he was, stalking toward her at the same pace as her other Sh'em. They would meet up with her at the same time. Alea's mind turned devilish as she looked forward and back, watching her husbands close in upon her, and as they did, they both unhooked and dropped their baldrics and then threw off their shirts.

Wait, she told herself. *Be patient... wait.* They were getting closer. *Wait... wait....*

Now!

With a heavy *oomph* Tren and Rjant slammed together as Alea leapt to one side. Literally, they bounced off of each other, and the looks of shock in their expressions made Alea burst out laughing.

"Vixen!" Tren bellowed and then he laughed too.

Rjant moved toward her eyeing her amorously. "You'll pay for that, She'mana."

"I certainly hope so," Alea answered through her chuckles as she backed away.

"Warriors..." she taunted. "Come out and play-yay...."

It was an old movie, but she loved that line. Never thought she'd ever get a chance to use it. If only she had a couple of pop bottles to clack together like they gang leader did in the film.

Tren and Rjant moved upon her, and in one, long leap, Alea was once again darting away from her Sh'em. But they were quicker this time. She was snagged from behind,

Rjant's arms sweeping around her waist, yanking her, locking her body against him. He backed up against the rocks, sitting on one of the formation's smoother surfaces that jutted from the wall, bringing Alea's bottom down to rest on his lap. Tren moved forward, and Alea brought her feet up, planting them on his chest, laughing, playfully trying to stop him, but with a sweep of his hands, he had her ankles shackled in his palms. Throwing one leg over each of his shoulders, Tren angled himself against the back her thighs, and braced his hands to either side of Rjant's head where he leaned against the facade of the rock wall. Tren then pressed his weight further on her, causing Alea to fold nearly in half.

Once again Alea was thankful for her extraordinary flexibility, as she was sandwiched in a v-shape between them.

"Interesting position." Rjant snorted, pushing Alea's thong aside. His fingers delved inside of her hollow and he was pleased to find that she was already wet for them. "Think we can make use of it?"

"I'm sure we can come up with something," Tren answered, lifting his hips slightly as he unfastened his pants, and then pushed them down his thighs. He looked down at Alea's thong and untied the strings that held it together at the sides, thinking how convenient the scanty little garment was. He rubbed the head of his cock between her labia, and then lifted her bottom from Rjant's lap so his brethren could free up his own cock. Tren focused on her pussy, his manhood swelling at the sight of the moist, but tiny, single opening, and he wondered how he and Rjant had both managed to fit without tearing her apart. His eyes dropped slightly to her other opening and he licked his lips. They would sample that little delight, as well.

Rjant caught the wave of Tren's thought as Alea was settled back onto his thighs and he grinned at his brethren wickedly, slipping his shaft inside of her vagina as she was lowered. Alea's breath came out in a raspy moan as she sank down on him. Her legs slipped from Tren's shoulders and her feet hit the ground. Rjant hooked his legs inside of

Alea's, and spread her legs wide open. His hand came around to play with her clit, flicking it back and forth with the tip of his finger and then rotating it in a circular motion. He removed his fingers lifting his hands to cup her breasts, his thumbs skimming her nipples, his shaft throbbing inside.

Tren dropped between her knees and he lowered his face to her pussy, sucking her clit between his lips, licking it languorously with his tongue. A frisson of heat and desire swept along Alea's flesh as she started rocking between them, Tren's tongue stroking, his lips suckling, her pussy clenching and riding Rjant's hard shaft.

"Don't stop," she pleaded, spreading wider, thrusting her hips and shuddering. "I'm cumming." And they both groaned at her words. She pumped her pelvis back and forth, rubbing her labia and clit against Tren's mouth, grasping his head, pressing her pussy harder to his face and shuddering as her vagina clenched tighter around Rjant's cock. Rjant grasped her hips and pulled her down tight against him intensifying her bursting orgasm.

Now? Rjant channeled to Tren.

Yes, now, he channeled back. *She's ready.*

Rjant lifted her hips and pulled himself free while Tren rose and hovered over her. He grasped her legs and placed Alea's ankles atop his shoulders again and then surged forward, sinking his cock deep inside of her, his way eased by the moisture of her streaming juices. Alea gasped at Tren's unrestrained plunge and even more so when she felt the tip of Rjant's cock poised at the entrance to her bottom. For a brief moment she tensed. The three of them had talked about this and Alea agreed that she would like to try it. She was ripe for it, but also afraid. She murmured a quiet protest.

"S-h-h, Alea," Rjant soothed, kissing her neck and whispering in her ear. "Relax. Let mc inside."

A slow, languorous breath of air escaped Alea's lungs and she leaned back against him, her muscles giving and he eased the tip of his shaft inside.

"We won't hurt you," he promised.

Tren slid back and then plunged forward again, slowly coaxing and bringing Alea back to arousal. "Only as much as you want, love."

Alea clenched. It was uncomfortable at first, but she willed her muscles to soften.

"Yes," she whispered, trusting them, her head falling back to rest on Rjant's shoulder. And he slid further inside. The position she was in allowed for only part of his cock to fill her, but they knew it was all she could take for now.

Tren stilled and groaned absorbing Rjant's telepathic thoughts, his cock growing harder at his brethren's aching lust. She was hot and tight and shuddering all around them. He started to move, stroking into her. His pelvis rubbing against her clit with every thrust and the pleasure inside of Alea began building again. Rjant held steady, not needing more than the gentle movements of Alea's bottom caused by his brethren's thrusting inside of her vagina and her spastic tightening as they filled both of her hollows.

Rjant closed his eyes and allowed it to all happen. It was a first for all three of them.

"Fuck me," she suddenly gasped out. "Harder."

Tren readily obliged slamming his pelvis, driving his cock harder and deeper, his breathing harsh as he started to cum. Alea clenched and cried out, her orgasm spilling free as well. She felt both her Sh'ems' cocks swell and pulsate as they simultaneously spewed their seed.

Alea slid her legs from Tren's shoulders and lowered her feet to the sand, though their still semi-hard cocks remained inside of her. Their breathing was heavy and deep, and Alea could feel her husbands' hearts beating solidly against her as her own thumped hardily in rhythm.

"Are you alright, She'mana?" Rjant finally asked.

"I'm wonderful," Alea replied on a breathy whisper.

"Well I'm squashed," Rjant returned with a chuckle. "And there's a piece of jagged rock piercing my ass cheek."

"I guess you got the raw end of the deal." Alea responded without thinking, as she considered Rjant's position on the bottom of the pile.

Tren and Rjant both snorted and Alea grimaced at her unintended pun. "I can't believe that just came out of my mouth."

"What would you like to do for the rest of this dawning?" Tren asked, lifting himself away from his wife and his brethren. Alea stood after him and Rjant followed.

"Don't you have to go back to the training fields?"

"There are advantages to being in charge, Alea," Rjant said as he leaned over her shoulder and nuzzled his cheek in the crook of her neck. "We delegated orders to one of our underlings and took the rest of the dawning off."

Turning, Alea looked at him askew. "We're not going to end up cleaning toilets again, are we?"

"Not this time," Tren answered. "How about a swim?"

He took Alea's hand and the three of them headed for the taw ocean.

"Let's have a picnic on the beach," Alea suggested, scooping up a handful of taw and splashing at Tren. Rjant dove through a rolling taw wave and disappeared beneath the surface. He came up in front of Alea, startling her and she shrieked.

"Perfect idea. I'll get my talon and go trawling for tirchin in the wading pool just down the beach."

"Mmm." Tren rubbed his stomach "I haven't had tirchin for awhile. We can roast it over a fire."

"Great!" Alea answered, wading out of the water alongside her Sh'em, eyeing the bevy of trees just beyond the rocks. "I'll go collect some firewood."

She had no idea what tirchin was, but was willing to try it. Alea discovered that most of the Tertian food was much to her liking.

Once on shore, Tren donned his clothes and replaced his weapon. He left to go retrieve Alea's hover cycle and the one he and Rjant arrived on.

"Now how's he going to do that?" Alea asked while adjusting her bikini into place. Her attention shifted to Rjant's body and her eyes perused his form. He stood next to her still unclad, his talon arc held in one hand. He looked sexy and wild as all hell, with both his weapons proudly displayed.

"Do what?"

"Huh? What?"

Rjant's mouth turned up on one side in a half-cocked grin when he realized his naked body was distracting her. His chest puffed up and his ego raised a notch. He never had much confidence in the way he looked, but Alea made him feel like a god. "You asked me a question, She'mana."

"I did?" Alea's eyes snapped to his face and she grinned. "Oh... yeah... how is Tren going to bring both cycles here?"

"The cycles have trackers in them," Rjant told her. "Tren will merely ride one and the other will follow."

It sounded simple enough. "Cool... I'll go get the wood." Alea finished straightening her bathing suit and trotted off toward the forest while Rjant headed for the tarn to catch their lunch.

"Ouch!" Alea pulled a stick from between her sandals and the sole of her foot. She definitely had on the wrong kind of footwear for this task. Having gathered a couple of thick branches and some kindling she started to head back to the beach. One of her Sh'em could get more if they needed it. They were dressed more appropriately than she was.

The sound of snapping twigs caught in her ear, and Alea stopped to listen. "Rjant, Tren?"

There was no answer, and Alea suddenly felt uneasy. What if it was some wild animal looking to fill its belly? Well, no sense in waiting around to find out. Quickly she moved from the forest and was relieved when she reached its edge.

"*Sherta abest tu,*" a foreign voice said from behind her and Alea stiffened.

"*Colsi perga!*" another voice said. "*Adsor shi corlfis enama tolt qi fa.*"

Alea turned around and dropped the wood, and then reconsidered her actions, bending to pick up one of the larger, heavier branches to use as a club, while keeping her eyes steady on the three unfamiliar warriors who had just surrounded her. The stick didn't make much of a weapon, but at least it was better than nothing.

She didn't recognize their uniforms, but they did look quite human.

Dormothians.

They probably thought she was a Dormothian, too.

"I would appreciate it if you would speak Tertian," Alea told them and waited for them to respond. They might not know the language, but then again, they were on the planet so she hoped that at least one of them did.

"Excuse our ignorance, female." A warrior answered her in Tertian as he brushed by one of the others and closer to her. Alea looked at him, feeling a bit intimidated. He had red hair and searing blue eyes and a physique that said, *Don't mess with me or I'll break you in two.*

"My comrade was just saying that you are a pretty little thing," he continued and took another step forward, his hands moving toward her hips.

Alea stiffened with worry. She didn't know much about the people from Dormoth other than their physical resemblance to earthlings. Alea took a step back, but not out of his grasp as he stepped even closer to her. She found herself trapped against the chest of a second warrior, who stood behind her. His hands came up to her shoulders and Alea opened her mouth ready to scream.

The one in front of her started to speak. "I told him that...."

"... that you're crossing a serious line here warrior," A voice finished for him--Tren. *Thank the heavens above.*

The blade of Tren's talon arc came up to the warrior behind Alea, its tip pressing into the flesh of his neck. A trickle of blood dripped from beneath it. Tren shot him a feral warning.

The laser end of another talon arc swept around and was planted between the eyes of the second warrior that held her in front. Alea heard a sizzle and smelled burnt flesh and the warrior howled at the burning to his skin, releasing her immediately. The third warrior dropped his weapon and held up his hands.

There would be no trouble from that one.

Alea blew out a relieved breath. She was safe now.

"Release our wife," Tren growled, his voice threatening but controlled. And the warrior with the blade at his throat dropped his hands and shifted cautiously. Rjant pulled Alea behind him and she willingly complied, her fear starting to subside, though her heart still raced in her chest. She peered from behind Rjant to see what was happening.

"We would not have hurt the wench," the redheaded warrior said. "I was just telling Zupol that she was not up for grabs."

"It looked like you were grabbing her to me." Tren shifted and the blade sank just slightly deeper into the warrior's throat.

The Dormothian swallowed and beads of sweat appeared on his forehead. "It would be unwise to kill the messengers of the king, Commander Tren ot Alea."

"Then drop the rest of your weapons," Rjant commanded and waited as they complied.

"Of course Rjant ot Alea," he replied removing his stunner from his holster, and signaled the redheaded one to do the same. Their weapons dropped to the ground with a clank.

"So sorry! So sorry!" Gorsch came scurrying along the beach and stood to his full height when he reached them. "Pardon sirs, but I told these sentries to wait for you in the main hall at the compound."

"Never mind, Gorsch. It wasn't your fault." Tren scowled at the three warriors. By the symbols on their jackets he knew they were part of King Dred's royal guard. "State your names and state your business."

The one held by Tren's blade spoke. "Zupol Egrin, First Baron of the royal court, planet Dormoth." He then held an upward turned palm toward his comrades. "This is Ivot Xalin and the other behind him is Hansit Brell, two of the king's guards who accompanied me here."

Brell and Xalin went rigid and presented the delta. It was a respectful gesture, Tren and Rjant both realized, as King's Dred's underlings typically greeted their own superiors with a high fisted salute.

"I've heard of you, Zupol Egrin," Tren acknowledged him. The warrior held a position high in the king's court. The other two, he didn't know. "What brings you here now and what gives you the right to handle our woman?"

Tren continued to hold his weapon at Zupol's throat while Rjant held his talon in offensive position, ready to strike if necessary. Alea still cowered behind Rjant. These men were intimidating and she didn't care if she looked like a coward.

Zupol Egrin glanced down at the blade threatening his voice box and then met Tren's eyes with a steady gaze. "Please accept my apologies for Xalin's most inappropriate behavior. He was trying to tell your She'mana, that Brell thought she was pretty."

Rjant snarled and lifted his talon higher.

"Please let me finish, Commanders."

Tren and Rjant both narrowed their eyes while Gorsch shifted around nervously. Alea just kept her mouth shut and listened. She had no idea who said what, since she couldn't interpret anything they said when she first encountered them.

"Continue," Rjant narrowed his eyes on the baron.

"I was reprimanding Xalin for putting his hands on her, but she was frightened and backed away. I was behind her and she backed into me. I merely put my hands on her shoulders to steady her."

"Is this true, Alea?" Tren peered behind Rjant's back at their wife.

Alea shrugged, there seemed to be a skew somewhere in the facts that he conveyed, but what else could she say? They really hadn't done anything to her other than frighten her. "I suppose that's true, Tren. They didn't hurt me." Still she had to wonder what they would've done if her Sh'em hadn't come along.

Tren reluctantly lowered his talon arc and Zupol Egrin visibly relaxed. "State your business, baron."

"The King is on Angard and requests your presence at a meeting he's arranged with the ISDS"

"Why Angard? Tren looked at him oddly. "Why so far

from Dormoth?"

"The Chief Arbitrator of the ISDS was planning on being nearby," Egrin answered. "It was mutually agreed upon. And since it's Tertani sentries who mostly guard the perimeter around the planet they felt that you should be involved."

"The planet is under quarantine for scanning, baron," Rjant interrupted. "How is it that the king and a crew were able to leave the planet?"

"The Arbitrator made exception," Zupol Egrin paused before continuing. "I assure you our entire crew has been scanned and none of us are tainted." And then he added to put their minds at ease, "The three of us were scanned on Angard as well, before holotransporting down here."

"Very well," Tren conceded. "Send a message to King Dred and the Chief Arbitrator that we'll be present."

Chapter Sixteen

"Again, I beseech you, Flomink." King Dred held his hands outward. "The quarantine has put my economy into dire straits."

"I understand your position, your majesty," the Chief Arbitrator answered. "But it's too risky."

Tren unfolded his compu-sheet and activated it, studying the incoming data. He handed the device to Flomink.

Flomink shook his head. "Only one quarter of Dormoth's inhabitants have come forth for scanning, Dred. Of those, a handful were tainted and removed from the planet."

Alea sat to one side of the conference room on Angard, desperately trying to not look at the king. He was a tall, but plump man with beady little eyes and he kept leering at her with a glare that was making her uncomfortable. And the way he kept wiping the spittle from the corner of his mouth with a single fat pinky was totally grossing her out.

"But our traders cannot enter and leave the planet and the shortages are causing much unrest among my people."

Yuk. He did it again--looked at her and drooled. Alea shifted in her chair, wondering why she even considered that these proceedings might be interesting. Tren told her he was in good fellowship with the king and she thought it would be cool to meet actual royalty. So she asked if she could accompany her Sh'em to this meeting. But now, she was sorely regretting that decision, wishing only for it to end. She'd rather be doing something else--swimming or hiking, cleaning even. Anything would be better than this.

Alea doesn't look happy, brethren. Rjant cast a sympathetic look in his wife's direction.

I noticed, Tren answered. At this very moment he was much appreciating their telepathic skills. *And I'm not entirely happy myself with the way the king keeps looking at her.*

The king is acting a bit odd... out of character. He's usually more congenial, Rjant replied.

His grim manner is understandable considering the state of his planet.

Rjant pondered that for a moment before responding. *I suppose. Shall I send Alea to the Angard plaza? She might enjoy some shopping.*

I think that's probably a good idea.

Rjant excused himself from the proceedings table and moved to where Alea sat. He whispered their suggestion to her and Alea's face brightened. She rose immediately and left the conference room.

Almost simultaneously, King Dred stood and approached one of his guards, passing unheard instructions to the underling. The guard nodded and left the room and the King returned to the table without anyone in the room regarding his actions. Kings were always giving orders about one thing or another.

Alea was glad to be away from the stuffy room and the boring arguments and the disgusting king that kept ogling her liberally. Angard was an interesting space station and she was eager to explore it. The market plaza had the most interesting of offerings, Alea noted as she strolled from booth to booth examining the wares that vendors had for barter. She didn't notice she was being watched by the warrior at the table in the café just a short distance away.

Tocol chuckled silently when he caught sight of Alea, thinking about the latest Earth game she had taught him-- thumb wrestling he believed she called it. It was better than hot hands because he could truly beat her at this game. His thumb was bigger and longer. Not that she didn't pin his thumb several times, much to his surprise, telling him it was all in the technique. She was an amusing woman there was no doubt, and Tocol much enjoyed her company. They were good friends.

Deciding he would walk over to say 'hello', Tocol stood from his chair at the cafe's table. His eyes drifted to the three uniformed Dormothian guards and he watched as two of them put their heads together to whisper something and then look Alea's way. If he could lend his mind to suspicion, it appeared as though they were following her, and he found that strange. Her Sh'em would use Tertani sentries if they wanted their She'mana guarded. Tocol lifted his hand to the telcom button on his belt. He would investigate the situation and find out if any of the Dormothian crew had been given leave or assignment.

No sooner had he thought to do that when he noticed the guards move quickly upon Alea and Tocol immediately stalked toward them ready to intervene. Alea turned just in time to see the guards advance on her and then Tocol step in between. Without a word one of the guards hit the holotransport button on his belt and in a flash of movement through the corner of his eye, Tocol saw a second guard's hand come up. A blinding pain to his head caused his vision to darken. The last thing he heard was Alea's muffled scream.

"Tocol... Tocol," the voice whispered and Tocol groaned at the throb in his head. "Tocol. Are you alright?"

Through the fog that was starting to clear, Tocol recognized Alea's voice.

"Alea?" He grimaced, but had yet to open his eyes. And somewhere in his sensible brain he thought he heard the murmur of engines and movement in the space around him, though he couldn't be sure. He'd received a blow to the head and that could be responsible for causing faulty sensations. Tocol lifted his hand to the back of his head and winced as he pressed into the knob that was swelling there.

Definitely a blow to the head. But why?

He suddenly became aware that his wrists were shackled by a short leash. He tried to shift his legs and realized his ankles were tied together.

"Wake up, Tocol! I'm scared."

Forcing his eyes open, Tocol attempted to focus and Alea's form materialized within his field of vision. His eyes crossed at that moment and he closed one eye, opened it and closed the other.

"What are you doing?"

"I'm trying to determine which one of you to focus on."

Tocol shook his head to rid himself of the unwanted dizziness.

A scent invaded his nose, forcefully tantalizing, bringing him to sharp alertness. His cock hardened and his eyes riveted to where Alea was. He became keenly aware that she was nude, her body veiled only by a thin covering. She was lying on a bed with her arms shackled to the wall behind her head. Alea was pale, her fright was obvious and from her dilated pupils he could tell that the drug was already starting to take effect.

"I think I've been poisoned, Tocol. I feel funny."

"Where are we?" Tocol tried to remain calm, steeling himself against the pheromones taunting him.

"King Dred forced me to drink something." Alea closed her eyes and arched her back her body diving into a confusing craving. "What's happening to me?"

"Listen to me, Alea." Tocol attempted to straighten against his bindings, gritting his teeth to tamp his growing arousal. "Listen carefully."

The door to the chamber slid open and Tocol clamped his mouth shut as King Dred stepped inside. The door slid closed behind him. Tocol knew immediately that something wasn't right with the king. His skin was sweaty, his pupils were like pinpoints and there was an uncharacteristic rigidity to his demeanor.

"What's this about, Dred?" Tocol demanded. "Why have you brought us aboard your ship?"

His majesty sniggered at Tocol without answering and moved immediately to the bed. "She's lovely, don't you think?" His hand leisurely massaged Alea's calf as he spoke. "Fertile too, I assume."

He looked at Tocol and laughed sadistically. "My seed will settle nicely inside of her."

Tocol bucked against his chains, shocked by what the king was saying. This made no sense, no sense at all. His majesty was a peace-loving sort and an ally to the Allegiance. His eyes snapped to Alea were she was writhing on the bed and his stomach churned at the thought of what was about to happen while at the same time his shaft was screaming with need.

"She is mated in a Trigon, Dred!"

The king turned a feral glare to Tocol. "She now belongs to me."

A stream of frothy spittle escaped from the king's mouth and Tocol nearly gagged at what that meant. Grimacing, he closed his eyes and turned his cheek to the wall. The king was tainted and there would be no reasoning with him now.

"Why, Dred? Why would you keep me here to see what you'll do to her?"

"I need a witness, Krellian, that I've mated with her, so her Sh'em will then cast her aside." His majesty's hand meandered up Alea's thigh. "Would you like to sample her when I'm done?"

"You sick bastard!" Tocol spit, his eyes narrowing on the king. He jerked against his shackles in a futile effort to get free.

Through the haze and confusion befuddling Alea's brain she heard the king's words and moaned her desire at the thought of being had by two men--and then her body seized.

"No!" Alea screamed, railing against her sordid thoughts, terror racing through her veins as she realized with clarity that she indeed couldn't fight her genes.

"It was rather convenient that you tried to come to her rescue." His eyes settled on Alea's covered breasts. He wiped away the foam dripping from his mouth and then settled his palms on Alea's hips. "You'll serve a dual purpose for me, Krellian."

"Meaning?" Tocol asked.

"Since the ISDS won't release my planet, I'll have to resort to making money by other means." The king stood and turned toward Tocol, releasing a guttural laugh. "You, Krellian will bring a fair price on the market."

"What in star blazing hells are you talking about, Dred?"

"The Krellian radicals are issuing great sums for the return of their wayward denizens."

"And how many Krellians have you sold, Dred?" Even as Tocol's mind was reeling from Alea's emanating pheromones, he had the clarity of mind to keep the king talking, thinking to delay the inevitable, knowing that the longer he held the king from Alea the greater the chance that the vessel would be overtaken by the ally sentries. Surely by now his Commanders were aware that he and Alea were missing, they had to be on their way.

Tocol barely clung to that hope.

The king furled his brow and it was clear that there was confusion in his brain. He wiped more froth from his mouth and then spoke. "Why... you'll be the first."

"Think about this, Dred. You can't defy the Allegiance or the laws. You and your people will suffer for this." Tocol was all too aware that trying to reason with an infected individual was nearly impossible, he would be adamant that his thinking was rational, but this plot of his was horribly ill-conceived. His majesty was no longer in control of his faculties. The king would be caught and severely punished.

King Dred suddenly went rigid and he grabbed his groin. "You distract me from my purpose, Krellian." With that he turned to Alea, crawled on the bed and hovered over her.

Alea felt the fire spread through her as she looked up at the king and then her body went cold, but not from lack of arousal for she was mightily aroused, her body was in great need.

"Ah, yes, lovely, you need my heat." The king smiled down at her.

"Yes," Alea whispered, her mind whirling in contradicting thoughts. She was still coherent enough to realize that she wanted to scratch the king's eyes out yet her brain was muddled enough to concede.

"Fight it, Alea!" Tocol jerked at his chains, the manacles cutting deeply into his wrists and he started to bleed. He would gnaw off his hands if he had to.

There was a commotion in the corridor outside--shouting and the sounds of heavy footsteps. The door to the chamber slid open and three guards rushed in. They moved to the king, jerking him off of Alea, and he was quickly subdued.

"Take him to the brig," one of the guards ordered.

"Release me immediately!" King Dred bellowed.

Ignoring him, the two guards dragged him through the door.

"Executed! You'll all die!" his majesty yelled, his ranting growing fainter as he was taken down the hall.

Tocol glared at the remaining guard, waiting to see what his next move would be. The guard stared at Alea who was whimpering on the bed and he adjusted his groin. Stiffening, Tocol opened his mouth to warn the man off when the guard turned abruptly and crouched down before him.

"Ivot Xalin, Chief." He pulled a key chip from the inner pocket of his uniform vest, inserted it into a slot on one of Tocol's shackles and then the other, releasing the latching mechanisms.

"The crew has gone into mutiny," he said moving to Tocol's ankles and freed them as well. "We follow Zupol Egrin now."

"I know that name," Tocol said, rubbing his wrists and wincing with discomfort from the slashes caused from his struggles. "He's one of the royal court's high barons."

Tocol stood and went to Alea. The color had drained from her flesh and the trembling had already begun. Her head thrashed from side to side and her body writhed causing the linen to slip down to her waist. Tocol grasped the edge of it, and even as the urge to pull it off of her and cover her naked body with his own assailed him, he instead pulled the linen to her neck to cover her. He grimaced knowing she was already in dire straits.

"Your king is infected with Brits Scorn, Xalin," Tocol said.

"We're aware of that," Ivot answered. "But he is... was our king. We could not, however, justify what he's done here. The crew realized he was out of control."

"How many on the ship are tainted?"

"The crew has been scanned. All are clean."

Tocol sat on the bed next to Alea and placed a hand on her shoulder. Her skin was cold when he first touched it, but warmed beneath his palm. She stirred slightly and her eyes fluttered open.

"How did the king get through the scanners, Xalin?" Tocol asked him as he watched Alea.

"Pft." The guard slashed his hand through the air. "The king has loyal followers, some see him as being above the law. In other instances, bribery works wonders."

Someone's head would roll for that, Tocol knew.

"He avoided the scanners on Angard," Xalin continued. "Because he never left the station."

Ivot's eyes drifted to Alea and he groaned at her scent of arousal. Tocol was equally affected if not more so since he had a genuine affection for his Commanders' mate. He wondered how he would fight this. "Open a com to Tertia and turn this ship around. We have to get her to her Sh'em immediately."

"We have already contacted them. The Stardancer is on its way, and the Commanders are on board. As for this vessel, I'm afraid it's incapacitated."

"How so?" Tocol asked.

"Not all of the crew was, shall I say, cooperative. There was laser fire aboard the ship and our controls have been significantly damaged. We're merely hovering in space."

Tocol blew out a disgusted breath and dug his fingers through his hair. "What's our position?"

Xalin relayed their coordinates and Tocol shook his head. It would take too long for the Stardancer to reach them. Again he looked at Alea. She was curled into a ball and not looking very well. "How far out are they?"

"Three dials at least," Xalin answered and his attention also went to Alea. "She'll need your help long before then."

The thought made Tocol ill. How could he? How could he not? "Can you open a comlink from this room?"

Xalin nodded and walked to a panel on one of the walls. He tapped a tile and a small door slid open revealing an imaging screen and then he turned and walked toward the door. Hesitating, Xalin looked over his shoulder. "I've posted four of my most trusted and sturdy guards down the hall to keep the weaker males away."

"Bring frozen taw, Xalin. A lot of it." Tocol paused,

another thought occurring to him. "Are there any females onboard who might service me while I help the She'mana Alea?"

"I'm afraid not, Chief." Xalin left the chamber, and when he returned a short time later with two buckets of frozen taw, Tocol was in a heavy discussion with the Sh'em ot Alea, his hand was riding up and down his exposed cock. Xalin placed the buckets on the floor and quietly left the room.

Tocol lifted glossy eyes to Tren's image on the com, and though the Commander couldn't see more than Tocol's upper body, Tren knew by the way the sentry's shoulder moved that Tocol was sexing himself while they spoke. He was relieved when Tocol's head dropped and his body went rigid. Tocol's climax would give him a bit of reprieve and keep him longer from Alea.

Rjant stood in front of the desk in the Stardancer's private consult room propping himself with his hands, his head hanging as he listened to the conversation between Tren and Tocol. It seemed like eons since he'd encountered the female whose blood was laced with megberry and he understood exactly how torturous such an experience could be. Tren was in his mind during that time, giving him the needed strength to resist.

But who would help Tocol now?

"How far gone is she, Tocol?" Tren closed his eyes and waited for an answer.

"Uch! She is curled up like a wounded fifon." Tocol responded on a heavy exhale, sexually satiated for the time being.

Tren opened his eyes to the sound of Rjant's fists slamming down on the desk top. He watched Tocol on the imaging screen as he moved to a bucket of iced taw, scooped a handful of it and dumped it down his trousers. Tocol turned back to the screen. "You won't get here in time, Commander."

Tossing his head back, Tren stared at the ceiling as if he might find answers there. His heart twisted. Something had to be done or he and Rjant would lose Alea. Megberry was a potent aphrodisiac that didn't just drive males erotically insane because of the pheromones it caused the female to release, but it also had devastating effects on the woman who ingested it as well. Not only did it cause extreme sexual arousal in the female, but it also pushed her body temperature to a life threateningly low level. Warming the female wasn't enough. The only way to bring her through the effects of the fruit was to help her to sexually climax repeatedly.

Tren gritted his teeth and Rjant's head snapped up as he caught the wave of his brethren's thoughts.

"Ka! Tren." Rjant's expression was strained as he turned toward him. He shook his head, vehemently denying what he knew had to be done. "What are you considering?"

Walking over to Rjant, Tren stood before him. His face clearly revealed his emotional pain. "We haven't a choice, Rjant. Alca is dying."

Rjant pursed his lips and nodded as Tren turned back to Tocol's waiting image. "Do whatever you have to do to save her, warrior," Tren told him.

The image on the screen faded and Tren turned away from it, picking up the crystal glass sitting on the desktop near Rjant. He looked at the liquid in it, swirled it and then threw it forcefully against the wall causing it to shatter.

Chapter Seventeen

The scent of female pheromones was driving Tocol insane. He was horny as all star blazers and Alea was dying.

He had to do this... he wanted to do this... he couldn't do this.

Tocol paced the room battling against his honor and his need, his friendship with Alea and her life, his self-control against the mind-blowing, cock-swelling effects of the megberry. He smashed his fist into the wall and bloodied his knuckles.

Tocol had never coveted another's She'mana.

Never.

But how could he help her without becoming unrestrained himself?

With absolute certainty he knew he couldn't fuck her, yet his burgeoning libido was urging him to do exactly that.

He had to fuck her. Tocol tucked his cock back in place and re-did the fasteners on his trousers. His shaft swelled painfully against his seam, threatening to burst through it.

Caress her. Maybe that will help.

Tocol moved over to the bed where Alea lay moaning and shivering. He leaned over her and reached out, touching her bluish, icy cheek with his palm. It flushed and warmed under his touch but paled again when he removed his hand. Alea stirred briefly and began to mumble incoherently.

Cold. I'm so cold. Alea felt like she was imprisoned in a block of ice. She couldn't move. *Why am I so cold?*

Was she dead?

"Help me," she muttered.

Her heart felt like black snow, her blood like frigid slush rushing through her veins. There was warmth on her cheek. And then it was gone, and she craved for its return.

Please, I need heat. Don't leave me.

Tocol knelt before the bed and paused, trembling, fighting his arousal, but as he shifted, his cock grew harder. Closing his eyes, he allowed thoughts of battle and torn flesh to purposely command his thoughts and when his erection started to shrivel, he lowered his mouth to Alea's, brushing his heated lips against her cold lips, before lifting his head to inspect the results.

Blue lips turned to purple and then to a healthy pink as blood rushed to them. But the color rapidly drained out of her. He rose and sat on the bed next to her and lowered his head once more.

Her mouth and tongue were like ice, but still his cock twitched and stiffened.

He suckled her lips gently, licked at them, then suckled again. Once more, pink flooded the blue. It was working. Alea's lips were blossoming, starting to warm.

Alea felt the hot breeze sweep across her face, a blanket of heat covering her mouth. "More. Please. I need more," she begged in a barely audible whisper.

Tocol rolled Alea to her side and she coiled into such a tight ball, wrapped herself so firmly in the linen, that he couldn't even peel it from her. The most he managed to do was uncover her back. On a heavy inhale, he removed his shirt and reclined behind her, molding his body around her and pressing his chest against her. A soft, pleading cry escaped Alea's lips, and Tocol stayed there for awhile before moving away to examine her. Her flesh was pink and warmed from the skin to skin contact, and he waited and watched as slowly she turned pale and cold again. Alea's body began to shiver and her teeth started chattering.

It wasn't enough.

Tocol pursed his lips, sitting up on the bed and leaning against the wall.

Divinities, forgive me, he beseeched as he lifted Alea and pulled her tightly contracted body between his legs, cradling her in his arms.

In that moment he loved her dearly--so he told himself.

So he had to believe.

He slipped a hand down the front of the linen, molding his hand around one of her breasts. It swelled with heat beneath his touch. Tocol's heart pounded. His cock throbbed, and he couldn't help but push against her bottom and grind his pelvis into her.

No, he told himself, fighting against the effects of the megberry. Alea was not his to take. He slammed his head backwards and felt the wall give way with the impact.

"Freakin' loving stars, that fucking hurt," Tocol grumbled. Well at least the pain caused his hard-on to go down. He continued to massage Alea's breast.

Alea stirred in his arms and her rigid body began relaxing. She moaned and turned her head to him, kissing his throat. Tocol sighed at the full, soft feel of her lips as they moved up along his chin, higher to his mouth. He tipped down his head and let the kiss happen.

Reaching around to her still tightly clenched legs, Tocol gathered the covering with both his hands and then started massaging her ankles, and then higher along her calves, and his hands slowly meandered upward, along her cold flesh. As expected, everywhere he touched, her skin became warm. Tocol groaned. It would be easier to resist if she stayed cold but as her body heated, her flesh became supple causing his shaft to become stiffer and longer. Her passionate responses urged him to touch her more.

Tocol bit down on his lip until it bled, growling at the pain it caused, swiping at it with the back of his hand. This time it was only a short reprieve before his cock began stirring once more, as Alea's scent saturated the room.

How in Hades' fires was he going to get them both through this?

Heat on my legs... heat on my back... warm air against my face and neck. "Don't leave me, Tocol." Alea's head fell against his shoulder.

"Yes, Alea. Take my heat." He turned his head away from her. She knew it was him, and she would be aware of what he would do to her. He knew Alea loved her Sh'em and he rued that she would hate him for this. But Tocol wouldn't let her die.

By the blasted gates of bloody, fucking hell, this is torture. Any other warrior would be ramming her pussy by now. But she was the She'mana of Rjant and Tren, his superiors, his Commanders.

Alea was his friend.

"More," Alea whispered. "Please, touch me."

Her legs fell apart.

Tocol sucked in his breath and held it. Her begging and carnal reactions didn't help avert the lust that continued to build inside of him. He needed release.

Reaching between her thighs, Tocol slid his hand upward until he found her clit.

It was icy hard.

He rolled it between his thumb and index finger, and felt it soften then swell with heated arousal. With his other hand he dipped two fingers into her vagina. Her moisture felt like frosty dew.

Incredible warmth spread through Alea's body. "Don't stop," she whimpered in a low cry.

"I won't, Alea," Tocol promised with a husky voice, his fingers moving more quickly now, manipulating her clitoris, while his other fingers plunged in and out of her vagina, faster and faster. Her body warmed within his embrace and she was cumming.

Every muscle in Tocol's body went into spasm. "Cum, Alea. Cum for me." And he meant it, wanted to see it. She was so beautiful in passion.

Alea turned her head toward his and parted her lips. He kissed her again, stroked his tongue against hers as she moaned her orgasm. Tocol held his breath as the muscles of her hollow gripped his fingers and wept its molten moisture into the palm of his hand. He ground his crotch into her backside, spilling semen into his pants, and then he sighed.

Relief once more, at least for a time.

Tocol gently lowered Alea down and backed off of the bed. He needed to replenish their fluids. At this rate, they would both be dehydrated soon. With an awkward stride he went to the sideboard, his balls swollen between his legs, his rod starting to rise again, making walking difficult. Tocol entered his choice into the pad and the holoplate shimmered to life. A large pitcher of taw and two mugs materialized.

"I'm thirsty, Tocol."

"I know you are, Alea." He spoke softly as he looked over his shoulder at her. Alea was sitting up on the bed and he could tell she was barely coherent. Already her skin was starting to pale again. Tocol poured the liquid into the mugs and turned toward her. But before he could reach her with the drink, Alea's body recoiled into a tight ball, the scent of her sexual arousal increased again, becoming overbearing.

Tocol ignored it with a mighty struggle and tipped up Alea's head, putting the rim of the mug to her lips. She turned her head away.

"Drink, Alea," he gently urged. Her lips parted and she took several sips. Tocol set her cup aside and drained his mug, cursing under his breath as he set it down next to Alea's. Her hips were already starting to gyrate even as her body trembled with cold. Tocol peeled the sheet from her body and separated her arms which were crossed over her chest. He groaned and turned his head aside at the sight of her lovely breasts. Turning back, he bent and suckled them.

"Yes." Alea's body heated and loosened. She arched up into his mouth. "More. I need more, Tocol."

Her cries were as much passion as need, beckoning him by calling his name, weakening his self-restraint. If her Sh'em didn't arrive soon he would lose himself completely.

"Tren, Rjant, where in the fucking evil, dark ditches are you?" he muttered, not knowing how much more of this he could take.

"Make love to me, Tocol," Alea rasped out, her eyes glazed. "I want to feel your cock deep inside me."

It was getting worse. She didn't know what she was saying. The megberry was now reaching its peak in her bloodstream, clouding her sensibilities, claiming her mind and body. Shifting lower on the bed, Tocol gently parted her legs and lowered his head.

Eons seemed to pass before the chamber door finally flew open. Rjant and Tren were met with the sight of Tocol sitting on his haunches between their She'mana's legs. He was stroking his rod with one hand while the thumb on the other hand rotated on Alea's pussy. Tocol threw back his head, the layers of his butter yellow hair flying off his face. He locked on their glares with heavily dazed eyes.

"I don't know whether to be grateful you have arrived or regretful." His voice was husky with his arousal as he rose up to his knees and took his hand away from Alea, his cock heavy and full, jutting from his trousers.

Fury seized Rjant and he lunged, pinning Tocol against the wall. "How many times did you take her?"

Tocol just stared at him and then blinked as the pain and lack of air from Rjant's hands squeezing his throat temporarily tamped his erection.

"How many?"

"None, but your arrival was timely." And Tocol was immensely thankful for it, or at least he convinced himself that he was.

"Then why is your cock free?" Rjant glared at him murderously.

"I needed to give myself release... again," Tocol barely choked out.

"I don't know whether to believe you or kill you." Rjant's hands tightened and Tocol started to gag. He didn't fight the Commander, his mind was too far gone and somewhere deep in his rational brain he felt he deserved it.

Tren had already pulled Alea in his arms, examining her, worry for her life overwhelming the anger he felt for what Tocol was forced to do. His eyes scanned the room and noted it was in chaos. There were holes in the walls and some of the furniture was splintered, but there wasn't one mark on Alea. Tren knew right then and there that Tocol waged a furious battle with himself and he was immensely grateful that his warrior had won.

"Release him, Rjant. Alea needs us."

Rjant's head turned and his grip on Tocol's neck

loosened. His heart wrenched when he saw his She'mana's pale, deathly blue skin. She was shivering and nearly unconscious. He then noted that the room was in shambles and turned back to Tocol.

The warrior was a mess.

His forehead was bleeding from bashing his head into the wall. His lips were swollen from biting them and his knuckles were raw from slamming them. The bones in his hand were unnaturally askew. He looked as though he'd been beaten up but Rjant realized his wounds were self-inflicted. Rjant lowered his hands and Tocol starting coughing as his lungs dragged in gulps of air.

"Latian?" Rjant called.

A uniformed, female sentry appeared in the doorway--a Krellian who had joined their ranks and one of the few female warriors who served with the Allegiance. Tren and Rjant were thankful she was on the Stardancer and equally indebted when she came to them to discreetly offer her services.

Latian approached the bed and took Tocol's uninjured hand. "Chief, take me as you need to."

Tocol didn't hesitate to consider what she meant. There was no misunderstanding. He sprang from the bed and was on her in an instant, stripping open her trousers and pulling them down to her knees. He spun her around and Latian braced herself against a chair nearby as Tocol grasped her hips and plunged his cock deep inside of her. In two strokes he ejaculated.

"I'm sorry," Tocol whispered in her ear, panting, riding out his climax.

"No regrets, warrior." Latian pulled free from Tocol's shaft when he was done and re-arranged her clothes. She took his hand again and started leading Tocol from the room, pausing to help him make himself decent. "There's a chamber for us on the Stardancer."

Her attention shifted to Tren. "I assume we're both on respite, Commander?"

Tren nodded and watched them leave the room, and then took the bedcovering and wrapped Alea in it. He rose with her and headed for the door.

"I've had the crew of both vessels moved far from the hatches and entry corridors to keep them from catching the scent. Calem is seeing that they stay put," Rjant assured Tren as his eyes spread over Alea, his concern for her apparent.

Tocol had managed to keep her alive, but it was far from over. The philter fragrance was intensifying, consuming them both, their cocks swelling to excruciating measures as they rushed with her from the king's star vessel to their own.

One full dawning and six dials they spent sexing their She'mana, one at a time to give the other time to replenish. They loved her with their mouths, their fingers, their cocks and she cried out their names, aware of their presence for fleeting moments, before slipping back into a stupor. Her body temperature rose with each climax, maintaining at healthy levels for longer periods each time until it finally stabilized and they knew she was safe.

Tren gazed at her as he held her, tears in his eyes. He couldn't remember when or if he had ever cried, but it was something he couldn't hold back now. Rjant was equally overcome, falling face down on the bed to hide his lamenting. They were both exhausted and relieved and near collapse when it was finally over, but Alea would live, and that's all that mattered.

"It feels like the flesh has been stripped from my cock." Rjant sat up on the bed leaning against the wall, watching Alea's chest rise and fall steadily as she slept. He was still nude, his knees bent and his feet planted on top of the mattress. His rod hung flaccidly between his thighs, reddened and raw from his sexual ministrations.

What do you think about when you watch me make love to Alea's body? he asked Tren mentally.

Tren shrugged. *Why do you ask?*

When I saw Tocol over Alea, I was enraged, Rjant told Tren. "I wanted to kill him."

I felt the same, Tren admitted.

Alea once asked me if I ever felt jealousy when I watch

you make love to her.

"Do you?" Tren asked aloud.

"I know no other way. It's natural that you're there."

Tren nodded his agreement. "The Tertian ways are unique, even in our own galaxy, I suppose."

"Our culture is the only one in the CalyTron galaxy that has two males marry with a single female." Rjant moved from the bed and sat down on the settee next to Tren. "Alea told me that on her Earth it's irregular and in some cultures, considered amoral and against their laws even."

Tren merely shrugged. *Before we joined with Alea, I had never sexed a female with another male present. It was never all that satisfying.*

It was the same for me, Tren, before we married with her. My prior affairs somehow felt incomplete. Rjant scratched his head and yawned, stretching his legs out in front of him. *I have overheard other She'manas speaking of how they've watched their Trigon males pleasure each other.*

I suppose it occurs in some Trigons, if the mutual desire is between them. According to our sacred dictates the bed is undefiled in marriage, all forms of love-making are just.

Rjant watched as Alea began to stir in Tren's arms. He reached out and took her hand, stroking it gently. *I'm focused on her needs, though I'm aware of yours as you are mine. And I'll admit your arousal enhances my own.*

Our bodies touch much during sexing. Tren pondered that for a moment and then said, *but my focus is also on Alea's pleasure.*

Tren drew his brows together as his eyes flicked to the flesh between Rjant's legs. *Do you think to have me pleasure you, Rjant?*

Rjant sat upright, his eyes going wide. "No!" he bellowed vehemently. He hadn't even been thinking in that direction.

Tren blew a relieved gust of air. "I thought for a moment our compatibility was in question."

Alea shifted in Tren's arms and she mumbled before drifting back into a slumber. Rjant bent and picked up his bunched up trousers that lay in a heap on the floor and slid them on, grimacing as the material scraped his sore groin.

He looked at their sleeping wife and lifted several strands of her hair, allowing them to fall through his fingers. "If anything were to ever happen to her I would be devastated." He lifted his eyes to Tren. "But my heart would suffer much if anything happened to you as well, my brethren."

"Are you trying to say you love me too, Rjant?" Tren couldn't hide his smirk, though he felt the same.

"There's no masculine way to say such a thing, brethren." Rjant snorted and slashed his hand upward through the air. "I would be quipped by our warriors if I ever spoke those words."

"Then let's not admit it together," Tren answered his expression going somber with his admission.

"Tren?"

Alea was speaking.

"Welcome back, love." Tren gazed down at Alea and then he lowered his mouth to kiss her. Rjant reached for her and Tren handed her into his brethren's arms.

"Where are we?" Alea asked, snuggling into Rjant's embrace.

"On the Stardancer," he answered.

There was no choice but to stay on their vessel when it docked at Angard. Alea needed their immediate attention and in addition to that they couldn't carry her through the weigh station to the sight of inquiring eyes and rambunctious libidos. A portable scanner was not an option either as it too would've been noticed by the visitors on the station. Tren and Rjant were trying to keep the whole disturbing incident as quiet as possible. Much to their dismay, Calem informed them that word had already leaked out, and the Allegiance was in an uproar over King Dred's actions. They would see to it that the king and all involved were justly punished.

"I had the weirdest dream," Alea spoke through a yawn and then she went still. "Oh."

Tren and Rjant watched as clarity swept over her and her expression grew pained. "Don't think on it, She'mana." Rjant tried to pull her closer to him, but she pushed away.

"Oh my God." Alea's hand went to her mouth as hazy memories seeped and then flooded through her brain. She crawled from Rjant's lap and sat between him and Tren, drawing up her knees and covering her face with her hands. "What have I done?"

Tocol had touched her and she wanted him to. He ate at her pussy and she came in his mouth. He fingered her, sucked her breasts, played with her clit and she liked it!

"Oh no, oh no, oh no," Alea cried.

She stroked Tocol's cock.

She begged Tocol to fuck her and he refused.

Alea groaned and shame snatched her. "I'm a whore."

Tren and Rjant looked at each other, bewildered.

"Why would you say such a thing, Alea?" Tren touched her shoulder and she shrank away from him.

"Don't touch me!" She looked at him and then snapped her head to look at Rjant. "How could he... how could I... how could you...?"

Alea was so beside herself she couldn't speak. And the king. Oh God, she'd wanted him too!

"It was the megberry, Alea," Tren tried to explain, his heart wrenching at their wife's horror-filled expression.

"No, you don't understand." Alea pulled at her hair and dropped her forehead to her knees, shaking her head from side to side. She had become like her mother.

"I should've fought it. And Tocol..." Her head snapped up, humiliation turning to anger. "How dare he!"

Rjant tried to reach for her but Alea held up her hands, her body stiffening, and he drew back away from her as he looked to Tren for help.

It was clear by Tren's befuddled expression that he was just as clueless as to what they could say to make Alea feel better about this. "Tocol isn't at fault, Alea. We told him to do what he had to in order to save your life."

Alea stared off into the distance and her breathing rate increased.

"Oh my God." She rose from the settee, grabbing the linen as she did and wrapped it tightly around her body.

"You gave him permission?" Alea barely whispered the

words, her voice coming out in a tremble. She turned to face her husbands, her eyes shifting back and forth from one husband to the other as she stared at them in shock and disbelief.

Did they watch and then take her afterwards?

She closed her eyes and turned her head away grimacing. *No.* She knew that wasn't the way it happened.

Everyone on both star vessels had to know about this, how could they not? They must've heard her climatic screams.

She remembered screaming.

"Alea," Tren pleaded. "You would've died from the megberry without Tocol's help."

"He has been nothing but honorable," Rjant added.

"Oh God! I can't hear this!" Alea felt disgusted and dirty. She had to run away.

"If you would just speak to him, Alea. He's as upset about this as you...."

"No!" Alea cut him off. "I never want to see him again."

She sank to the floor and started to sob. Rjant reached her first and this time she allowed him to hug her, but there was nothing he could do to soothe her.

"Take me home now," she told them.

Tren knelt down in front of her and she fell into his arms, tears rolling down her cheeks in sorrowful streams and Alea wept quietly.

"Of course, love," Tren answered. "We all need to rest a bit. Our chambers at the compound will be much more comfortable."

Alea lifted her face to him and shook her head. "Not to Tertia."

She paused, her expression growing somber and then stern. "Earth. Take me home, now. I don't want to be here anymore."

Even as she said it, she knew she didn't mean it, but heaven help her, Alea would never have sex again. She would go back to her own planet where she didn't belong and live out the rest of her life in quiet, celibate silence.

Chapter Eighteen

Alea leaned against the door frame leading out to their private garden, drinking warmed *chim*, a brew similar to tea, and watching the various miniscule creatures scurrying about. On the ground, a triple of purple *jugis*, about the size of her finger hopped quickly across the moss. Above her head she heard the chirping of *crobans* coming from the branches of the *parberry* tree. A small horde of *riklies* was digging in the pocket of a nearby rock searching for minute vermin to eat.

Small, insignificant little pests, Alea thought dryly.

What was it about bugs that made one feel so powerful and why was it so gratifying to call someone that?

King Dred was a bug.

Alea mentally squashed the slime with her foot.

For the last three weeks the garden served as a sanctuary for Alea. She spent hours each day there, absorbed in her thoughts, refusing to leave the dwelling. Well, she did venture out once last week, but it turned out to be a disaster. Syrat showed up on her doorstep and convinced her it would do her some good to get out. Almost simultaneously, Karen contacted her by comm from Terta Minor, suggesting the very same thing. Alea accused them of a conspiracy but relented. She made it as far as the compound's community dining hall, when she and Syrat overheard two of the residents snickering and joking about Alea's illicit liaison with the Commanders' chief warrior. Mortified, Alea turned on her heels and scampered back to her dwelling.

"They're just being ignorant," Syrat attempted to soothe Alea. "Everyone knows how potent megberry is. Anyone with a piece of brain in their skull would know you had no choice."

"Does it matter?" Alea snorted, though her mood was far less than humorous. "Through most of adolescence and all of my adult years, I fought to keep my life on a certain level of decency, and I was successful at it too. I let down my guard, Syrat. Now I'm the laughing stock of an entire galaxy and my husbands look like fools. I've made a mockery of my marriage and all I've struggled to control."

Alea paused, her expression impassive. "I am brazen and wanton."

Then she told Syrat to leave her alone, and numbly watched her friend's caring façade turn sullen as she left the room, shaking her head. Alea should've felt bad for being so harsh, but she didn't. Nor was she remorseful for rudely ignoring her mothers-in-law who appeared after that. She didn't want to hear the comforting words of two virtuous women who had no idea what it was like to be brazen and wanton. And then to make matters worse, all four of her fathers-in-law showed up, telling her what a wonderful She'mana she was and how happy she made their sons, and they numbered all of her talents....

Talents? Alea just rolled her eyes at that. Apparently her only talents were getting drunk and falling off chairs and of course being brazen and wanton. Ileg did mildly catch her interest when he mentioned that he'd been exposed to a poisoned female while in battle and she asked him what happened. He casually waved his hand in the air and said. "Ka! I resisted the woman of course."

His response earned a slap upside his head and a comment similar to *shit for brains* from Tonor for being stupid.

Sure, Alea thought. *Everyone else seemed able to resist the effects of megberry.*

Everyone except her, because she was--Alea didn't need to say it again. She knew exactly what she was.

As for Rjant and Tren, they treated her like fragile crystal, but Alea was far from ready to break. In fact, she was building an iron wall around her heart, flatly determined to never let anyone near it again.

Alea sighed. She missed her morning runs, but running was too risky and it was also cruel since it excited her Sh'em too much. It was a small sacrifice to make if it meant keeping Rjant and Tren at bay. She should return to the pool. Teaching the children would at least be an innocuous task. But Alea didn't feel like it. She didn't feel like doing anything.

Except eating. In fact Alea felt like she was eating the compound out of house and home. It seemed to baffle Tren and Rjant until she told them that on Earth, some people refuse food when they're depressed. Others devour it. Apparently she was the devouring sort. That explanation seemed to satisfy them.

Melancholy.

That's what the Pontiff Jer called it. A common result of the megberry ingestion, and he said that it would pass. He came to council her shortly after her ordeal on the King's ship, and she listened to some of his advice politely, blocked out other things he had to say, knowing he was only trying to help, but there were just some things he was telling her that she couldn't listen to--didn't want to deal with at that moment.

Alea knew the truth. She couldn't overcome the genetics her mother passed to her and though she understood that one might succumb to the effects of the herbal aphrodisiac, a woman who had any morals surely would've fought against it.

Alea grimaced. She didn't fight it, and that frightened her. How could she ever trust her wayward libido again? It was one of the real reasons she refused to see Tocol. What if he turned her on just by looking at her? The other reason was that she was still angry with him for touching her, and embarrassed, not to mention the resentment she harbored that her husbands had given him permission to go ahead and do it. Tocol should've resisted. He was a trained warrior after all, and he should've waited for her Sh'em to arrive.

Alea didn't think she could ever forgive them or herself for being so weak in character.

And there was another problem as well. Her desire for Tren and Rjant was dulled. Her body seemed to be rejecting the affections of her Sh'em, when before they only had to be nearby for Alea to be turned on. Oh, she still loved them with every ounce of her being, but what if they weren't enough for her anymore now that she'd gotten a taste of variety? What if she did let them have sex with her and she couldn't cum or worse, what if they bored her? For many days afterward, Alea thought about this and even found the courage to mention it to the Pontiff. He told her that sexual impotence was another side effect of the fruit once it left the bloodstream, but she didn't believe him, and it was an area that Alea was firmly unwilling to explore. She would not hurt her husbands. It was much better they thought that she'd been too traumatized by the incident to respond to them.

Alea inhaled a long breath and took twice as long to exhale it. She took another sip of her tea and watched as an unusual looking insect fluttered around a flower that grew near the garden entrance. She held out her arm and it floated to rest on her open palm. It resembled a large butterfly. Its body was thick and fuzzy like a bright red pipe cleaner, and it had four wings, two to either side of its body, and spanning nearly six inches each. They were beautiful, translucent except for the shimmering yellow veins that ran through them. If Alea let her imagination blossom, she could almost imagine that it was some kind of faerie come to greet her.

Alea swallowed a sob. She could use a little magic right now.

"She's an exotic creation. Is she not, Alea?" a voice spoke from behind her. It was Tren. His hands came up to her shoulders and he leaned in to get a better look at the arthropod that sat contently on Alea's hand.

"Rarely seen by the mortal eye," he added.

"I've never seen one," Rjant said as he came to stand beside them. "It's written in the ancient scripture that if one ever encounters the pixie it is a sign that the divinities find favor with that individual's house."

Alea pursed her lips in a near smile at the name, but it quickly disappeared. It was the closest she'd come to smiling since all of this happened.

"You aren't just trying to make me feel better, are you?" She watched as the pixie gently folded and opened its wings repeatedly.

Tren answered. "Of course we're trying to make you feel better, Alea. But the story of the pixie is still the truth."

"And she allows you to hold her," Rjant added. "It's a blessing that is two-fold. To my understanding they are skittish little creatures and avoid mortal contact."

A smile did crease Alea's lips this time, but it was small and bittersweet. She couldn't let herself believe in fairy tales or dreams come true.

Not anymore.

And she had never been much of a spiritual person either. Alea always favored the rational side of reality though her studies in philosophy often had her questioning life's greater truths.

And one of those truths was that running away from problems was never the answer to solving them. It was a pattern in her life that she wanted to break. Because of that, and much to her Sh'ems' relief, Alea agreed to stay with them, although she had the feeling Rjant and Tren wouldn't have taken her back to Earth regardless. Besides she really didn't want to leave Tertia. She didn't want to leave her Sh'em. Alea felt like she belonged in this world. And aside from that, there was another reason for her remaining, a reason she wasn't quite ready to reveal yet.

"Her mates come for her," Tren whispered softly, drawing Alea away from her thoughts. Her attention drifted back to the pixie in her hand. Two plum colored creatures, similar in form but half the female's size descended and circled around her before making contact, one to the front of the pixie and the other to her back. Their wings fluttered like the petals of a blooming flower caught by an easy breeze, and the triple lifted from Alea's palm and floated away, blending into the garden foliage.

Rjant took Alea's hand and ran his thumb over the area where the pixie had just sat. He lifted her palm to his mouth, pressing his lips against it. His eyes closed briefly and then he met her gaze. "Her mates would be nothing without her, Alea."

Oh. Alea's heart wrenched. Their patience with her was unbending. Where they should be angry with her by now for her detachment, her Sh'em were nothing but loving and kind. Alea lifted her head, turning to where the pixie triple vanished and she wondered about the legend. Maybe she was truly blessed.

"She'mana, there's something we have to show you."

Alea shifted her eyes toward Tren, furling her brow at his grim expression. Still holding her hand, Rjant led Alea back inside, urging her to sit on the sofa in their den. Tren pulled a compu-sheet from his pocket and started unfolding it. Alea eyed him warily as he set it at an angle on the foot table in front of them.

"Why do I have a feeling I'm not going to like this?" Alea commented, observing as Tren sat down in the empty space next to her and keyed a code into the device. He didn't respond to her question.

With Rjant on her other side, Alea watched as a video appeared on the screen. It showed a laboratory of some sort and there was gurney in the middle of the room. A woman was curled up on it and she was being attended to by the healthtcks in the room. She was shivering uncontrollably yet she kept kicking at the blankets her aides tried to cover her with.

"What is this?" Alea looked from Rjant to Tren, feeling a bit confused.

"She's passing on, Alea," Rjant answered, his expression was strained. "From the effects of megberry."

The woman released an agonizing moan and Alea shuddered remembering her own anguished cries while she was under the influence of the aphrodisiac.

Alea sucked in her breath.

"I don't want to see this," she gasped out and started to stand. Tren and Rjant each grabbed one of her arms and forced her back down to the sofa.

Are you sure about doing this? Rjant threw his thoughts toward Tren.

What other choice do we have, Rjant? We can't let her go on thinking she is somehow at fault.

"You need to see this, Alea, so that you'll fully understand," Tren firmly told her, his expression sober.

"I won't watch someone have sex with her!" Alea spat venomously, standing abruptly, ready to walk out of the room. "I don't need to be reminded that I'm…."

"We know, we know, She'mana!" Tren bellowed. "Brazen and wanton. Now sit down!"

Alea's body jerked, startled by his tone of voice.

Well, she thought bitterly. *So much for patience.*

That was real smooth, brethren, Rjant admonished Tren for his reaction. He reached toward the compu-sheet and put it on pause.

Tren gritted his teeth. He didn't mean to yell, but he was frustrated. They hadn't made love to their wife for three sept-dawnings. Alea wouldn't even allow them to kiss her lips, though he was relieved she at least let them touch her on this dawning, even if it wasn't in the way they desired. What made it even worse was that she wouldn't allow them to speak to her about it. If he or Rjant even broached the subject Alea shut down. The Pontiff Jer advised them to give her time and they tried to do that, but nothing seemed to be changing and now time was of the essence. They had yet to tell Alea that they were summoned to battle and were leaving soon. They needed to resolve this issue with her before they were gone, wanting no regrets to surface if either or both of them did not return alive.

Tren gentled his words when he next spoke. "Alea, that is not what happens here. Trust us, please."

Alea studied the tense expression on Tren's face and then turned to Rjant. Though he sat quietly, his expression told her that he was as equally stressed as Tren, and she suddenly felt guilty about everything she was putting them through. Alea did trust them, and she knew they would never purposely hurt her. Nevertheless, she had to wonder what good watching this video would do. She was already depressed enough as it was, and seeing someone else go through what she had couldn't possibly ease her distress about it.

Did they think that misery wanted company?

Alea bit her lip, her anxiety apparent. "Why? How can this help me?"

"The image was recorded by ISDS several phases back, when megberry was first being used," Tren answered.

And Rjant added, "We knew very little about it then, Alea, other than the effect it had on the male and female libidos."

She stared at them, her eyes blinking rapidly, hating that she was letting herself drift from them, that she'd been so numb and far removed. And damn, if they didn't look like two, sad, little boys who couldn't find their puppy. Alea sighed forlornly, grieving for innocence lost. If only she could turn back time to days not too long ago, when she made love to her husbands in ignorant bliss.

"Alright." Alea finally relented. If she didn't like what she was seeing she could just disconnect it. "I'll watch, but it goes off when I decide."

Tren and Rjant both nodded and then Rjant leaned forward and set the image on the screen in motion.

Slowly, Alea sat back down and forced herself to view the recording. The first thing she noticed was that there were only females in the room.

"Why only women?" she asked.

"The males were kept away, for their and for her sake," Rjant answered and then continued. "And only female healthteks, those with no desire for their own gender, were assigned to attend to her."

The woman on the gurney screamed and her body went stiff. Her skin turned a sickly shade of purple and then blue, before becoming nearly white, as all of her blood seemed to drain from her. Alea brought her hands to her mouth, watched in shock as the attendants attempted to warm the woman with the blankets.

I looked like that, she thought.

From the sweat dripping on the healthteks' brows and the dampness apparent in their hair and skin, Alea assumed that the temperature in the room had to be hellishly high. One tek forced the woman to drink a liquid, while others attempted to massage her stiffened limbs, and yet, nothing they did seemed to be helping. Alea shivered, remembering the pain of being frigidly cold, of being tormented by the bleakness consuming her.

From the imaging screen she heard the sound of a slowing heartbeat coming from an unseen monitor, and it was apparent the woman was dying.

"Help me," the woman cried.

"Oh God." Alea trembled at hearing the woman echo the very words she had spoken to Tocol. She closed her eyes, but they snapped open again. It was a hard thing to witness, yet Alea couldn't drag her eyes away from the screen. A deep ache filled her and she watched in horror as the poisoned woman's life began to slip away. Alea remembered the terror of death coming to call.

"Why doesn't somebody help her?" Alea sucked in a sob as the rhythmic heart sounds slowed even further until there were seconds between every beat. Blood began streaming from the woman's nose.

"There's no antidote, Alea." Tren looked at her sadly.

Tears welled in Alea's eyes, as the simple nature of the megberry and what it had done to her came surfacing to the light. She turned to Rjant. "Surely there must be someone willing to do for her what Tocol...."

The thought froze in her head.

Tocol had saved her life.

"Turn it off." Alea's shoulders slumped and Tren wrapped his arms around her pulling her close. Rjant immediately shut down the compu-screen and slipped his hands around her waist, resting his cheek on the back of her head.

"At that time no one knew how else to help her," Rjant said. He glanced at Tren hoping that doing this hadn't been a terrible mistake.

Reality slammed Alea harder than a fist to her gut. If Tocol hadn't been there, she would've died. Either that or the warriors on King Dred's vessel would have....

Alea willed the alternative from her brain. That much she would not let herself think about. It's what Tren and Rjant had been trying to tell her, what the Pontiff and Syrat and her in-laws attempted to explain. Yet Alea refused to listen. She'd blocked out what she thought was just their contrived excuses, convincing herself that she was to blame.

It wasn't her fault. It was nobody's fault. Well, it was the King's fault, but he would suffer for that in the long run as Brits Scorn devoured his mind and body.

And Tocol....

Alea frowned. She remembered how battered and bruised he was, inflicting wounds on himself to keep his arousal cowed. He'd done that for her. Alea squeezed her eyelids shut, filled with shame of a different sort. She'd been so selfish, concerned only for her own feelings, disregarding the impact this had on others. People she cared about-- people she loved.

Slowly Alea lifted her head. "I need to talk to Tocol."

Tren nodded. "I'll have him come this eve...."

"No." Alea cut him off. "I want to talk to him now, and alone."

Tren and Rjant said nothing for several moments. Alea had become so familiar with her husbands' behaviors over the last few months she knew they weren't communicating with each other. Each was absorbed in his own silent thoughts. Finally, Tren rose from the chair and walked over to the commlink on the wall. He activated it and a male voice transmitted through.

"Yes, sir?"

"Locate Tocol and have him meet me in the compound garden in half a dial," Tren instructed.

"Yes sir." And then the commlink went silent.

Tren turned to Alea. "Before you say anything, She'mana, I should tell you that if Tocol thinks he is meeting with you, he may not show."

Alea inclined her head to one side, drawing her brows together. "Why?

"Let's just say that he is as uncomfortable with all of this as you are."

Rjant pulled her closer. "He's requested a transfer to another military sect, one that is located on the far perimeter."

"But this is his home." Alea pulled back slightly so she could look at Rjant and shifted to look at Tren, her expression growing troubled.

"Yes it is," Tren answered. He was disturbed by it as well. Not only was Tocol his third Commander in line, and a damn good one at that, Tren and Rjant were also immensely grateful that Tocol had saved Alea's life. He should be rewarded for his actions. Instead he was being forced from Tertia as though he were being punished for an injustice he did not commit.

He doesn't deserve this, Alea thought. Tocol was her friend, and Alea shirked that friendship because of her own selfish ideals. Alea frowned. She'd assumed that because he was a man, what happened between them would be a notch in his belt. It wasn't, and Alea understood that now. She stood abruptly and then smiled gently, lovingly at her husbands, studying their features for the first time in days and days. Tren's eyes sparkled turquoise green, enhanced by the gold surrounding them. His beautiful, silky black hair framed his masculine face, which was slightly shadowed with morning whiskers. Her eyes grazed his body, large and strong and firm.

Her clit twitched.

Alea's gaze descended on Rjant where he sat on the sofa, his riveting, gold encircled, aqua eyes meeting hers, his beautiful wavy, blonde hair falling over his muscular, bare chest. Alea's eyes moved lower to his narrow hips and the outline of his shaft beneath the trousers he wore.

A rising heat simmered between her legs.

Alea was becoming aroused. The Pontiff had warned Alea that her libido would likely return with a vengeance, and at the moment she was becoming so horny that Alea thought she might explode. At first she was astounded by the carnal sensations flooding her and she just stood there as every nerve in her body came to life and began screaming to be satiated. She looked from Rjant to Tren, her thoughts narrowing down and focusing on just one thing.

"I need sex." Alea stated it simply though her pussy was seething with a wonderful craving, her soppy juices flowing into her panties and begging out her need.

Rjant and Tren stared at her in stunned silence, neither sure they correctly heard her words.

"Well?" Alea said, her body jerking as her arousal soared to near volatile proportions.

"Now?" Rjant asked. Already his scent was filling the room, but he held back, not wanting to rush his She'mana.

Alea caught the pheromone fragrance in her nose, and Tren's aroma quickly rose up to meet and mingle with it.

Tren looked at her questioningly. His cock shifting and bursting to life between his legs, yet just as Rjant, he didn't want to push Alea too soon. "But Tocol?"

Alea crooked a brow at him. "Haven't you ever heard of a quickie?"

If they didn't start humping her soon she was going to blow apart

Neither of her Sh'em had to be asked twice. They were on her in a flash and clothes were flying, bodies were grinding, mouths were tasting, voices were moaning and climaxes were bursting through. A quarter dial later, the Trigon of Alea lay in an entangled heap on the floor, arms and legs entwined, hearts beating furiously with their exertions, all three of them panting for air.

Alea slid from between Rjant and Tren gathering her clothes and donning them. She nearly laughed at their stupefied but satisfied expressions as they both lay limp on the floor. Alea allowed her eyes to scrutinize their cocks, glistening from her cum and still semi-hard.

She smiled broadly at them. "I feel so much better!"

Her Sh'em both expelled relieved breaths in unison, and Alea bent down and gave each of them a kiss on the lips.

"I'll be back soon," she told them, closing her eyes briefly, an easy smile curving her lips. Alea stood and headed for the door. She was starting to feel whole again.

Chapter Nineteen

The outside corridor was quiet, and Alea was glad because she didn't feel like dealing with any of the compound's residents at the moment. Most of them had been kind, sending words of sympathy and well wishes to her quarters. One of the cooks even attempted to make a pizza for her and Alea did get a mild chuckle from her attempt. The entire concoction was various shades of blue. It didn't taste half bad though. This morning, however, Alea was focused on a different agenda, getting her amity with Tocol back in order.

The compound garden unfortunately was not as empty as Alea would have wished. Calem and Merse were there, off in one corner, sitting at a small table, eating their morning meals and conversing. Calem saw her first and nodded his head in greeting. Merse twisted around to see who Calem was looking at and then waved a hello to Alea. Their acknowledgement of her was casual--no mocking glares or sniggering, and Alea was relieved. She waved back. Merse turned back to Calem and they resumed their conversation.

Reasa however, was a different story and Alea groaned when she caught a glimpse of the woman heading in her direction, knowing she would be less than tactful about the fact that Alea was out in public.

"Alea!" Reasa yelled loudly, drawing the attention of other visitors in the garden.

Oh just great, Alea grimaced at Reasa and the young, Tertani widow that followed close behind her. Her name was Cormsei and she was a known busy body.

"Are you feeling better?" Reasa asked, coming to a stop in front of Alea. She took one of Alea's hands. "We were all so worried that the megberry was still affecting you!"

"Is it still affecting you, dear?" Cormsei asked, and Alea could swear that a glimmer of eagerness shone in her eyes as she waited for Alea to answer.

Alea winced. *Could they possibly talk any louder?*

"I'm fine really," she stated dryly.

Though Alea hadn't grown as close to Reasa as she had to Syrat, Reasa was still a decent friend to her and Alea knew that Reasa was genuinely concerned. Cormsei's intentions were another matter. She was likely looking for gossip to spread around the compound. On more than one occasion Cormsei had tried to engage Alea in her tittle-tattle or Alea had overheard the woman relaying and often embellishing on stories that were nobody's business. It irritated Alea that Cormsei was blatantly trying to dig her way into Alea's private affairs.

Private affairs... poor choice of words, Alea thought.

"Well I heard..." Cormsei began her blathering and Alea's hearing instinctively started to muffle. She looked beyond the two women, not hearing a word of what Cormsei was saying, and saw Tocol entering the garden. Their eyes met, Tocol blinked impassively at her a couple of times and then turned to leave.

"Tocol!" Alea called to him and started forward. *So much for discretion.* "Wait!"

He stopped abruptly, tossed a glance over his shoulder at her and Alea waved him over. He hesitated but then began heading toward her, his expression becoming taut with apprehension.

Alea shot a stern glare toward Reasa and her cohort, willing them to go away. They stared at Tocol and then Alea, and she could pinpoint exactly when Reasa's understanding of Alea's unspoken meaning dawned.

"We'll talk later," Reasa said and started to walk away. Cormsei stayed right where she stood as though she were glued to the spot.

You've got to be kidding me. Alea crooked a brow at her. Did the nosy woman really have the audacity to think she could hang out while Alea and Tocol talked?

"Let's go, Cormsei." Reasa yanked on her arm.

"But…" Cormsei started to say, nearly tripping over her own feet as Reasa started to drag her away.

"Not now, Cormsei," Reasa scolded.

"I wouldn't mind spending a day romping with that one," Cormsei commented, passing Tocol as he approached, her eyes roaming up and down his body, and her neck nearly twisting around backwards as Reasa continued to pull her along. They made themselves scarce, but Alea was sure they wouldn't be too far, waiting to pounce on her at first chance. At this point, she didn't care anymore. It was more important that Alea make things right with Tocol.

Tocol shook his head in apparent irritation at Cormsei's comment as he came to a stop in front of Alea.

"Did you need me for something, Alea?" He grimaced at his own words and tipped his head downward, glad the two women were far enough away by now not to have overheard him. "I didn't mean to imply,…"

"No, don't," Alea said and took his hand. "Come with me."

He let her lead him to an alcove secluded by brush, and Alea indicated for Tocol to sit on the bench there. With obvious uncertainty written on his face, he sat down, and Alea angled herself on the bench beside him.

For several moments she didn't say anything, wondering how she should begin.

"So, how have you been?" she asked tentatively.

There, that was a nice easy start.

"Fine, and you?"

"Okay, I guess."

An awkward silence filled the air between them. Tocol's eyes darted to and fro, looking everywhere except at Alea. Her eyes moved over his face, studying his features. He looked thinner--tired. There were fading purple-yellow bruises on his forehead along with a purple scabbed-over cut over one eyebrow. She looked down. His left hand was splinted, the fingers protruding from it a darker gray than normal and swollen. Alea's heart twisted at what Tocol had done to keep himself from her. She remembered it well, although at the time she had difficulty making sense out of it.

"How's Tehali?" Alea asked, her attention returning to his face. She was referring to the female who was with Tocol at her wedding celebration. Over the past few months his relationship with the woman had blossomed, and they had become quite close. Alea was quite sure they would eventually marry.

Tocol shrugged, his eyes glancing at her briefly and then shifting elsewhere. His tension seemed to thicken and Alea was suddenly inundated with the urge to run away.

She would not run. Not this time. Alea scratched the back of her head, her lips thinning as she pondered what next to say. By his expression all was not right with Tehali.

"What happened?" she asked him. "Is Tehali okay?"

Finally, Tocol met her gaze. "You shouldn't be bothered with my personal problems, Alea."

"Yes, I should, Tocol," Alea said, her voice holding an adamant tone. "We're friends."

He shot her a sardonic look. "Are we?"

Alea didn't miss the bitterness in his tone, and she couldn't be quite sure as to why he might be feeling that way, though she could surmise that it probably had something to do with Alea's determination to avoid him. Tocol had made several attempts to visit her over the past couple of weeks but she insisted he be turned away.

"I care about you, Tocol. Please talk to me."

Tocol blew out of gust of air and dragged the fingers of his uninjured hand through his hair. "That is something I'm not convinced of at the moment, Alea." His expression went vacant.

"If you really must know," he stated blankly. "Tehali couldn't deal with it. The rumors, the gossip, the fact that I had touched you. She thought it would be for the best if we parted."

Alea's shoulders slumped. "That really sucks, Tocol."

Her hand came up to rest on his forearm. Tocol stiffened, and he moved his arm away. "I'm so sorry," Alea told him, apologetically. She felt terrible and understood if he felt she was to blame.

"There's nothing for you to be sorry for, Alea." Again Tocol looked away but his body visibly loosened.

"I would do it again if I had to, and I was honest with Tehali about that," he murmured.

And then he did something very adorable. His smooth, gray, skin flushed a deeper gray and his head dropped to a bashful pose. He was blushing and Alea couldn't help but laugh. Tocol's head snapped up in confusion. "What is so amusing, Alea?"

"I would think you'd be bragging about the fortunate position you found yourself in." She tried to hold her smile, but her mouth pulled back to a frown. "You know, another notch in your belt."

Although her comment was an attempt at making light of the situation, it was very ill-timed. Abruptly, Tocol grabbed her at the shoulders and jerked her forward.

"I would never touch you inappropriately!" he barked. "It was torture, Alea!"

"Oh..." Alea's face fell, her embarrassment apparent, and she could feel heat rushing to her cheeks. "I didn't realize you found me so repulsive."

This conversation wasn't going very well at all. Not that Alea wanted Tocol to be attracted to her but it stomped her ego to think he might find her unpleasant.

Tocol loosened his grip on her. "That came out all wrong."

He rubbed his brow and then stared at her for a moment before speaking again. "This is awkward, Alea. I'm not sure of what to say."

"Try," she told him, taking his healthy hand between hers. This time he didn't pull back from her.

Tocol sucked in a hearty breath and then pressed his lips together before expelling the air in his lungs slowly. He stared where Alea held his hand and then pulled his hand away. His expression sobered. "The sentries here, they make a mockery of it. Some have been rude enough to ask me if the megberry made you wild and if I enjoyed it.

Some snickered behind my back wondering how many times you came."

He rolled his eyes in disgust. "Some of the females here who were once in my acquaintance now look upon me with contempt."

Pausing again, Tocol drew in another breath, his nostrils flaring as air passed through them. "Only those who have experienced an onslaught of megberry offered me a respected regard."

Alea pressed her lips tightly together and wrinkled her brow, not knowing what to say. He looked so angry--so offended.

What he said next made her feel even more terrible than she was already feeling. "I couldn't hide my face as you did, Alea. I had duties to attend to."

The sting of his words cut through her deeply, and a guilty lump formed in Alea's throat at his sour tone.

Run... no.

She forced herself to stay put, but averted her gaze from his as he continued speaking, feeling his eyes boring into her.

"I am Krellian, already a strike against me. My kind is not accepted with easy trust as Brits Scorn was first conjured amongst my people." Tocol snorted cynically. "I've put in for transfer and I will, as you wish, go away."

Alea opened her mouth to say something but decided against it, snapping it shut. She swallowed hard as she lifted her head to meet his eyes. The resentfulness Alea read on his face was more than understandable. Her Sh'em told her none of this--about the hearsay, or how Tocol was being taunted by his fellow sentries. She wondered briefly why Rjant and Tren kept this from her, but realized immediately that in her distraught state of mind it wouldn't have made a difference. In fact, if she'd known about all of the rumors spreading about, chances were, Alea would have withdrawn deeper into herself.

"Well, I have nothing else to say," Tocol said and started to stand. "And neither do you obviously."

Alea shook her head from side to side, she couldn't let him leave with so much unsettled. She had to make this right between them, so she grabbed his hand, trying to keep him from departing. Unfortunately it was his injured one and he yelped with the pain, further entrenching Alea's mind with what he'd gone through at her expense.

"Oh God, I'm sorry." Alea released his hand at once. "Please sit back down."

Tocol's expression softened at the distressed look on her face, his fondness for her overriding his disdain. For a few tense seconds he didn't move, but then he slowly lowered down to sit on the bench. His eyes searched hers as he waited for her to speak.

"So tell me, why didn't you bother to mess up this hand too?" Alea lightly touched his other hand and then managed a slight smile.

"I needed a healthy arm in case I had to fight my way out with you."

Alea finally decided that her attempts to find his sense of humor were futile, and the more she thought about it, the greater was her realization that King Dred had put them both in a dire situation.

Alea's demeanor became serious and her brow furled. "You saved my life. Why would anyone consider it was anything but what it was?"

"Your reaction told all that you thought otherwise, Alea. And then you refused to see me. Some even questioned that you weren't given megberry at all and that you were hiding because you were ashamed."

Choking back a sob and closing her eyes, Alea considered her words carefully, knowing fully well she wanted him to understand why she reacted the way she did.

Squaring her shoulders, Alea looked Tocol directly in the eyes. "I was ashamed," she whispered, and then added before he could respond. "But not of you."

Alea had to make sure he knew that. "Well, at first I was angry. I couldn't even comprehend why you would... why my Sh'em would allow...."

Stammering over her words, Alea paused, and then said, "It doesn't matter anymore. I now know that it couldn't be avoided. I would be dead if it weren't for you, Tocol."

Simply put and he could read the gratitude in her visage. Her expression then grew distant and Tocol looked at her questioningly. He could ascertain that she wasn't just accepting the fact she was poisoned by a potent aphrodisiac that could've killed her. There was more beneath the surface than Alea was revealing.

"Tell me, Alea." Softly he urged her on. "Something more is bothering you."

Alea chewed at the inside of her lower lip and shifted uncomfortably on the bench. A pit formed in her belly and she suddenly wasn't sure that she really wanted to talk about it any more. Especially with a man. She cast her gaze downward for a few moments as her heart started hammering in her chest. She had to, and Tocol wasn't just any man. Male or female it didn't matter, he really was her friend. Swallowing hard and then taking a slow, deep breath, Alea let her eyes drift upward to look at him once more.

"My mother was a whore."

There, she said it, out loud, for the very first time in her life.

Tocol's eyes widened and his brows went up. He stared at her for a few seconds before speaking. "And that has what to do with you precisely?"

"I have her blood," Alea answered wryly.

He shot her an expression of disbelief. Alea was a Tina when her Sh'em claimed her. It was no secret, a fact known to all. So she had the blood of a tart, but that didn't make her one. Understanding shot through him suddenly. If Alea believed that what happened on the king's ship was the result of her own weaknesses, then her over-reaction to the event made quite a lot of sense.

"And your mother was that vile?"

Alea sat quietly for a few moments, allowing distant memories to drift through her brain. "I was only twelve when she suggested I sell my body. Yes, she was vile."

"Your mother insisted you follow her ways?" Tocol understood that some females were ruthless, but for a mother to push her mere slip of a child--her own daughter-- to engage in such acts, to him, was beyond belief.

"She said people like us don't get many opportunities in life and we have to use what assets we have to survive." Alea stopped talking, recalling more of her mother's words. "She stroked my hair and told me I was pretty, that I could use that to get what I needed from men."

"So you became a whore?" Tocol already knew the answer, but he wanted her to say it.

"You know I didn't, Tocol," Alea admonished.

Tocol rubbed his hand along his jaw as though there was more about this to consider. "I see, but still she tried to corrupt you."

"Yes." Alea agreed.

"So instead of selling your body you became... what? A murderer instead?"

"N-o-o-o." Alea emphasized the word. "Don't be ridiculous."

And then she paused once more. "But I'd like to wring Dred's stumpy little neck."

"I would whole-heartedly join you." Tocol snorted. "But you're not a murderer."

"No," Alea responded.

"But you are violent?"

"No."

"Mean-hearted... unkind?"

"No."

"I see. So you lived a deplorable life as a thief." He stated this smugly, but there was mockery underlying his tone. "Uch! That must be it. You became a thief."

"Uh, I stole some food once."

"Doesn't count. You were probably hungry."

"What's your point, Tocol?"

"I'm not sure," Tocol admitted. "What else did your mother say?"

You're very intelligent, my darling daughter, use what is innately yours wisely. Alea looked at Tocol with surprise, repeating her mother's words out loud, as she took new perspective on the things her mother had been saying. "She was telling me I had choices."

"I think that she was a good mother to raise such a fine daughter as you."

"But only for twelve years."

"Enough to impress both your personality and your morals."

"I never thought about it like this before." Alea then waved her hand through the air, dismissing the regret that was now filling her. She never really did find out exactly what the truth was because the next day she ran away, and never saw her mother again. If she miscomprehended her mother's intentions it was something she would need to examine later. And make peace with it.

"But I used to listen to her... uh..." Alea stammered over her words. "...servicing the men, and I wondered what it would be like. My thoughts worried me."

"They're natural thoughts, Alea."

"Well, I didn't think so." Alea shrugged and continued on, telling Tocol about some of her bawdy imaginations as she was growing up and explaining some of the bawdy situations with men that she fled from.

"So when your Sh'em came to claim you, you resisted them, as well?"

"Well, no... I... uh...."

Tipping his head sideways, a smile starting to curve on his lips he then asked, "Why not?"

Alea pursed her lips and pondered that for a moment. She wanted to have sex with Tren and Rjant because it felt right. But wasn't that the way all relationships got started? It didn't matter that it was against most Earthly viewpoints and she was light years from her planet's cultures and beliefs. Her beliefs and the ways of this world were her only concerns. Alea's relationship with her Sh'em was meant to be.

"Okay, okay. I get your point." Alea snorted and Tocol's smile broadened.

"I'm sorry I was so cruel after what happened." Alea placed a hand on his shoulder. "Thank you."

Leaning in closer, Alea tipped her head upward and touched her lips to Tocol's, less than passionate, but not quite platonic either. Tocol responded in like manner, moving his mouth with hers, but refraining from touching her with his hands. Alea felt the warmth of his lips, but nothing else. There was no heated passion, no sexual craving or emotional desire. It was merely a kiss.

Tocol withdrew his head and smiled at her. "You just had to know, didn't you?"

Smiling in return, Alea nodded.

One of Tocol's eyebrows rose questioningly. "And?"

Alea smacked her lips as though she was tasting them, her eyes went upward and askew. "It was like kissing my brother."

Tocol bellowed out a loud, relieved laugh before calming himself into a relaxed pose. He wouldn't acknowledge that he too needed to explore the possibility that he might also harbor sexual desires for Alea, something he'd worried about after their episode together, forced by the hand of King Dred. But this kiss proved to him as well, that Alea was merely a friend.

"I have obligations to see to." Tocol pulled his time crystal from the inside pocket of his uniform vest, checking the mark of the dial. He slipped it back into place and took a deep breath.

"In all seriousness, Alea, do your Sh'em know about these fears you've been hiding?"

Bligh's story came to Alea's mind, relayed by Cormsei during one of her spells of gossip. Alea took interest in this particular tale because Bligh's plight seemed so similar to her own and she thought perhaps it would be comforting to have a friend she could relate to. But when she asked Tren about it, his revulsion toward Bligh's mother was apparent. It dissuaded Alea from not only seeking out Bligh's friendship, but from telling them about her own mother's doings.

"They know most of it. I just never told them about my mother."

"I think it's time you did so." Tocol leaned forward and gave Alea a quick peck on the cheek before standing. "I'll see you soon."

Alea watched him disappear from the garden alcove. He was right. With a calm resolve, she stood and went back to her dwelling in the compound to find Rjant and Tren. She told them everything, save for the kiss she gave Tocol. Some things were better left not said. Rjant and especially Tren accepted all she had to tell them with unconditional regard and she made love to them with her heart much lighter, wild and free--like a woman finally released from a lifetime of bondage.

Chapter Twenty

"You've got to be kidding me!" Alea paced the den in their quarters, her eyes wide with fear, her heart thumping woefully.

"We have to get the planet under control, Alea." Tren winced at her reaction though he wasn't surprised that she was so upset.

This was so not happening! Finally she gets her shit together and her Sh'em tell her that they must leave--*no*-- not just leave. They were going to fight a war. She halted and watched Tren latch his black trousers and then slip on his jerkin. He pulled it straight before donning his baldric, the talon arc sheathed in it at his back. Despite her upset Alea couldn't help but to suck in her breath at how sharp and handsome he looked in his Tertian uniform. His presentation articulated every bit of his leading command and power. He was a true warrior in the sense of the word.

"Oh," Alea cried, her brief perusal of Tren interrupted by reality. She flopped down on the sofa, dropping her face into her hands.

"Dormoth flew into civil war when news of their king's actions reached them," Rjant said as he kneeled down in front of Alea. He frowned at the worry they were causing her. "They're without leadership and various sanctions on the planet are fighting for supremacy."

He and Tren exchanged glances, regretting that they would have to leave her so soon after her recovery from the megberry poisoning.

"Zupol Egrin put out the distress call to the Allegiance six dawnings ago," Tren added. "And with Brits Scorn now tainting the planet we have no choice but get it under Allegiance control."

He sat down next to her and took her hand. "Already the Krellians are driving their vessels into the Fourth Ward attempting to gain access to the planet. They're attacking our sentry patrols stationed around the perimeter."

"But both of you? Why can't just one of you go?" Her eyes shifted from one husband to the other.

"Which of us would you have stay, Alea?" Tren tried to reason with her. "Which of us would you have go?"

Alea's question was really a stupid one. She couldn't possibly give up one for the other. Not that she had much of a choice. They were both going whether she liked it or not--whether they liked it or not. They were duty bound, first and second Commanders, and neither of them would shirk their responsibilities. The Allegiance had summoned the regiment that they were both enlisted with and Alea recognized the fault in having both her Sh'em assigned to the same military unit. She recalled the terrible story of the five Sullivan brothers, all members of the United States Naval force, all assigned to the same battleship. During World War II, their vessel, Alea couldn't recall the original name, was sunk by enemy invaders during the Battle of the Solomon Islands. All five brothers died. In order to avoid having such a tragedy occur in the future, the United States government passed a regulation stating that members of the same immediate family could no longer be stationed on the same vessel. The ship itself was eventually salvaged and renamed *USS The Sullivans* in their honor and was now docked in a naval museum on one of the U.S.'s Great Lakes. Alea saw pictures of it while surfing the internet, doing research for one of her classes, and the story rent at her heart. She remembered thinking how awful it must have been for the parents of those boys to have the blessing of so many children only to lose them all in a single instant.

Was she about to suffer a similar loss of her Sh'em? Would the children she bore to Tren and Rjant be possibly faced with the same fate?

Over my dead body, Alea affirmed solidly. She was going to do whatever it took to protect any children she ever had.

"It's not fair." Alea closed her eyes, biting back the anguish shredding her nerves. She had never felt so helpless. Women on Earth had been seeing their men off to battle for centuries. Many returned badly maimed, others never returned at all. Would the grief be greater if she were to lose two men? Alea took a deep breath and pushed the thoughts away. The CalyTron Galaxy had been fighting this war for epochs now. It had been a way of life for generations of inhabitants across the star system's Wards. One squawk from her wasn't going to change a thing, at least for the moment. Her Sh'em had no choice but to continue on as they always had before--fighting to save the galaxy, in order to keep the civilized, untainted races of people who dwelled in it from becoming extinct. There were other possible consequences, as well. If the Krellians and their diseased rebels conquered the Allegiance forces they could bring devastation throughout the universe. It might mean annihilation of her own planet, Earth. They had to continue this war, and it was imperative that the Allegiance be victorious.

Alea steeled herself against her panic as her stomach churned uneasily. She couldn't let her husbands leave with their last thoughts focused on her emotions being in a state of upset. She had to be strong, so their heads would be clear during battle--so they could each come home healthy and in one piece.

Alea blew out a gust of air. Reaching forward she stroked Rjant's cheek and then ran her hand down his neck before grazing her fingers through the golden hairs on his chest, visible beneath his undone jerkin. She pressed her lips into a forced smile and then latched up the jacket for him. When she was done, Alea gently kissed his mouth.

"Please be safe," she whispered against his lips. She reached around him and snatched a leather thong from the foot table and told Tren to turn around. He did so and Alea combed her fingers through his dark hair, breathing in the clean scent of it from his recent shower and reveling in the silky feel of it. She gathered it together, wrapped the thong around the mass tying it back in a queue and then ran her fingers down the length of it, examining her work.

Tren preferred his hair pulled back most of the time, while Rjant liked to wear his hair down. Rjant told her once, while smirking at Tren, that gathering his hair back as such was a conservative act practiced by aging warriors and Tren responded with a scowl. Alea laughed at them both. She loved her Sh'em no matter how they wore their hair and would continue to do so even if they had none at all. Jokingly, Alea proposed shaving it off, suggesting that bald men could be very sexy. She snorted when they both paled. Occasionally, Rjant and Tren disagreed and they did like to banter, but that was one thing they vehemently agreed on. The hair would stay put.

Alea slipped her arms around Tren's waist and pressed her cheek against his back. His hands came up to caress her arms where she held him. Shifting, Tren faced her and cupped her chin, tipping her face up to look at him. She showed no tears and managed to wipe away the stress from her face, though inside she felt like dying.

"Be strong," she bade him and he lowered his mouth and kissed her.

Rjant stood and went to the wall where his weapon was hanging. He slipped into the baldric and secured it into place.

"There are advantages to being linked in the Trigon during a melee, Alea," he said. "Sometimes during the noise and confusion, it is difficult to warn one's comrades by vocal means. Tren and I will be able to watch each other's backs, advise each other without spoken words."

"Yes, I know you'll be able to do that." Alea nodded, swallowing hard. "It would be safer if the two of you fought side by side."

The commlink on the wall chirped, interrupting them, and Alea recognized Calem's voice coming through. "Commander, the sentries are gathering at the platform."

"We're on our way," Tren answered.

Alea's chest squeezed tight at his words. She would see her men to their warships and bid them goodbye. Hopefully it wouldn't be for the last time. Standing, she followed her beloved Sh'em out the door.

The platform was bustling when they arrived, a sea of plum-colored uniforms filling the area as sentries, hustling to complete their assignments, prepared to make their leave. They were mostly males, but Alea noticed that there was also a handful of sturdy looking females amongst them, as well. Six mighty war vessels, including the Stardancer, were being prepared, last minute maintenance checks and supplies being loaded. Alea learned that fourteen more battle cruisers from various regiments of nearby Wards were gathering at Angard waiting to begin their journey. They would join twenty-two more star fighters as they traveled across the galaxy. This wasn't just a conflict between a couple of countries or one planet or even a single solar system. An entire galaxy was at war. Alea attempted to visualize the Milky Way and its vastness, and was instilled with a bit of awe at the magnitude of the situation.

It was a massive undertaking. Many, many lives could and probably would be lost.

Alea shook her head as she scanned the area. Her attention went to one end of the platform where a large number of sentries were assembled--a briefing area of sorts. Tocol was there checking star flight patterns with the pilots. He acknowledged her with a quick wave of his hand before returning to his tasks. Just a short distance away Calem stood before a large compu-imager, about the size of a slide projector screen reviewing ground battle maneuvers with the Chief at Arms. Alea briefly watched the three-dimensional images on it before turning her attention elsewhere. Rjant and Tren had left her momentarily to attend to their duties and were presently speaking privately with Tren's fathers. Her mother-in-law, Dmor was somewhere about, as Alea had seen her on the platform earlier--not to see her own Sh'em off however. The Sh'em of Dmor were now retired from their enlistments, but they still counseled the sentries regularly. It was the same for Rjant's fathers too--retired from battle duties. Along with Pel'r, they returned to Terta Minor to council a regiment that was joining the Allegiance forces. Alea took a deep breath and sighed, impatient to wait for that day when her own two husbands could adjourn from the battlefield.

Sadly it seemed a far way off. Tren was still young and Rjant was even younger. Rubbing her forehead, Alea pushed the miserable thought deeper into her brain, just as her ears caught the laughter of children.

Turning toward the sound, she spotted Syrat. Five of her children were romping about, the sixth, and youngest was clinging to her thigh. Alea made her way to where she stood, amongst other families who were milling about. As Alea strode up and stopped by Syrat's side, she noted that the Tertani woman's face was void of expression.

"How many times have you seen them off to war?" Alea asked her.

One of Syrat's shoulders lifted into a shrug, as she watched the activity around them. "I've lost count."

The slight twitch in her cheek told Alea that Syrat was not as emotionally unaffected as she pretended to be.

"What if only one of them comes back?" Alea gulped at the thought, but her tone was deadly serious.

Syrat's head snapped around and she glared at Alea. "Don't even think such a thing!"

Her anger was apparent in her eyes. They darted back and forth across Alea's face as though Syrat was determined to bore a hole into her.

Alea glared right back undeterred, her lips thinning in an anxious clamp. "But my Trigon will be broken if that happens."

Upon seeing the angst on Alea's face, Syrat's expression softened. "The triple is dissolved, though the remaining male and female do not separate. They merely become a couple."

Somehow that seemed so unnatural to Alea. Each of her Sh'em completed her in their own unique ways. Rjant in all of his youthful glory fed her carefree and wild side, while Tren kept her grounded and reassured. One without the other would be a devastating loss.

"Sometimes another male is called to the Trigon, sometimes not," Syrat continued, her tone casual as if it were an option she wouldn't even consider. Alea didn't want to think about it either, but there were things she never thought to ask. Things she now needed to know.

"And if the She'mana dies?" she asked.

"That, my dear, creates an odd situation." Syrat snickered and reached down to rub the top of her youngster's head where he snuggled her leg. "If there are children they are by edict, bound to stay together. Sometimes they are blessed with another mate of the divinities' choosing, and sometimes not, but the transdelta link between them remains."

"That's really sad, Syrat. It would mean that they could be alone forever."

"Not really, Alea. Some prefer it that way, but truthfully, most Trigon males find new mates."

Syrat's attention shifted, catching at a point across the platform, and a smile spread across her mouth. "If there are no children their mind link dissolves and they often go their separate ways."

Alea's chest felt heavy at the thought. Her Sh'em were so compatible not just with her but with each other, and they seemed so content within their Trigon. She couldn't imagine it all falling apart.

"This is all so complicated," she said as her gaze followed the path of Syrat's attention to where Merse stood among his fellow warriors. His eyes were locked on his wife, and where Alea had always pictured him as rigid and intimidating, the expression on his face at the moment could be interpreted as nothing but adoring. The love he held for Syrat was clearly apparent in his gaze.

"It's all a matter of the heart, Alea, grief and happiness are universal, no matter where in the galaxies you go," Syrat answered while continuing to admire Merse, and then shrieked when her other Sh'em suddenly grabbed her from behind, nuzzling her neck. Syrat giggled and then bent to pick up her smallest child. Turning, she handed him to Alea, before allowing her Sh'em to drag her away from the crowded platform, probably to a more secluded place to privately say goodbye.

"Daddies fight." The little boy Alea held stared at her with wide, innocent eyes while pointing toward the sentries at the platform. His name was Hanjek and he was a little clone of his mother. Alea hugged him close finding more comfort from him than in giving it, wondering about her own yet to be born child.

Matters of the heart. Syrat's words rang in her ears, and she wondered if widowed Trigon males resented being shackled together with children to care for. With sudden realization Alea understood. It didn't matter if there were two males or one in such a case. Or if it was one female alone or a woman and her remaining mate. The feelings of loss were still the same.

Ugh! Alea was sick of thinking about it. She needed to find her happy place and keep the faith that both her Sh'em would come home, or that she wouldn't croak and leave them behind. No, all three of them would live on together and drop dead of old age--at the same time.

"I'll take him." Two hands reached up toward Hanjek. Alea looked down at Syrat's oldest child, Cordalise, who at the age of ten stood nearly a foot shorter than Alea. Blue, gold-rimmed Tertian eyes blinked up at her. Alea was reluctant to hand over the child who was filling some basic, motherly need in her.

The battle horn blasted suddenly and the sentries began scurrying, falling into place for role call and inspection. Alea's heart sank at the meaning. The hour for her Sh'em to depart into the war zone was near. She handed Hanjek to Cordalise and waited.

"All ranks!" Tocol roared and the loud thump of clicking heels echoed across the platform as thousands of well-trained sentrymen stiffened to attention, presenting the delta and bowing their heads. An ominous silence filled the air as Tren and Rjant stood to the front of the regiment eyeing the warriors who would fight by their sides. Something akin to pride surged through Alea, mixing with her worry, as she watched her beloved husbands take command. She glanced around to see how the other onlookers were reacting and located Dmor standing next to Reasa. Tren's fathers stood nearby. Dmor was bawling her eyes out and Alea turned away, swallowing a thick lump that seemed to lodge in her throat. The sight of her mother-in-law's tears was encouraging her own and Alea was adamant that she wasn't going to cry.

The Mahatma Tribunal moved onto the platform and the Pontiff Jer began the mantra blessing, leading the group in prayer. Alea prayed as well, though at the moment she didn't know who she should be praying to. The last few months prompted many questions about religion and beliefs and she was no longer sure about what might be real. To be safe, she prayed to God and to the divinities and to the cosmos and any spiritual creature out there that might be listening, asking--begging for them all to watch over the Allegiance fighters and to end the foray of Brits Scorn throughout the galaxy.

When the prayer chanting eased and then quieted there was another silent pause before another blast sounded and Tocol yelled out once more. "Embark by order!"

Alea didn't understand what that meant, but by the way the multitude of warriors fell out of position and moved purposefully and immediately to specific areas of the platform, she assumed that it was a pre-organized method of getting them all on board the vessels as efficiently and quickly as possible.

One by one the warriors began entering their assigned battle cruisers, their presence and accountability verified with an identity scanner held by a sentry stationed at each vessel's hatch. The device looked like a laser price checker used at many of the supermarkets on Earth. Alea   didn't bother moving to an observation deck where many of the bystanders were gathering to wave their good-byes and yell out their well-wishes. Instead Alea parked her rump on a nearby bundle wanting to be alone. Closing her lids, she attempted to gather her thoughts. Rjant's arms slipped around her waist and she felt him settle behind her on the sack she sat on. She was acutely familiar with his inimitable scent and knew his touch without looking-- distinct from Tren's but equally as pleasurable. Alea turned her head nuzzling her cheek against his. "Here you are," Rjant whispered, wrapping his arms further around her and drawing her closer. He cupped his hand under her chin and tipped her head back to kiss her. His tongue swept inside of her mouth and Alea's insides crumbled as she relaxed into his embrace. A small whimper escaped her and Alea wished there was time to make love to him once more. She leaned into him, one of her hands pushing through his hair and Alea kissed him harder, gulping back her need to cry, determined to take as much of him as she could until he boarded his ship. Rjant's hand slid up along her rib cage and he molded his palm around her breast, gently kneading and massaging it until her nipple peaked, pushing through the material of her top. He stroked the bud with the pad of his thumb, groaning disappointedly as he pulled back from her, knowing he had to stop.

It wouldn't look good for one of the lead Commanders to cause a delay in the fleet's departure because he was busy tupping his woman.

"No, that wouldn't look good at all," Tren said as he approached, catching the wave of Rjant's thought. "And now it's my turn to say goodbye to our wife."

Rjant snorted at Tren before turning back to Alea. He pressed his lips to hers once more before standing. He then strode up to Tren, stopping to give him two thwacks on the shoulder blade. "I'll be at your tail on every turn, brethren."

The two of them exchanged glances, communicating unspoken words, and Alea noticed that their demeanors had changed. There was something different about the way they were conducting themselves. It then dawned on her. Rjant and Tren had their game faces on. They were getting ready to rumble.

Rjant took one more look at Alea and smiled slightly before heading toward the platform. He signaled Calem, and they spoke briefly. Rjant then boarded the Stardancer while Calem boarded her companion ship, the Cosmic Springer. The two vessels would fly side by side when in formation, as they navigated across the stars. In some ways, Alea wished her Sh'em were traveling on separate ships. It would lessen the chance of them both being blown to smithereens should they come under attack, but it would also mean that they would fight separately while on the ground, a catch twenty-two any way Alea construed it.

"Come to me, woman," Tren said to her, and Alea walked into his open arms. He buried his face into her hair as he held her tightly against him, dragging in a large breath, taking in her essence.

"Promise me something, Alea."

Alea craned her head back to look up at him. "Anything."

"This endeavor may be over quickly or it may take some time. I don't want you withering away in our dwelling the entire time we're gone. Promise me you will keep yourself occupied with the things you enjoy."

For a moment Alea just stared at him, and then she finally answered, "I'll try."

Tren's eyes roamed her face as if he were mapping every curve of her features. His hands came up to cup her head and lowering his mouth to hers, his lips slowly slid along Alea's mouth before he moved to plant kisses on her chin, her neck and then back up to her eyelids and forehead. Rjant's goodbye held passion, while Tren's was filled with tenderness, and she adored both their ways of saying farewell.

Another sound blasted, and Tren slowly backed away from her, the palms of his hands sliding down her arms, taking her hands and enclosing them in his own. Without another word, Tren released her and turned, heading toward the platform, the last to board the Stardancer. He stopped as he entered and stood just inside the hatchway of his vessel, giving Alea one last glance. A heartfelt *I love you* formed on his lips in unspoken words and Alea mouthed the words back to him. The hatch on the Stardancer slid down and Tren was abruptly gone from Alea's sight and she just stood there, committing her last vision of him to memory.

A hand closed around her wrist snapping Alea from her thoughts. She looked down and then up to find Tocol standing there. "You need to get off the platform, Alea."

He didn't wait for her to answer, but instead pulled her along until they reached a safety area and the place where ground control attended to their duties.

"Aren't you afraid someone might talk?" Alea looked down to where Tocol's hand closed around her wrist and he released her.

"There are more important things to be concerned with at the moment," he answered.

Alea tipped her head up and studied his face. His expression was tight with annoyance. Because of his injuries, Tocol was left behind, and his overly rigid stance, and the way he craned his neck back and forth revealed that he wasn't too pleased about it. At least he had cancelled his transfer. She was so very glad he was staying on Tertia.

"All systems ready," Rjant's voice transmitted through the commlink. Apparently he was piloting the Stardancer. "Awaiting clearance."

"Clear, Stardancer," one of the ground crew answered. "Begin launch sequence."

The engines on the star cruisers whirred, and Alea sucked in an anguished sob.

"They wouldn't have earned their present ranks if they were not highly trained, Alea," Tocol responded without looking at her, his eyes fixed on the control panels in front of him. His words did little to soothe her. Alea wasn't foolish enough to believe that capabilities were all her Sh'em needed to survive. One wrong move, a single lapse in concentration, or merely being in the wrong place at the wrong time could be all it took to bring a soldier to his demise. Though skill and experience were very important in battle, in most cases it was luck that held the upper hand. And the possibility of such a bad turn in fate is what fed into Alea's dread.

"Lift in progress," Rjant reported, and the voices of the pilots on the other ships came through the communicator as they confirmed their status and readiness. Alea focused on the six war vessels docked at the platform. At the same time, a final signal warned all personnel to vacate the vicinity immediately. A series of booming tones rang forth and a countdown followed. In unison the battle ships lifted and zipped away, vanishing into the Tertian skies.

Chapter Twenty-one

Over the next couple of days Alea made every attempt to hide away in the dwelling, despite her promise to Tren. She paced restlessly back and forth for what seemed like hours. At other times she tried to sleep but only managed to toss about in a restless stupor.

Alea was agitated and anxious, and not functioning very well--tolerating was a word she could apply to herself more appropriately. Finally feeling like she might go stir crazy, Alea decided to run, and found that it made her feel better. She eventually returned to the pools and continued her swimming lessons with the children, and she frequented the temple to pray along with many of Canyon City's residents, finding a smidgen of comfort in being around other people who were as worried as she was.

Two weeks came and went and no word came from her Sh'ems' regiment. That, in and of itself was disturbing, and Alea thought she might go insane if they didn't receive some information soon. Ileg reassured her that communications from the fleets were kept to a minimum due to risk of interception by the radicals. The Allegiance was never sure where the enemy might be lurking, and that no news was good news.

"If some calamity had befallen the Tertian ships," he told her. "We would've been notified at once and the dead bodies would be returned for the burial ceremony."

Alea paled at his reference to the bodies and Ileg once again received a slap upside his head from Tonor.

"You must be sitting on your shit for brains," he told Ileg.

Bantering between them ensued and Dmor, recognizing Alea's distress, towed her from the compound garden, where the whole incident had taken place. She took her into the dining hall to get something to eat, hoping that some good food and light conversation would put Alea's mind at ease. Once inside Dmor chose a table and then ordered an array of Tertian delicacies, which appeared on the holoplate. She scooped the various foods onto a small platter and placed it in front of Alea so she could sample them.

Alea ate and ate and ate with no concern for the pounds she might be gaining, drawing several sidelong glances from Dmor who wondered where her daughter-in-law was fitting it all. Between shoveling bites into her mouth--damn she was hungry--Alea described some Earth foods to Dmor piquing the woman's interest in tacos and buffalo wings and milkshakes.

"I think we'll consult with the cooks to see if we can't reproduce some of that cuisine," Dmor decided. "It sounds delicious."

Alea sighed contently at that, as she scraped up the last remaining crumbs from her plate, resisting the urge to lick it clean. Tertian food was delicious, but she missed some of her favorite, earthly junk chow.

"That sounds like a wonderful idea, Dmor," Syrat said as she approached, overhearing a portion of their conversation. She was accompanied by Bligh and both women joined Alea and Dmor at the table.

"My palate is always craving new tastes," Syrat said while tapping an order into the holoplate keypad and then waiting for her food and drink to appear. She then rubbed her belly.

"Your pallet is always craving... er odd tastes, Syrat." Dmor glanced at Syrat's parturient midsection, recalling that with her last pregnancy Syrat had a bizarre penchant for mixing sour flavors with spicy concoctions. It was rather disgusting.

Dmor chuckled. Like Pel'r, the girl seemed to be perpetually pregnant meaning she was sexed a lot by her Sh'em, or her Trigon was extremely fertile. Either way more children on the planet was always cause for much celebration, especially if they were fertile females, since the galaxy was suffering from a shortage of them.

"Being on an outpost, I had the pleasure of tasting a variety of foods from across the galaxy," Bligh commented, removing her own platter from the holoplate. "And when my mother wasn't fucking the men, she would sneak me to the kitchens and teach me to cook."

She tossed a glance at Alea. "I am quite proficient with flavors and textures. I might quite enjoy trying to reproduce some of your planet's foods. Where did you say you were from again?"

Alea blinked at Bligh, *fucking the men* sticking in her brain, the words spilling casually from Bligh's mouth like it was a fact of her life--and really it was, wasn't it? Alea had to admire Bligh's simple acceptance of her past. She was no more at fault for her mother's behavior than Alea was for own mother's. Someday, Alea decided, she was definitely going to get to know Bligh a bit better, perhaps over conjuring recipes.

"I think it would be a blast trying to create some of my favorite foods with you, Bligh," Alea answered. "I look forward to it."

She ignored the question about her home planet. Only a handful of people, including Dmor were privy to that information, and Alea would keep her origins a secret for as long as necessary, protecting Earth at all costs.

"They're back! They're back!" Reasa came running through the hall, heading for the front entrance of the compound. Dmor rose quickly from her chair and blocked Reasa's forward progress.

"Who?" Dmor grabbed Reasa's arm. "Where?"

"The warships have returned. They're docked on Angard!" Reasa shrieked. She jerked her arm from Dmor's grasp. "Let me go!"

Alea rose slowly from her chair, her heart thumping erratically in her chest as terror seized her. The hall was quickly clearing as residents began rushing to the doors.

"What do you know?" Alea grabbed both of Reasa's upper arms and pulled the Tertani woman around to meet her eyes in a pleading glare.

"The Cosmic Springer was destroyed," Reasa's brow furled as she spoke. Her eyes began filling with tears. Her Sh'em were on that particular vessel and the fret was clear on her face. "The Stardancer went to Angard for a quick scanning, but the ship is now bringing the wounded down to the planet."

Reasa pulled free from Alea's grip and without another word she ran from the hall. Dmor exchanged glances with Alea and then looked at Syrat and Bligh. The four of them hurried from the hall, hailing one of their hover vans once they were outside.

The platform seemed to be in chaos when they arrived. Dmor went one way and Alea went another. Bligh found her Sh'em immediately and Alea was relieved for her. The Stardancer was already on the platform and the first thing Alea saw was that a corner of it was a mass of jagged, charred metal where a hole had been blown into it. The opening had been sealed shut with a patchwork of sheet metal in an obviously hasty repair job.

"Oh God," Alea gasped, her eyes darting all over the platform. Shrouded bodies were already being lined up along one side of the docking area and the sounds of wailing were piercing her ears. "No, please."

She rushed forward searching the hover gurneys that held the wounded, as one by one they passed her by. Healthteks were pushing her aside as they swiftly moved the most badly injured to the health complex. There was no sign of Tren or Rjant, but Alea would be damned if she would check the corpses--not yet.

She heard a high pitched cry, and turning toward the sound, Alea saw Reasa sitting on the ground near the deceased, her hands were covering her face and she was shaking her head back and forth.

"Oh no... no," Alea muttered as she hastened over to her. She knelt down in front of her and pulled Reasa's head to her shoulder, hugging her, giving her comfort.

"They're not here," Reasa said, and Alea then understood that her cry was one of hope not sorrow. Alea closed her eyes as she expelled a breath, firmly latching on to her own hope.

"They're on Angard for debriefing, Reasa."

Alea's eyes flew open.

Rjant.

He was kneeling down beside them. "They're safe and well," he said to Reasa, and a tender smile spread on his mouth as he shifted his gaze to look at his She'mana.

Alea nearly crumbled with relief. And she was so overjoyed at seeing him alive and walking that she threw herself into his arms with such force she knocked Rjant onto his ass, missing the pained grimace that flickered across his face. He was injured, but Rjant wouldn't tell her that right now. First, he needed to warn her about Tren's condition.

The thought came belatedly.

As Alea held Rjant, her arms wrapped around his neck, she looked over his shoulder and her eyes flew wide, locking onto a gurney that carried Tren.

"Tren!" she yelled and rose immediately, running to his side. His uniform was tattered and he was a bloody mess and he looked dazed, but he recognized her.

"Damn it," Rjant muttered as he trailed after her.

"Alea, I'm fine," Tren rasped out and tried to take Alea's hand as she jogged alongside the gurney.

She followed the healthteks from the platform and into a waiting emergency vehicle where other injured sentries were also being loaded. Rjant climbed in behind her. During their two minute ride to the medical complex she held Tren's hand, afraid to touch him yet wanting to hold him tightly. Amidst her frazzling nerves she barely heard Rjant saying something to her, but there was so much noise inside the vehicle as the staff attended to the wounded, that she couldn't decipher his words.

Inside the medical building, Tren was moved from the gurney to a bed and the staff began cutting off his clothes. Rjant pulled Alea to one side so the team could attend to Tren and she turned her head aside, not wanting to see how severe his wounds were.

"He's going to be alright, Alea, I assure you." Rjant wrapped his arms around her.

Briefly, Alea's mind went numb, but then she stepped back from Rjant, her attention suddenly fixated on his form. Her eyes darted all over him. He was clean. His hair was neatly combed. His clothes were unmarked and fresh.

Alea's temper seethed. There wasn't a mark anywhere on him.

"Where in hell were you when he was getting hurt!" she yelled.

"She'mana, don't." Tren spoke from behind her, but Alea ignored him.

Her features grew taut with fury. "What did you do, Rjant? Run away like a little girl leaving Tren to fend for himself!"

That was cold. And Alea knew her words were biting, but her distress was overriding her rational thinking.

"Alea..." Rjant reached for her.

"Don't..." Her body stiffened and she held up her hands. "...come near me."

Rjant's chest convulsed.

In the lashing of her words he felt young and stupid and unwanted. He accepted that she was worried about Tren but to accuse him of retreating like a coward. He was a warrior by the heavens. He would never do such a thing!

Rjant shook his head once and he backed away, his heart cracking in two as he watched his beloved She'mana turn away from him and go to Tren, a string of *I love you's* flowing from her lips as she rested her head on Tren's chest. She tossed Rjant a scathing glare and suddenly he felt like a stranger to them, separate from what they were sharing... alone.

In that moment Rjant understood Alea's description of jealousy, and over his own brethren, no less. The feeling took him quite by surprise. He'd never heard his fathers speak of such emotions and he wondered if he was the first to feel them. Then again, his and Tren's fathers were married to Tertani women. Perhaps the possibility of the woman preferring one mate over the other was a risk that

Trigon males took when mating with women who weren't
Tertani natives, though he never heard others in such a
marriage talk of it. Maybe they kept these feelings as
private unspoken thoughts.

Rjant would've never believed it could have happened to
him though, and yet, there it was.

His chest clutched tighter as other sensations crept in--
hurt and betrayal. Without another word he departed from
the area feeling isolated and very disturbed.

Alea pulled the covers higher on Tren and then retrieved a
cloth from a bowl of taw that had been placed on a nearby
table. She squeezed the excess from it and began to clean
the blood from Tren's face. Having finished with him, the
medical staff moved on to the next patient leaving them to
their privacy.

With her concern so focused on Tren, Alea was scarcely
aware that Rjant had gone, and she was completely
oblivious to the angst she caused him. But Tren was acutely
cognizant of how her verbal blows affected Rjant. Not only
had he heard Alea's every word, the crushing impact they
had on his brethren was delivered directly into his mind and
his heart.

"Alea," he spoke softly to her and then started shifting his
body.

"Shh, don't try to say anything," she said softly as she
continued to wipe him with the cloth. "Lie still. I won't
leave you."

Tren attempted to sit up, but his eyeballs crossed and he
fell back onto the mattress with a groan. His nostrils flared
as he inhaled a breath and then released it quickly. "I am
sorely angry and disappointed with you, Alea."

Alea features turned confused. "I don't understand."

"Your words to Rjant were bitter and cruel."

"But I didn't mean...."

"Hear me out, wife," Tren interrupted her, forcing his
voice up an octave. "I felt every thread of pain it caused as
it shot through him."

Alea pursed her lips and continued to listen.

"I am reclined because if I were up and walking I would be tripping over my own feet and bumping into things."

"Why?" Alea frowned noticing that he was having trouble focusing on her.

"I hit my head, rather hard I might add. My brain is in a bit of a muzzle."

"You have a concussion." Alea nodded. She suspected as much. "How did it happen?"

"Rjant pushed me."

"He pushed you?" Her eyes grew wide.

"Out of the way of an oncoming blaze thrower's blast," he told her. "I would be dead right now if Rjant was without foresight to act quickly."

Alea's expression fell as she listened to him. "And for his troubles he was slashed in the back by a radical who had cut through our line..." Tren paused and gave her a stern look. "Luckily he had the fortitude to stay on his feet long enough to bring his attacker down."

"But he looked...."

Tren lifted a finger to her mouth. "Let me finish."

"The wound to my thigh is nothing. The blood you see on me is mostly Rjant's."

Alea lifted her fingers to her mouth. She didn't realize Rjant was hurt.

"The techs onboard the ship had sentries that were more critical than I was," Tren continued. "Since standing may be dangerous to my health, Rjant forced himself from his bed in the ship's health triage intent on making himself fit to be seen. He didn't want you to be frightened by the shower of blood plastered on both of us."

"How badly is he injured?" Alea replayed what she said to Rjant. Now that she was calmed down, Alea was beginning to realize how cruel she'd been to him.

"Oh my God," Alea gasped. "What have I done?"

How the hell was she going to fix this?

She turned to look for Rjant and then remembered that he left. "I didn't mean to hurt him, Tren."

"He's gone home, Alea." Tren lifted his palm to her cheek and stroked it. "He needs you more than I do right now. Go to him."

Alea kissed Tren on the forehead and left the medical complex, grumbling when she got outside, because she didn't have any transportation and their dwelling was at least a half of an hour jog away. The hover van they brought might still be at the platform and that was about a ten minute run, so Alea did a few stretches and then darted off in that direction.

Dmor was coming off the platform.

Alea had forgotten about her mother-in-law with all the confusion and expected her to be frantic, but was surprised that she seemed calm.

"Tren is at the health building." Alea waved and yelled to her, as she spied their hover van parked off to one side. "He's okay, but I have to go home!"

"I already heard," Dmor yelled back. "One of the sentries told me that my son was fine. I'm heading there now. Is everything alright, Alea?"

"I'll talk to you later." Alea waved one last time and climbed inside the vehicle, thankful that she didn't need keys. The control panel inside was activated by personally assigned codes and she had access to this one. She entered the proper combination and the hover van's engines hummed. Alea revved the vehicle and sped off toward the compound, determined to find her husband and undo the damage she caused.

Chapter Twenty-two

The complex seemed deserted when Alea arrived home, with the exception of a few unmated warriors milling around the communal dining hall, drinking. They looked like they were already half way into their cups. Alea assumed that some of the absent residents were celebrating quietly and she didn't want to think about those who might be grieving. Tomorrow, when things were a little more settled there would be happiness mixed with sorrow. At that moment Alea became acutely aware of how fortunate she was.

When she entered the dwelling, the first thing she did was trip over Rjant's boots, which were haphazardly thrown by the entrance. His empty baldric was lying in the middle of the blue carpeted floor in the den, and his uniform jacket was tossed over a chair. The shirt he wore beneath it was crumpled by the hygiene chamber door.

Alea walked into the room and grimaced. Rjant's trousers were on the floor alongside a large, blood-soaked bandage and the wet towel he used to dry off after the taw shower he evidently had taken.

But where was Rjant?

She left the hygiene chamber and looked across the den and out toward the garden.

Rjant loved the garden. He often took naps there atop the soft, plum moss.

Sure enough, that's where Alea found him, sitting butt naked on the top step of the terrace. His back was toward her and he didn't stir when she approached. His hair, a mix of dry and wet strands, was blowing casually in the warm breeze. His elbows were propped on his bent knees, his forehead on his clasped palms. The talon arc rested across his thighs.

Alea's heart leapt at his solemn beauty.

And he was beautiful to her despite the gash that marred his skin obliquely from his right shoulder to the left side of his waist. It was deep and looked horribly painful, and it was partially split open where some of the stitching had broken loose. Alea thought that she might have caused that when she'd knocked him over at the platform. She swallowed a gasp and a series of sobs and blinked back the tears welling in her eyes.

Alea went to him and knelt down at his side, sitting back on her haunches and facing him. Gently, she touched his shoulder. Rjant didn't look at her, but instead picked up a buffing cloth and began polishing his talon arc.

"Does it hurt?"

Rjant stilled briefly but said nothing. He then continued polishing his talon arc, rubbing it even harder and more quickly, his lips thinned and pressing tightly together, as though he was venting his pent up anger on the weapon.

For a moment Alea let the silence fill the air. It was thick with tension, heightening Alea's shame at the terrible things she said to him. She wanted so badly to put things right between them, to make him understand how deeply she cared.

"How bad was it?"

Rjant lifted his head and his hands went still. For a fleeting moment his face was stricken with anguish. It vanished as quickly as it appeared. He turned his head away from Alea and gazed out at the garden.

Talk to her, Rjant. Tren's channeled thoughts filled Rjant's brain.

"Please talk to me, Rjant." Alea shifted, positioning herself between his legs, kneeling upright and facing him on the step below the landing that he sat on. She took the talon arc from his hands and set it aside.

Rjant took hold of her hands and held them, stroking his thumbs along the tops of them. He shook his head. "You don't need to know about the atrocities."

"I'm not made of glass, Rjant."

His lids lifted and he looked her directly in the eyes. After taking a deep breath he released his hold on her and dug the fingers of one hand into his hair. "No, you're not."

Alea held her palm to his cheek and he nuzzled into it. He looked so drained and despondent.

"Tell me about it," she said.

"Innocent lives are in shreds." Rjant's fingers curled around Alea's and he lowered her hand away from his face. He leaned back, craning his neck back and forth and stretching his back. He winced at the pain the movement caused him. "If the Allegiance had waited even one more dawning, it could have become a hopeless situation for the citizens of Dormoth. The radicals nearly overtook the planet."

"The king's behavior was very reckless. He risked the lives of his people," Alea commented.

"It's the nature of the virus, She'mana, stealing all sensibility from an otherwise honorable man."

Alea nodded slowly. She finally understood that what King Dred had done didn't just affect her personally. His irresponsibility, putting himself at risk to catch Brits Scorn, and then not reporting it--allowing the disease to run rampant through his mind and his planet, was an unforgivable act against entire nations. "I want you to tell me about the battles you fought, Rjant."

Rjant shuddered, the terrible cries of the dying, women and children among them ringing through his brain, and the horrible dead silence of stumbling onto the scenes of blameless, lifeless bodies. "It was the worst I have seen."

His reply came out in a hoarse whisper, his voice breaking with the sound of sorrow.

It slashed deeply though Alea's soul.

"I saw men slaughtered in the very chairs where they sat at the dinner table, still sitting upright," Rjant continued. "There was a massive slaying of the Dormothian men."

"And women?"

Rjant nodded. His expression went blank in an attempt to harden his emotions from what he witnessed. "Women and children," he said with a detached comportment, though inside his stomach churned.

"But you stopped them."

"After a difficult battle we were able to take out the radicals' space fleets, but then we had to move to the ground. There were a vast number of radicals already invading the planet--tainted radicals. They were berserk in battle, having no regard for the lives of others or their own lives, as well. They are the most dangerous of enemies to face."

Rjant wearily rubbed his temple. "Please don't ask me more. It's over for now. Tren and I will deal with the effects of it in our own way."

Alea paused. Truthfully she really didn't want to hear any more. She didn't need details to comprehend that her Sh'em had seen horrible things. "Tren told me how you were hurt."

"There was no need to tell you that."

Yes there was.

Shut up, Tren.

I don't think so.

"Any warrior would've done the same." Rjant's throat squeezed tightly as he recalled Alea's harsh words, and he had difficulty swallowing.

She loves Tren and loathes me, he thought. "Tren will recover, Alea. His injuries are minor."

"What about yours?"

"Don't concern yourself."

"There was a lot of blood on Tren. It frightened me."

"Yes, and none on me." A bitter anger stretched across his face as he recalled her scathing expression at the health complex.

"I was just as worried about you when I arrived at the platform, Rjant."

"Yes, I believe you were." He glared at her. "Until you saw Tren."

Alea's attention dropped to the ground. She closed her eyes and shook her head. A tear fell from the corner of her eye and meandered downward. "I'm so sorry. I wasn't thinking straight."

Unconsciously, Rjant's hand lifted. He smoothed the pad of his thumb over the drop on her cheek and then hooked his fingers under her chin, tipping her face toward him. He ran his thumb along her mouth.

Will you kiss her already! Tren bellowed the unheard message into Rjant's brain. *I need some sleep.*

So go to sleep then.

What and leave you to your own wits? You're too high strung for you own good, Rjant, and I won't rest knowing you might screw this up.

Thanks for the vote of confidence.

Fix this between the two of you. Alea's happiness in our Trigon depends on the mental well being in all of us.

But that was just the problem. At the moment Rjant wasn't so sure it was true. Did he contribute to Alea's happiness as much as Tren did? It was something he needed to find out. On top of the pain in his back and the post battle stress he was experiencing, his heart was aching, and it was that sensation he liked the least. The others he could deal with.

Rjant studied Alea's face for a moment, thinking that she never looked so radiant. His demeanor began to soften toward her, but then he drew up his emotions and glared at her with steely eyes. "If you prefer Tren, I'll try to understand, though I won't like it."

Alea pulled back from him slightly, giving him a befuddled expression. She stiffened.

Prefer Tren? Was he kidding?

After all those years she'd spent in libidinous confusion, only to become more confused when they entered her dreams and then to finally have all her desires fulfilled when they both came for her. Alea blew out a harsh breath and carefully considered her words.

"Remember the day when you and Tren came to claim me?"

Rjant didn't say anything so Alea continued. "I saw you first, before I even knew Tren was there."

Alea glanced down between Rjant's legs and admired his half stiffened cock and then looked up again. "I nearly fainted at the sight of you, Rjant. No one man ever turned me on like you did. I thought you were the most delectable man I'd ever seen." She cupped his balls and felt his shaft twitch. A devilish smile crossed her mouth. "I was hoping it would bust through your pants."

Rjant snorted. "It nearly did after I caught a glimpse of you, Alea. I thought you were magnificent and I craved you with a passion so fierce I thought I might die from it."

Aw, now isn't that special.

Jealous, Tren?

Of you? Hardly.

Do you have to rub it in?

Snicker... what else are brethren for? Someone has to keep you on your toes.

May I remind you, dear brethren, that if I hadn't been on my toes during that melee, you would be cosmic dust right now?

Ah, of course. I forgot to thank you for cracking my skull.

I should've cracked it harder. Now will you shut up?

Snort.

"You knew us equally then, She'mana." Rjant refocused his thoughts on Alea. He couldn't help the pained expression that passed over his face then. He removed her hand from his cock. A muscle ticked in his cheek before his features sobered again. "Time passes and feelings grow, or they don't grow. You love Tren and I accept that."

Alea's brows lifted. "Whoa! Back up the ice truck here. Is that what you think?"

"What's an ice truck?"

"Frozen taw carried in the back of..." Alea slashed a hand through the air, interrupting her own explanation. "Never mind, it's not important."

Her mind went back to his words. Did he really think she only loved Tren? Alea's shoulders sagged as she looked into Rjant's despondent eyes, and absorbed his sadness.

"I love Tren with all my heart." She touched his cheek with one hand. "As much as I love you with all my heart, Rjant."

Alea took his hand and pressed his palm against her belly. "You both will be wonderful fathers."

Rjant stilled. Then reality hit like a cosmic storm. His heart thumped and warmth came flooding in. Alea was carrying their child and she had just told him for the first time that she loved him. He had never felt faint in his life, but he did now.

Did I understand that correctly?

You heard me correctly, Tren. We are to be fathers.

If a swelling heart could be channeled, Rjant could surely feel Tren's. Rjant took Alea into his arms and kissed her passionately.

Finally! It's about time.

Will you get out of my head!

Do you really want me to?

Pause....

No. You've sort of grown on me.

I do have that affect sometimes.

Yeah, like a blister on my ass.

Now there's a visual I didn't need at the moment, brethren.

"Tren is in your head right now, isn't he?" Alea was studying Rjant's face and it was clear that there was communication going on between them.

"Tren is always in my head." Rjant rolled his eyes.

"Well ask him what he thinks of this." Alea's head lowered. She took Rjant's cock into her mouth and he groaned with the pleasure of it.

Ka!

Are you in pain, Tren?

I am getting a hard on, and yes I am in pain! Aren't you?

Perhaps I should close my thoughts to you?

Try it and you will find yourself in the bed next to me.

I'd like to see you try and put me there.

Ugh!

You just attempted to sit up. Got dizzy, didn't you?

No.

Liar.

Rjant slid his arms beneath Alea's and then around her, lifting and drawing her tight against his body. Alea leaned in further and his heated, thickening cock pressed at her belly. She lifted her arms and rested her palms on his chest, savoring his firm muscles as they rippled beneath her touch. She wanted to hug him, but she couldn't. It would mean wrapping her arms around his wound and she knew that would be painful.

"Tell me something, Alea."

"Sure. Anything."

"What is feelusoffy anyway?"

Alea smiled warmly. She loved the sound of his voice and the way he mispronounced the word. She loved him. "It's the study of nature and reality, the search for knowledge based on logical reasoning rather than experimental proof."

Rjant crooked an eyebrow at her rote definition. "And did you find what you were looking for, She'mana?"

"Make love to me and I'll let you know."

Rjant didn't hesitate. He lowered his head and her mouth opened immediately for him.

She's so damn sweet, he groaned, and somewhere in the back of his head he heard Tren groan too.

With quick and nimble fingers he stripped the clothes from her body and then turned her toward the terrace. Alea moaned with anticipation as Rjant placed her on her back and then climbed over her. He briefly gazed at her naked form, breathing deeply, reveling at how splendid she looked and how her skin seemed to glow with her impending motherhood. Her breasts were fuller and her nipples peaked and he noticed the very subtle swell beginning to form at her belly. He lowered his mouth and began a slow, steady lick with his tongue from one nipple to the other. Alea arched her back and cocked her hips, overcome by the rush of urgency coursing through her, not wanting to wait for her pleasure. Sensing her intense need, Rjant moved directly to her pussy and began licking and sucking her clit. She rocked her hips against his ministering lips, slowly at first, then more quickly, rubbing at his mouth and crying out as she gave in to her passion. Her orgasm came hard and fast and she screamed. Rjant growled low as he lapped at her passion juices, thrusting his tongue into her vagina and sucking and tasting Alea's flavor like she was a rare, desirable treat. He then shifted, moving to kiss her lower belly, and nuzzled his cheek against her, atop of the place where their child was growing.

Alea spread her legs wide, her clit throbbing as Rjant moved upward kissing a path along her body, urging her passion higher.

Tren bucked in his bed at the medical complex as Rjant plunged his cock into Alea, knowing how tight her pussy was and riding the thought sensations darting from Rjant's brain to his as their minds meshed together.

She's so tight! Milking my cock, squeezing around me.

Alea pumped her hips faster. Her hands tightly clenched Rjant's ass pulling his pelvis tight against her pussy while she frantically rubbed her clit against him. Her vagina clenched and she felt a shift in his cock as it grew harder inside of her. Her back arched then as the waves of ecstasy seized her with such force she cried out once more.

She is coming all around me. I... am going to....

Rjant began slamming his hips, riding his woman, lust driven by the shattering orgasm Alea was having as he sank into her. His thrusts swelled to a feverish rhythm, as he slid in and out of her slick, hot sheath. Words became numb to his brain and he lost control of his channeling thoughts, though they continued to mesh with his brethren's. Rjant was mindless with his sex, his penetrations pushing deeper and deeper, his shaft growing thicker and thicker, his lips in a frantic seeking caught hold of one of her nipples and he ravished it with his mouth.

Rjant roared and his cock pulsated. His cum spurted into Alea's womb.

A grunt from Tren seeped through Rjant's brain.

Are you alright, Tren?

Silence. And then....

The healthtek is none too pleased with me.

Why?

He came rushing in. He thought I was in distress and lifted the blanket to check my wound.

Another pause.

I came all over the supplies he set to my side.

Rjant snorted. *Hangin' a little to the left this dawning, brethren?*

No, to the right.

They shared a channeled laugh.

"What's so funny?" Alea asked, noting the humor in his expression. "You're sharing something with Tren, aren't you?"

Rjant nodded and rolled to his side, pulling her into his arms. Alea sighed, not asking what transpired between them. They were entitled to their private thoughts at times.

Alea smiled happily as she began to doze in Rjant's arms, suddenly missing Tren and wishing he was with them as well.

And there it was, the simple reality. Alea was blessed with the love of two men, and she had plenty of room in her human heart to love them both, and there was nothing unnatural or weird about it.

Epilogue

Alea looked down at Krista and stroked her tiny head as the baby girl continued to suckle at her breast. It was early in the dawning and Alea was comfortably cradled between her Sh'em, Rjant behind her and Tren to her front. After being married to them for some time now, Alea learned that Rjant preferred to sleep on his left side and Tren preferred his right with her quite conveniently cocooned between them. Oddly, or perhaps appropriately, they rolled away from each other when she wasn't there. Alea herself could sleep on either of her sides, which to her benefit, allowed her to nuzzle up against either of her husbands.

She sighed with contentment as her gaze drifted to her now sleeping daughter. It was a great relief to Alea when she was informed by her mothers-in-law that the female by tradition chose their offspring's name. Rjant wanted to call their new daughter Booger after a pet he had as a child. But Alea stood firm. She didn't care if Rjant's pet was adorable. There was no friggin' way she would call her daughter by that. She insisted he search his earth translations to get an interpretation, so he did and it was the end of that name.

Tren, on the other hand, preferred Slika after a star in a solar system he visited some phases back. He told her the name meant bright and beautiful. Alea answered him with a solid *no*. In the end, she chose Krista, for no particular reason other than she liked the name, and there was no argument from either of her Sh'em because they both liked it too.

If only life could always be that simple.

Alea's eyes drifted shut and she began to roll. Tren's hand came up to her shoulder and he stopped her.

Alea opened her eyes. "What?"

"You were about to crush Krista."

"Oh." Alea attempted to shake off her drowsiness as she watched Tren's eyes close. Within a few minutes his deep breathing told her he was back to sleep. Her eyes started to drift shut again and as before, she started to roll. This time Rjant's arm scooped around her preventing her, once again, from falling on top of their babe.

"Do the two of you sleep with one eye open?"

"When it comes to protecting those we love?" Tren mumbled.

"Always, She'mana... always," Rjant finished for him.

Such was the nature of the Tertani males.

Such was the nature of the Trigon.

The Trigon Rituals
Basics and Definitions

Flaunting--the initial self-introduction of the Trigon males to their chosen female mate to intrigue her. During the flaunting, the males spar with each other, to demonstrate their masculine prowess, and to peak her interest in accepting them as her *Sh'em*. The exhibition is performed using the *talon arc*.

Talon arc--a curved thin weapon, similar to an archery bow, approximately four feet in length and two inches in diameter, made of a highly resistant smoky colored metal. A talon or claw shaped blade with a single barb is attached to one end. The other end throws laser orbs that can be set on stun or kill. Contact with this same end will cause and shock that when set to high drive will render its victim unconscious for hours. Set on low drive it merely delivers a minor jolt that's uncomfortable but not damaging. The handle is made of a thick leather cord, wrapped to a length of twelve inches. The talon arc is sheathed at the warrior's back and is attached to a baldric belt. During the flaunting, only the clashing of arcs, similar to a sword fight, is demonstrated, and because the Trigon mates are in constant telepathic link during the flaunting it is highly unlikely either of them will be hurt.

Trigon--type of marriage common on the planets Tertia and Tertia Minor consisting of two males and one female.

Tina--virgin female

Sh'em--the two husbands/betrothed males of the *She'mana*.

She'mana--term given to the wife of Trigon males once she has been breached.

Trigon males--Interchangeable with *Trigon mates*. The two Tertani males who have been mystically brought together for the purpose of claiming a mate. The males of the Trigon refer to each other as brethren.

NOTE: In the Trigon, the males take the name of the female. For example if the

She' mana's name is Alea as in the book, her mates, Tren and Rjant will be known collectively as the *Sh'em ot Alea*, and the union as the *Trigon ot Alea*. The *Sh'em* also attach their female's name to their own birth names after they marry, dropping their own mothers' names, i.e., *Tren ot Alea*. Their offspring will also carry the name of their mother attached to their first names.

Edification--the preparation of the virgin female by her Trigon mates to decrease her apprehension and intimidation of the upcoming Triconjugal consummation. During the first sexual encounter with her *Sh'em*, a female will frequently become overwhelmed by two overpowering warriors intent on ravaging her body. She may become hysterical. The edification helps to increase her trust in her mates and to ease her fears.

Triconjugal Hunt--The pre-wedding, predatory ritual during which chosen married females, and the claimed Tina, flee from their mates, to be hunted and captured by them. The Triconjugal prowlers, once they have captured their females, are expected to fornicate, to diminish their frenzy, before witnessing the breaching of the virgin female.

Triconjugal Prowlers--The wedded males who are invited by the betrothed Trigon males to participate in the Triconjugal hunt. The hunters must already be mated. In the early days of the planet's history, while the males lived in organized and domesticated encampments, the females banned together in packs, roaming freely and untamed in the savannas. Despite their lack of civility, the females were quite cunning about eluding their males. Even so, when their pursuing mates did manage to outwit her, the female's extraordinary running speed and agility often allowed her to avert capture. Because of this, it was the Trigon prowlers' duty to assist the Trigon males in tracking their Tina through telepathic linking, informing them of her location.

Triconjugal Ceremony--The sacred ritual of marriage mating, following the capture of the Trigon males' female. The Triconjugal Prowlers, after having mated with their own She'mana, bear witness to the consummation. During this ritual the male Prowlers encircle the new Trigon sitting cross-legged around them and with their hands held in Delta position. They chant the ancient words that bring health and fertility to the new triple. At this time the transdelta within the group is broken, but not the mental thought sharing that occurs between males of the same Trigon. That blessing remains intact. The Trigon females are not present, but gather in a separate location to continue the celebration and await their males' return. The wedded males are usually quite randy after bearing witness, much to the enjoyment of their females.

Transdelta Link--the blending of two Tertani male minds. Males of the same Trigon are constantly linked. During the Triconjugal Hunt, the prowlers' minds are linked during a Transdelta meditation ritual. It dissolves once the Tina is claimed and sexually mated. Tertani females do not have this capability.

Tertian--the word properly used to refer to any inanimate objects of the Tertia and Terta Minor planets.

Tertani--the word properly used to refer to the inhabitants of the Tertia and Terta Minor planets.

Delta--The position the hands are held in during meditation and during sacred ceremonies including the Triconjugal Ceremony, often bringing forth a transcendental manifestation.

Mahatma Divinities--ancient mystical spirits of the Tertia and Terta Minor planets.

Mahatma Tribunal--court of law and law makers consisting of twelve Tertani males brought by mystical summoning similar to the way that Tertani men are called to the Trigon. Members of the Mahatma Tribunal are celibate.

Credics--the universal monetary device used throughout the CalyTron Galaxy. Each individual had his or her disc and could transfer or receive funds with it. The disc keeps record of all transactions and credit balances and is the means to buy and sell.

Wards--the six districts within the CalyTron galaxy

consisting of fifty-two inhabited planets and many uninhabited.

First Ward: Location of the planet Geminus (Home of Windi Britny) and the planet Krell (Place of Tocol's heritage)--native planet of the prince Jonhi, who raped Windi Britny

Second Ward: Location of Puratan--the satellite colonies established for those infected with Brits Scorn disease and the planet Junpar (Gorsch)

Third Ward: Location of the sister planets Tertia and Terta Minor

Fourth Ward: Dormoth (King Dred)

TIME MEASURES
Min--star minute
Dial--star hour
Dawning--one star day
Septdawn--one star week or seven dawnings
Lunar Cycle--one month, four Septdawnings
Phase--one star year
Epoch--century/one hundred years

Printed in the United States
66297LVS00001B/47